ABOUT THE AUTHOR

Andrew Batty is an Architect by day designing all kinds of schools for all kinds of people. By night he is generally asleep. In the tiny gap between day and night he finds time to write stories that keep him amused, and hopefully others as well. He was born in a small village near Rugby, where he had so much fun, he forgot about schoolwork, failed his eleven plus, and ended up in a secondary school, instead of the grammar school up the road. Every day the school bus went past a posh private school. The posh kids looked so different to the kids around him. That contrast provided the inspiration for *The Boy and the Briefcase... and the Moose.*

ANDREW BATTY

THE BOY
AND THE
BRIEFCASE...
AND THE
MOOSE

The Book Guild Ltd

First published in Great Britain in 2021 by
The Book Guild Ltd
9 Priory Business Park
Wistow Road, Kibworth
Leicestershire, LE8 0RX
Freephone: 0800 999 2982
www.bookguild.co.uk
Email: info@bookguild.co.uk
Twitter: @bookguild

Typeset in 11pt Minion Pro

Printed on FSC accredited paper
Printed and bound in Great Britain by 4edge Limited

ISBN 978 1913913 731

British Library Cataloguing in Publication Data.

A catalogue record for this book is available from the British Library.

To love and laughter

This is a story inspired by my experience of school in the seventies. The thoughts and ideas are my child's eye view of things as I found them. I hope you can forgive the innocence, ignorance and occasional insanity of Andrew Baker and enjoy his courageous attempts to right the wrongs and get the girl. Let's be thankful he has friends such as Winston and Josephine to keep him on the straight and narrow.

1 THE BOY AND THE BRIEFCASE

Winston was:
A kid
A big kid
A big black kid
And he was strong
Maybe the strongest
No one really knew. He
Never fought
Never punched
Never got punched.

It's not that he was chicken
It's not that we were scared
It's just
No one had a gripe
No one had a grudge
No one had a good reason to punch Winston.

It would be fair to say he was not an obvious target.

He wasn't: girly, stupid or weak; nervous, timid or shy; creepy, slimy or strange.

He didn't have: pizza pox, pig smell or a twitch; weird hair, a funny voice or annoying habits.

He was sound.

He was normal.

He was not an obvious target.

But then again, neither was I, or so I thought, but I still got into scraps, I still got beaten up.

I annoyed.

I needled.

I pushed.

Eventually, someone's gonna push back.

Winston wasn't like that.

He didn't wind people up.

He got on with everyone.

He always said the right thing.

If someone pushed in front of him in the dinner queue, he wouldn't say, 'Get back, d**khead,' like I did. He would say something clever. The kid would happily go back to his place in the line, and everything would be okay. No threats, no aggravation, no fight after school. No being beaten to a pulp before the RE teacher found me and broke it up. I wasn't wary enough.

Not that anyone would have dared to push in front of Winston. He was after all a big, strong kid. Big, strong and black, although I don't think being black made you more, or less, likely to get into a scrap at my school. I never noticed any aggravation between black and white. We seemed to get along just fine. There was just one incident I remember, one incident everyone remembered.

2

The school had its own black role model. Janet Johnson was head girl. She was tall and athletic with a smile full of teeth. I guess she was good-looking, maybe great-looking, but to a fourth year like me, she was just scary. Occasionally we'd see her, on her own, training on the playing field. One day she'd be in the Olympics, but at school she was really known for being a black belt in karate. Once, when we were queuing for dinner, Janet came down the corridor. 'Hey,' a kid shouted out, 'he called you a "black b*****d".' She put her hand on the back of the offender's neck and he crumpled to the floor, crying like a baby. I never heard anybody call anyone anything after that.

For me, Winston was well on the way to being the next Janet Johnson. He wasn't a saint; no halo, no prayers, no eyes turned to heaven. That would have been weird, even if the school was Church of England. He wasn't perfect; he was just good. He never fought, never even threw a punch. We really wanted him to. We wanted to see the piledriver those big shoulders could pound; to see the other guy after being hit by that. We never thought it would happen.

Winston did have one quirk, one oddity that set him apart. He carried a leather briefcase. A good-quality leather briefcase. The sort with a clasp at the top. You popped the clasp and the top popped open. This was at a time when the only school bag was a sports bag, with a zip. Adidas was the big name, and the three stripes were everywhere. A briefcase was unheard of. Any other kid who came to school with a briefcase would have left without it. But somehow, with Winston, it added dignity, and a certain authority. I don't know why he had a briefcase; I never asked.

2 BOYS AND BRIEFCASES

Actually, to say I never saw another kid with a briefcase was a lie. I saw them every day. Loads of them. The school bus passed by Rugby School, one of the poshest private schools in the country, and every day I'd watch those kids striding across the grounds, briefcase in hand, eagerly anticipating the first lesson of the day. It was a confident stride, spine ramrod straight, nose held aloft, pointing the toes of their patent leather shoes as they passed by. It was the walk of someone who knows where they're going; it was the walk of a winner; it was the walk of wealth. They were being groomed for the boardroom, and it was clear from their immaculate appearance, the boardroom demanded a lot of grooming.

It would have been a whole lot sweeter passing by Rugby School every day if we beat them at rugby. Then we could have jeered at them through the windows. Unfortunately, the posh private school always won. I guess there was a lot at stake for the school that invented rugby. Winning was the only option. It was a matter of honour. If they lost, they were probably whipped senseless and sent to bed without any brandy. Only our first team got to play them. I was in the seconds, so I never got to see that perfectly drilled military machine march to victory.

I never understood how they managed to beat us. I had one game for our first team, and I was more scared of our players than the opposition. It's not like I was small either. I was a second row forward, tall enough to jump in the lineout and strong enough to push in the scrum. I just wasn't nasty enough. I didn't have their killer instinct. I was more geek than gorilla. My pale, pasty complexion; thin, gangly physique and nervous disposition certainly fitted the stereotype. My teammates, on the other hand, were grizzled, ugly and volatile. They were so pumped, I got the impression that a gentle prod in the wrong place and they might explode.

The bus to the match was like being in the back of a guard van, full of inmates on their way to a high-security prison. As we got closer, they got more and more aggressive. They became wolves baying for blood, whilst I became a poodle cowering in the corner. Their hormones must have kicked in earlier than mine because I could have sworn a couple of them had beards. Winston was there, of course. The perfect prop. A steady rock amidst stormy waters, totally untroubled by the crashing waves of testosterone. We won, but I didn't care about the score. I was just glad to get home in one piece. I was second team; I knew that then and was glad of it.

Rugby School and our school. Two different schools; two very different worlds. Both schools would have happily gone on living their parallel lives, ignoring each other, if it wasn't for the experiment. A social experiment. For three weeks, two students from one school would swap with two students from the other. This was a bigger challenge than you may think. Our school was a secondary school. The grammar school down the road had already creamed off all the intellectuals; all the pupils that one day would be the accountants, lawyers and managers serving the boys on the way to the boardroom. It made sense for those schools to swap, as they were likely to meet in the future. We were destined for the factory floor. The boardroom boys were only likely to see us at a distance, through their binoculars, from the balcony overlooking the production line. This was a clash of cultures, and no one was sure how it was going to work out.

Two pupils from our school were carefully selected for their mastery of the four Fs. The ability not to fight, fart, fiddle or say f**k. The pupils selected were so bland, they were invisible. No one was sure they had ever been to our school. There was a rumour they were the headmaster's nephews, though this was never proven. They were both male, of course, because, although we had a healthy mix of boys and girls at our school, the private school was strictly boys only. Girls were clearly a dangerous distraction, too great a risk to the high grades they had to get. Maybe they were right. Our selected students were kindly donated a posh private school uniform, complete with patent leather shoes, and dumped on the doorstep of Rugby School. Only the Adidas sports bag gave away their true origins.

The two replacements were eagerly awaited. We had heard they were arriving by car to the staff car park. We lined up along the fence to catch a glimpse. They were dropped off in a chauffeur-driven silver grey Mercedes Benz. The chauffeur got out and opened the rear doors in turn. The new arrivals emerged into the sunlight, like rock stars on their way to the stage. In theory, they were wearing our school uniform; in practice, it was something else entirely. The blazer was the right colour with the school badge emblazoned across the breast pocket, but I had never seen a jacket so well tailored, such a perfect fit. The trousers had a crease as sharp as a scalpel. The tie was the perfect length and the knot just the right size, not too big, not too small, and the shoes, they were so shiny you needed sunglasses to look at them.

They turned to face us and waved. Now it's quite possible it was a nervous wave, an uncertain attempt to say hello, but from our side it looked like they were waving to their adoring fans, or so they thought. It did not go down well. At their side was a black leather briefcase. A sly smile, a raised eyebrow and a gentle nod sent a silent message between us. It read *those briefcases are ours*. They scanned the unfriendly faces and their gaze settled on Winston. They smiled briefly. I think they sensed some affinity. Maybe it's because he wasn't scowling. Maybe it was the briefcase. Winston smiled back. Whether it was a smile of friendship, reassurance, or challenge, I just wasn't sure.

They were greeted on the steps of the main entrance by the headmaster and taken inside. Next time we saw them would be in assembly. We entered by the tradesman's entrance, dumped our bags in the cloakroom, filed into the main hall and filtered into one of the rows. Our school was a modern school built in the swinging sixties, when optimistic architects designed schools to be filled with daylight and fresh air, and the window walls certainly let the light flood in. However, the thin panes of single glazing in their ill-fitting steel frames also let the heat out. We were freezing cold in winter, and in the summer we were roasted alive, basted with sunshine. No one opened the windows in winter, so we were all gasping for air, and no one closed them in summer, so balmy breezes blew across your desk, taking any paper with them. It had its faults, but it was modern, and we liked it. At least it wasn't, dark, dank and miserable.

Rugby School, on the other hand, was old. We had no idea how old, but it had all the things old buildings have: spires, domes, bays, buttresses, turrets, cloisters, tracery, towers, giant chimneys and lots and lots of stone. It was vast, more like a small town than a school. There were buildings all over the place, and in between, mile after mile of perfect parkland, with that fuzzy felt grass people normally play bowls on. The word excessive was invented to describe this place. It was an enchanted land for charmed lives. For those with the right inheritance, the magic starts here, and never stops. We ordinary mortals lived in blissful ignorance of the vast chasm between our mundane world and the magical spires in the distance. Whilst they were learning to be statesmen, we were living it up on the state. No one knew how the other half lived. No one needed to know, until the other half arrived at our school.

Our school must have seemed as alien to the new arrivals as Rugby School appeared to us. However, early morning assembly was probably all too familiar. A long hall with row after row of students facing a high wooden stage, on which sat the teachers, and at one end, the two new fresh faces from Rugby School. Centre stage, occasionally waving a cane around, like a mad conductor in charge of the most unruly orchestra, was the headmaster.

Canes were the teacher's equivalent to a wizard's wand. Teachers would occasionally nip to London and slip down a narrow alley behind the Teacher's Lament Inn, where they would find Swish and Chuckle's Cane Emporium. There they would spend hours discussing the relative merits of Elder or Ash, before Swish or Chuckle would find the cane that perfectly matched their temperament and status. It is probably no surprise that our headmaster had a very long cane with knobbly protrusions where lesser offshoots had been gently trimmed away. It was a flamboyant cane suited to an overly dramatic, artistic temperament. In his booming baritone, he would roundly condemn students for smoking behind the bicycle sheds or dropping litter on the drive, whilst the cane bent and flexed as he drew great arcs in the air. The deputy head, on the other hand, had a short, straight, smooth cane which rather suited her short, sharp personality, if not her stubby appearance.

Pointing with his cane, the head directed stragglers to the remaining empty spaces like God completing a jigsaw. He patted down the coughs and laughs and murmurs to an even silence. With the last awkward pieces in place, he looked out over his creation and saw that it was good. He raised his arms, ready to address the faithful.

'Welcome, welcome, welcome.' He greeted the audience and those on each side of the stage in turn. 'It is lovely to see you all on this bright and sunny morn. Firstly, I would like to congratulate Susan Dorm on winning the WI paint-your-lunch competition. Spelling out sixty years of WI in chips was a masterstroke. Congratulations also to John Bullivant, whose marrow stole the show at St Marks harvest festival.' Pleasantries over, it was time for the pep talk. Like a vicar and his sermon, this was the head's opportunity to shine. Many years of amateur dramatics had provided the perfect grounding for a man that liked to put on a show.

'This school is a new school, a modern school, a school born of the white heat of technology. You... you are forged in that heat, ablaze with new ideas and burning with confidence, driving this country ever forward and never looking back. You are part of a great new tradition, a new way of doing things, and a new world waits for you!' There was a slight pause at this point. I think he half expected us to cheer and throw our caps up in the air, but cheering and cap-throwing require free thought, spontaneous action and a cap. We were cap-less drones, taught to obey orders. "Initiative" wasn't on the curriculum. He cast his eye over the blank faces, sighed wearily, shrugged his shoulders, re-girded his loins and boomed once more: 'But there are other, older traditions; traditions that have shaped our past, traditions rooted in the history of this great country. Today, on 6th October 1975, these two traditions meet for the first time. I am truly delighted to hold out the Harribold hand of friendship to these two young students from Rugby School known as—'

'Tossers!' someone cried, and a wave of helpless laughter washed over the audience and broke upon the stage. The maths teacher, Mr Samson, guffawed, panicked, and fell off his chair as he wrestled the convulsions into a muffled cough. The head span round so fast he almost thrust his cane up the hapless teacher's nose. The head turned back to face us. He was not happy. His eyes narrowed, mouth twitched, and his cane did several involuntary twirls. He scanned the innocent faces for tell-tale signs; a nervous glance or a sly smile, anything that might reveal the free spirit, the nascent creativity, so that it could be suitably strangled at birth. After all, you can't have free will in a secondary school. I'm not saying the teachers were evil or heartless; they just did what teachers did. They wrote words on a blackboard that pupils wrote in a book and later wrote in an exam. We weren't debating ideas, exploring options and creating solutions. We were taught to conform and were disciplined when we didn't. Imagination and inspiration were out in the playground, in the games we played, the jokes we told and the fights we fought.

The head spoke slowly, emphasising each word, steel in his voice, daring anyone to challenge his authority. 'As I was saying, these two courageous young students from Rugby School will be with us for the next three weeks. I would like to welcome our latest recruits, Tarquin Palaster and Quinlan Weston-Smythe.'

A tidal wave of laughter threatened to sink the stage, but King Canute stood firm, and eventually the wave subsided.

'As... I... was... saying... Tarquin and Quinlan will be joining us this term.' The head's laser eyes scanned the audience. Everyone knew; any laughter and they would be as clearly identified as the barcode on a can of beans. Fear muffled the mirth and silence returned.

'They will be joining form 4F and will be attending tutor group from tomorrow morning. Please make them welcome. And could Winston Grahame, Andrew Baker and Josephine Carter, please report to my study after assembly. Finally, we shall conclude with the hymn *All Things Bright and Beautiful*. As the strains of the parting hymn echoed around the hall, I looked at Winston, and Winston looked at me.

There was a standard list of offences that required a boy and a girl to attend the headmaster's study, together. These included: inappropriate use of the nature reserve, inappropriate use of the bike sheds, inappropriate use of the area behind the temps and inappropriate use of the secure store, although I think the last offence was a one-off. One afternoon, a sloppy admin assistant left the door to the store unlocked, then, realising her mistake, returned to lock up, accidently incarcerating overnight two over-amorous students. The problem was... or should I say, the other problems were... the secure store was used to store exam papers, and it was also used to store the secret staff wine cellar. This was where they kept celebratory bottles for the end-of-term parties, unbeknown to the head. When the door was opened the following morning, two very ill, very dishevelled students fell out onto the floor and promptly threw up, over the shoes of the deputy head. There had been so many breaches of protocol – the unlocked door, the wine, students locked in and exam papers open to view – that nobody was formally reprimanded, and the whole thing was quickly brushed under the carpet, apart from the vomit, which was promptly removed by mop and bucket. As far as the school was concerned, the incident had never happened, and thus, a mountain of paperwork was avoided. When the details finally dropped out of the rumour tree, it was not the night of passion I couldn't believe, it was that they didn't find the time to read through the exam papers. Clearly, in my case, testosterone had yet to addle my brain.

When it was announced we had to report to the headmaster's study, I shot an enquiring glance at Winston, because I knew I hadn't inappropriately used the nature reserve, bike sheds, behind the temps or the secure store, so it must have been him, but he shot the same look back at me. We both shook our heads and shrugged our shoulders. So, what had we done wrong, and what part had been played by Josephine Carter?

At this stage in my education, girls were still an unknown phenomenon. I don't remember any of my friends having a girlfriend. In fact, I don't remember any boys my age having a girlfriend. Surviving the general day-to-day lunacy of existence was difficult enough, without a girlfriend to cloud your judgement.

Mixed education was a misnomer. Girls and boys never mixed, well, rarely, and mainly in year 5, when they were making inappropriate use of various locations around the school. Girls were viewed from afar; an incomprehensible alien race. The boys were too busy trying to figure out what it was to be a boy to even attempt figuring out what it was to be a girl. The dinner queue was the only time we talked, and in the rush for food there wasn't the opportunity for like-minded souls to gravitate to each other, timid with timid and scary with scary. Timid could easily find themselves next to Scary, and there were some scary girls at our school; girls that talked about dubious stuff I just didn't understand. Girls were weird, and we just weren't ready.

The only time boys found girls entertaining was in a fight. Girl fights were the scariest thing on the planet. Girls would grab each other's long hair (short hair for girls had not yet been invented) and scratch each other's eyes out. I only learnt two things about girls in this period: never ever get into a fight with a girl, and keep your hair short, in case you get into a fight with a girl.

To be honest, I did sort of know Josephine Carter. We went to the same village primary school. She was in my class, and when you spend every day in the same room as someone, you can't help but get to know them a little bit. I was even invited to her birthday party once, although I can't remember much about it. I was more interested in the quadrophonic music centre than anything else. In the white Warwickshire village in which I was born and raised, she was the first black person I had ever seen. She was tall and slender with big eyes and a bright smile, emphasised all the more by her coffee-coloured complexion. She didn't like her natural tight curls and wanted straight hair like everyone around her, so it was pulled back away from her face into a tight bun, which further revealed her elegant features. Even as a kid mostly interested in model railways, I knew she was beautiful. She was nice too; a girl you could talk to, a girl with intelligent eyes. It was a shame she ended up here, with the rest of us rejects. She should have been at the grammar school up the road. Maybe those eyes weren't quite as intelligent as I'd thought they were.

3 BEAUTY AND THE BRIEFCASE

We lined up outside the headmaster's study in silence. Winston, Josephine and me. Without the angel in the middle, me and Winston would have tried to work out what this was all about, but unfortunately Josephine had tied my tongue in knots. I had spent the last three years avoiding conversations with girls and I was out of practice. It would have helped if she was fat and ugly. I might've had the confidence to speak to her if she was fat and ugly. But she wasn't. The years hadn't lessened her beauty or diminished her grace; instead, they'd added curves and contours that were both sensual and seductive. I was struck dumb by conflicting feelings of inadequacy, embarrassment and attraction. I felt strangely sick. I knew these were natural feelings, but I hadn't had them before, and I didn't like them. Why couldn't she be a bit… plainer, a little less appealing, a bit uglier? A troll would have been better than this. I closed and opened my eyes, but trollification had not taken place. She was just as beautiful as before.

'Are you okay?' she asked.

'Er, yeah,' I mumbled. 'Why did you ask?'

'You were scrunching up your eyes. It looked like you were in pain. I wondered if you had something in them.'

'No, no, nothing in them. I've… er… got dry eyes. I scrunch them to moisten them,' I lied, and scrunched them again as if to demonstrate.

'I don't remember you having dry eyes,' Winston chipped in.

'I don't have them all the time, just when—'

Winston cut me short. 'Just when standing outside the head's study, or maybe just when talking to a lady.' He bowed to Josephine as if she was royalty.

She smiled. 'Hi, I'm Josephine.'

'I'm Winston, and the eye scruncher is Andrew.' Winston gestured in my direction. I winced with embarrassment.

'I know Andrew already,' she said, flashing me a smile.

'You already know the eye scruncher?' he queried, looking at me with incredulity, as if I had been hiding a dark secret.

'We were at primary school together.' She frowned. 'I don't remember you scrunching your eyes then.'

'It's a recent thing,' I said, and scrunched them once more for good luck.

'Very recent,' Winston added.

'Let me have a look. You might have an eye infection.' She reached out and guided my head round to hers and drew closer to have a good look. I was forced to look deep into her big, beautiful eyes. I could feel her warm breath against my lips. Any closer and her breasts would brush against my chest. I felt light-headed. I thought I might faint. Shit! Shit! Shit! Shit! Shit! What was I going to do?

'I think you're all right,' she said, pulling away. 'Your eyes aren't red, but you are sweating a lot. Are you sure you haven't got a fever?'

The increase in distance allowed the stomach residing in my throat to return to its original location. I managed to regain some composure.

'I… I'm fine, thanks,' I said, stumbling over my words.

'Are you sure?' Her soft, soothing voice washed over me like warm honey.

'Yeah, yeah, I'm doing fine… thanks.' I looked away and took a few deep breaths.

She turned to Winston, who was his usual unflustered self.

'Do you know why we're here?' she asked. Winston pondered his list of misdemeanours.

'I dunno. I don't remember doing anything wrong. Nothing major anyway. Nothing you could prove. Nothing to warrant a trip to the head's study. Have you done anything?'

'Nothing I can think of.' She chewed her lip to help her remember.

Winston looked across at me. 'Have you done anything recently, apart from scrunch your eyes?'

'No!' I answered sharply. I was getting a little pissed off with Winston's jibes.

'Maybe,' Winston said with a smile, 'maybe we've not done anything wrong. Maybe we've done something right. Maybe we're here to get an award.' He rubbed his hands with glee.

'Don't be daft,' I said, 'they announce awards in assembly, and anyway, I may not have done anything wrong, but I'm pretty sure I've not done anything right.'

'Maybe it's something to do with the two new guys,' Josephine pondered. She nibbled the nail of her little finger. Deep thought required more than a chew of the lip.

'The rich kids from Rugby School?' Winston replied.

'Yeah, the rich kids,' she said, nodding gently.

'Maybe, but what?' I said, chewing my thinking finger in sympathy.

Josephine shrugged her shoulders. 'Maybe we have to look after them while they're here, show them round, take them to classes.'

'That might be the case for us two,' said Winston, pointing to me, then him. 'We're both in 4F, their new tutor group, but why you? You're not in 4F, you're in...'

'4H. I'm in 4H. Maybe... maybe I'm the best girl for the job,' she said, adopting the elegant pose of a leading lady.

'Why have a girl at all?' I said.

'Why just boys?' she snapped back.

'You've got to have a girl,' Winston advised. 'It's the only thing that makes us massively different to Rugby School. It's what makes us modern and them ancient history. The head can't boast about exam results, but he can boast about... girls.' He opened his arms and bowed graciously to Josephine, as if presenting her to a ball. She fanned herself modestly.

'It is only natural I should be the centre of attention,' she said, 'but why not choose a suitable girl from 4F?'

'I'm not sure we've got a suitable girl,' I replied, honestly.

'There's got to be at least one,' Josephine answered, defending her gender.

'Well, I dunno.' I turned to Winston. 'Which girl would you chose from 4F to show them round?'

'Hmm.' Winston interlaced his fingers round the back of his head and gazed into space, his mind running a slide show of all the girls in our tutor group. 'Not Macy or Jane, they're as thick as a brick, and Jude's not much better. Caroline and Stacy are rough; rougher than a badger's arse. They wouldn't give a good impression, and Martha... Martha is just plain nasty. What about Beth?'

'Beth? She stinks,' I said, wincing. 'I wouldn't want to sit next to her. Evy's okay though.'

'Yeah, but could you put up with that crazy laugh? She screams like a banshee. Sounds like someone shoved a red-hot poker up her arse.'

'There's Jo,' I suggested.

'Jo's so depressing,' Winston replied gloomily. 'She moans all the time. She sits behind me in maths. She goes on and on about periods and stuff. It's no wonder my marks are so low. I just can't concentrate.'

'Suzy would have been okay,' I said, 'but since she split up with Angus in year 5, she keeps bursting into tears. What about Samantha?'

'Samantha's never there. She's always ill. I'm not even sure she's here today.'

'Karen's nice,' I suggested keenly.

'What, Ugly Karen? Karen with the face like a bag of spanners?'

'You can't say that,' Josephine cut in sharply. 'It's derogatory.'

'It's not derogatory,' Winston replied, 'it's descriptive. Her face looks like a bag of spanners. How can that be derogatory?' Josephine lifted her eyes to heaven.

'She may be ugly,' I said, 'but she's easy to talk to.'

'So's a bag of spanners,' Winston said abruptly, then softened his objection. 'She's okay, but she moves like a snail. She never gets to a lesson on time, she's always late.'

'Aggie's clever,' I pointed out.

'Yeah, but she's Scottish,' Winston replied dismissively.

'What's that got to do with it?' Josephine interjected.

'The accent. I had no idea what she was saying for the whole of the first year,' Winston confessed.

'That only leaves Mandy,' I said. 'She's okay.'

'Yeah, she'd be fine,' Winston accepted. 'She looks okay, talks okay, and she's clever.'

'What, Mandy Aicart?' Josephine queried, looking doubtful.

'Yeah. Mandy Aicart,' Winston replied, surprised by the response.

'Randy Mandy with the... cleavage?' You've got to be kidding,' Josephine said, shaking her head in disbelief.

'What's wrong with Mandy Aicart?' I said, equally confused.

'Randy Mandy? She's slowly working her way through all the boys in year 5. She's obsessed. She's already been done for inappropriate use of the nature reserve twice this term. I don't know why she bothers wearing knickers because they spend so much time on the ground. She would *really* look after the rich kids. They'd go back with smiles on their faces and a rash between their legs.'

'Josephine!' I said, repulsed. It wasn't the character assassination that got me, it was Josephine. The image of innocence from primary school was well and truly shattered.

'I'm just saying. You can tell by her nickname she's a bit of a slapper,' Josephine said with contempt.

'Why? What do they call her?' I asked.

'Tramp! They call her "Tramp", and with good reason.' Josephine sneered.

'Tramp? As in, "a tramp"?' I queried. 'That's not such a bad nickname.'

'Tramp! As in, short for trampoline,' Josephine explained curtly, even giving a little bounce, just in case we'd never seen a trampoline.

'Oh! Okay!' I said. 'But what about the boys? They're all willing to jump on her. Doesn't that make them trampolines too?'

'It doesn't work that way,' Josephine made clear.

'That's not fair, is it?' I said.

'Look, girls have higher standards than boys when it comes to this kind of thing. We just don't like to see one of our own letting the side down,' Josephine explained.

'Oh, come on,' Winston cut in. 'You love it really. Bitchin' about the bad girls. It gives you good girls an opportunity to look down on them from your moral high ground.'

'You can't have kids… doing it, all the time,' Josephine responded angrily. 'There'd be broken hearts and babies all over the place. It'd be mayhem.'

'You can't know they're... actually... doing it,' I tentatively suggested.

'That's what John Bollocks said,' she reported confidently.

'Don't you mean Hollocks? John Hollocks? The tall guy, with the greasy hair?' I queried, wondering what the hell he'd got to do with it.

'I think she was closer to the truth with Bollocks,' Winston proposed.

'Hollocks, Bollocks, whatever! He said they were... her and him...' She lowered her voice to a whisper and drew us in close, as if the next word, if said out loud, could bring the walls crashing down. 'He said they were... shagging.'

'Sh-sh-shagging?' I whispered back, hardly daring to say the word myself.

'Yes! Shagging,' she repeated, far too loudly for my nervous disposition.

'Probably bragging, more than... shagging,' Winston suggested.

I checked the corridor for inquisitive ears then whispered once more, 'Bragging or brainless. It's just that half of all boys believe a peck on the cheek counts as... er... shagging, and the other half would claim they'd been... shagging, anyway.'

'You mean he might just have been talking...' Josephine looked around. 'Hollocks?'

'Probably,' Winston agreed.

'Are boys really that stupid?' She sighed.

'Yup,' I confessed. 'I've said some pretty stupid things to big myself up or avoid embarrassment in the past. Haven't I?' I looked to Winston for support.

'Yep! Very, very stupid things,' he confirmed. 'Look... Hollocks might be right, he might be telling the truth, but it's far more likely to be bragging or ignorance. He probably doesn't understand the strict definition of the noun.'

'It's a verb,' I quietly informed him. 'You know... I shag, you shag, we shag, they all shag.'

'Sounds like a hell of a party,' Winston joked.

'Surely everybody knows what... shagging... means,' Josephine said.

'Not necessarily,' Winston replied. 'Look, my mum told my sisters about... er... sex... really early, so they wouldn't get pregnant. Nobody told me. I had to figure it out for myself. I reckon it's the same for most boys. We're a few years behind.'

'Most of us learn about it by reading glossy magazines,' I admitted. 'Terminology is often vague.'

'Boys can read?' she said with mock surprise.

'To be honest, we don't read, we just look at the pictures,' I said, feeling more and more uncomfortable with the direction of the conversation.

'Hey!' Winston interjected, much to my relief, 'we've forgotten about the top contender for the job of female representative for 4F. The only one who could possibly knock Josephine off her perch.'

'Who?' I asked, curious.

'Mary!'

'Scary Mary?'

Winston nodded.

We all shuddered at the thought.

'They wouldn't,' I said, horrified. 'They couldn't. They really couldn't. Could they?'

'No! Never! Never in a million years. Nobody's that stupid.' Winston dismissed the idea with a shake of the head. 'But, even if she's not looking after them, she'll still be there, in the class, doing something... disgusting.'

'She's been here five weeks. Five weeks! That's all. Everyone is terrified of her,' I said.

'Not everyone,' Winston corrected.

'Everyone apart from you. Somehow you're immune.'

'Where did she come from?' Josephine asked.

'The deep, dark depths of Hell,' I said. 'Probably let out for bad behaviour.'

'She can't be that bad,' Josephine said.

I put my head in my hands and moaned. 'She keeps grabbing me by the balls and saying things like "They're coming along" and "Give them a few months and I'll be paying you a visit." I'm on tenterhooks in tutor group. I don't know what she's going to do next.'

'She once asked me if I wanted to read her tattoo,' Winston confided. 'It was horrible.'

'A tattoo?' I queried. 'It can't have been that bad.'

'It's not what it was, it's where it was.' He clearly did not want to explain any further.

'Has she sat on your lap?' I squirmed.

'Once! She wrapped her arms around me and tried to snog me. I don't want to see that tongue ever again. Blurrr!' He pretended to retch.

'I try to be the last one to sit down now,' I admitted. 'It's ridiculous. We're all dancing round the desks waiting for the bell to stop and the teacher to walk in. It's like musical chairs.'

'That's bonkers!' Josephine stated. 'Why don't you say something?'

'Oh, come on,' Winston snorted. 'Complain about being harassed by a girl. Do you think anyone would do anything? Do you think anyone would listen? We'd be ridiculed. They'd laugh us out of town.'

'You ought to try being a girl,' she murmured, as if we didn't know the half of it.

'Why? What do you mean?' I asked indignantly.

'You only have to deal with one tricky girl, just one, and you can't cope. We have to deal with loads of troublesome boys. Lewd suggestions and wandering hands... are all par for the course.'

'Yeah, but Scary Mary. There can't be any boys like that. Can there?' I said, looking doubtful.

'Maybe not a Mary,' she accepted, 'but they can be pretty bad.' A frown flickered briefly across her brow before she brightened once again. 'So, you're short of suitable girls to look after the little rich kids, but why, out of all the boys in 4F, why did they ever choose you two?' She shook her head as if it was incomprehensible.

'Excuse me! Are you suggesting we're not the obvious choice?' Winston responded indignantly.

'Just wondered,' Josephine replied snootily, looking us up and down.

Winston thought for a moment then put forward his theory. 'Well, I reckon Andrew got chosen because he won the maths prize last year. Ninety-eight per cent in the exam, as he never stops telling me.'

'Impressive,' Josephine mocked.

I blushed.

'And he plays the clarinet, so they think he's a cultured intellectual.'

She looked me up and down again. 'Well, I guess there has to be one in the school,' she said, 'but what about you? Why did they choose you?'

'I assume you are ruling out cultured intellectual,' Winston replied.

'I am,' she agreed.

'I'm the rugby captain. I think they want me as a minder, a sort of bodyguard. If I'm on board, they probably reckon the rest of the rugby team won't do anything stupid.'

'And are they right?' Josephine asked. Winston shook his head in despair.

'Have you seen our rugby team?'

'No!' she said inquisitively.

'If you had, you'd know,' he said. 'They escaped from a zoo.'

'They're not wild animals,' she said tersely, but Winston kept right on with the notion.

'They were roaming the nature reserve in a pack till last week. They had to be lured out with toad in the hole and slices of Manchester tart.'

Josephine crossed her arms stiffly, like a parent listening to a tall tale from a five-year-old. Winston continued, undeterred.

'I'm not really a captain. I'm more of a lion tamer. Keeping them in order is like herding cats... big cats obviously. They'll do what they want. They've already got their eyes on the briefcases.'

Josephine's ears pricked up.

'So you think they'll nick those fancy briefcases?' she asked.

'They won't last the day,' I said, knowing I'd have willingly taken part myself.

'Can't we do something?' she urged.

'Why?' Winston asked. He crossed his arms and shrugged his shoulders. 'Why should we?'

'Because we're nice. At least I am,' she said smugly. 'And, nicking a briefcase is not a nice way to treat someone new.'

'We must be able to do something,' I said, as much to myself as anyone else. Winston sighed.

'Yeah,' he said reluctantly, 'I'm sure we can do something. If we must.'

'Great,' she said excitedly, reaching out to Winston, who sidestepped a potential hug with consummate skill, before addressing the obvious question.

'And so, m'lady, apart from being nice, why are you the Number 1 candidate for this job? I'm sure it's not just your obvious sophistication and refinement. It can't be just because you speak posh.'

'I'm not posh. I'm normal, I speak normal,' she snapped. 'Why does everyone think I speak like a princess?'

'Maybe it's because you look like a princess,' I said, and blushed again whilst Winston rolled his eyes.

'I'm just normal, all right!' She looked at me, daggers drawn. We had obviously touched a nerve.

'Okay! Okay! No need to get so uppity,' Winston responded, 'but it's a fair question. Why should you get the job?'

'There's lots of reasons,' she advised curtly.

'And they are?' Winston prompted. Josephine clearly had a list for just such occasions.

'Well, I work hard. I'm good at most things. I'm good at French, I came top in French.'

'And they do speak French all the time at Rugby School,' I joked.

'I'm also good at English, in case they speak that as well,' she advised.

'Very useful,' Winston agreed.

'And I'm the netball captain, although I don't think they need me to keep the netball team in order.'

'I don't know,' I pondered, 'two handsome rich kids, you might have to fight them off.'

'Very true, but I'm first in line,' she said. 'I'll have both of them wrapped around my little finger, before the rest of the team get near.'

'I can believe it,' I muttered.

'Well done, Madam,' Winston announced, 'you've passed the interview with flying colours. The job's yours.'

'Thank you kindly, sir,' she acknowledged graciously.

At that moment, we saw the head turn the corner at the end of the corridor with the two rich kids in tow.

'Uh-oh, the royalty's arrived,' I declared.

They paused by the trophy cabinet. Presumably, the head was pointing out the tiny maths cup I had won, amongst the giant trophies for netball, hockey and of course, rugby. There was no doubting the school's priorities. They turned and headed towards us, the head in his traditional long black gown and, either side, the smartest students the school had ever seen.

Tarquin, to the left, was a modern-day matinee idol; tall, powerful and tanned, with jet black hair and handsome features. Quinlan, on the other side, with his long wavy blond hair and piercing blue eyes, was more Californian beach bum done good. From the confident stride, immaculate hair, easy smiles and haute couture, they could easily have walked off an advert for Man at C&A.

'I didn't know you could get our blazers from Savile Row,' Josephine quipped.

'Is Savile Row one of the roads off the high street?' I asked.

'Has fashion completely passed you by?' she asked. I think it was a rhetorical question; it didn't need an answer anyway. It would be true to say fashion had not yet found its way to the sleepy little village I lived in. Like the children in *The Sound of Music*, I would have happily gone out to play in clothes made from curtains. The only time that fashion impinged on my life was the infamous pink jumper fiasco.

We had a "wear your own clothes day" at school as a charity fundraiser. I dressed in the average, everyday jeans and T-shirt like everyone else. It was a bitterly cold day, so I picked out one of the jumpers Grandma had knitted me and set off to school. Now I know that jumper was knitted with kindness, I know that jumper was knitted with love, and I should be grateful, but it was also knitted in various shades of bright pink. I'm pretty sure most pupils, like me, had absolutely no concept of fashion. However, there was one principle that united them all; one thing they all agreed on and one line that should never be crossed: boys DO NOT wear pink. They made it their mission to explain this principle to me. I was bullied mercilessly until I tore off the jumper and shoved it in my bag. I almost turned blue in the bitter cold, but hypothermia is a small price to pay for fashion.

4 BRIEFCASE AND BAGS

'Hello, you three,' the head greeted us cheerfully. 'Come on through to my study.'

He ushered us into a large room with one wall of full-height windows facing out over the playing fields. To one side, in complete contrast to the brutal modernism of the school itself, was a large, elaborate, carved oak desk with green leather inlay, and to the other side, a group of padded lounge chairs covered in washable vinyl and framed in black metal.

'Please take a seat.' The head gestured towards the comfy chairs. We filed in around the coffee table and dropped down onto the low seats. The head dragged over an enormous oak chair from behind his desk and perched on the edge, looking down on us, like a king addressing his subjects.

'Tarquin and Quinlan, let me introduce the three students who are your guides and constant companions during your short stay at our school,' he said. The three of us glanced at each other and nodded; we had guessed right. 'Winston Grahame here is our esteemed rugby captain. He is responsible for maintaining order and discipline within the rugby team, ensuring the kind of… unworthy behaviour that plagues so many teams *does not* occur here.' His stare conveyed a thinly concealed threat. Winston nodded his understanding. 'Josephine Carter is our netball captain, although you are unlikely to play netball. We are modern but not *that* modern,' he joked. We all laughed politely. 'Josephine can introduce you to the breadth of talent amongst our ladies.'

'That would be just wonderful,' Tarquin responded, rather too politely.

'Delightful,' Quinlan agreed courteously.

This time, the head's stare indicated the breadth of talent should be suitably restricted. Josephine also nodded her understanding.

'Andrew here is the winner of our maths prize, a regular wizard with numbers, and a clarinettist, I believe.' He smiled disarmingly at me. 'He will be able to help you with any academic queries.' Then he gave me a stare and I too nodded my understanding, although, unfortunately, I had no idea what covert instruction the stare was intended to convey.

'Good, good, good. I think that's everything,' the head concluded cheerfully. He turned to us escorts. 'Could you please take Tarquin and Quinlan along to the second lesson of the day. You're a bit early, but I'm told the classroom is empty, so please go in. It will give you time to get to know each other. I do hope you thoroughly enjoy your first day at Harribold School.' He waved us out of the room.

'Er… excuse me, Headmaster,' Josephine said, looking somewhat confused.

'Yes, what is it?' he said, leaning back in his chair, hands behind his head, mind already on the next engagement.

'I'm not in 4F, so I can't take them to lessons.'

'Ah yes, very good, well done for reminding me. We thought it wise to have someone from another tutor group, someone who knows pupils outside of 4F, someone who can introduce Quinlan and Tarquin to a wider range of students. You, Josephine, are that someone.' He smiled as if that was that, and was about to wave us out again when Josephine pointed out the obvious.

'But, sir, I still can't take them to lessons,' she said. 'I'm in 4H.' The headmaster leaned forward, elbows on his knees, fingers interlaced.

'Hmm, yes. Well, you can now,' he said. 'For the next three weeks, you have been swapped with Mary Tideswell from 4F.'

In the background, me and Winston mouthed 'Yay' to each other and celebrated with a thumbs-up. We weren't so much cheering Josephine's addition, which was, I admit, a minor benefit, rather Mary's subtraction, which was a massive gain. There wouldn't be any dancing in the aisles when 4F heard the good news; we'd been doing that for the last five weeks. We'd finally be sitting down before the bell went.

'But, Headmaster, all my friends are in 4H,' she grumbled.

'And they are still your friends, but now, you also have the wonderful opportunity of making a whole new set of friends in 4F,' he said, as if she should be overjoyed.

'But… but…'

'Don't argue. Run along.' He waved us off for what he thought and probably hoped was the final time. But before we went, I felt it my duty to raise the business with the briefcase.

'Er… before we go, Headmaster, I thought… er…'

'Spit it out, man,' the headmaster replied impatiently.

'Er… well, I thought I should just mention the… er…'

'For goodness' sake, Baker. What is it?' the Head growled, like an old bulldog.

'The… er… briefcases,' I finally divulged.

'What about the briefcases?' he grumbled.

'They make the rich kids… er… Quinlan and Tarquin, a… er… target, sir,' I said nervously.

'A target? What do you mean… a target?' You could tell the

notion was clearly preposterous by the way the head waved his hands in the air.

'The briefcases might be viewed as... a... a... trophy, as the... er... spoils of war.'

'Spoils of war? Spoils of war? This is a school, not a conflict zone, Baker,' the headmaster barked. I nervously tried to explain.

'Y... yes, sir, I... er... know, sir. It's just that they are so... so... very attractive and expensive-looking.' I gestured towards the shiny black briefcases, with their polished sliver clasps and leather wrapped handles. The headmaster rested an elbow on the arm of his chair, his chin on his hand as he pondered the luxurious luggage.

'I see. Hmm... well, what do you suggest we do about it, Baker?' he said, expecting an instant solution.

'I think... I... er... I... er...' I had absolutely no idea, and then, in a flash, it came to me. 'I suggest... we swap them for two bags in lost property, sir,' I said, rather pleased with my hasty proposal.

'Good idea, Baker. Good idea,' he agreed cheerfully. 'I always knew you were the brains of the bunch.' Winston and Josephine looked at me as if they knew better. 'Please ask Mrs Goodfellow to show you the collection.' He waved us to the door once more, but Tarquin had other ideas.

'I am sorry, Headmaster, but I simply cannot swap my briefcase,' he advised haughtily. 'My father says a briefcase is essential to any civilised society. I would feel like a scruff without it.' The headmaster sighed. He had rather hoped he had finally got rid of us.

'I'm not sure they are truly... essential, Tarquin,' the headmaster professed with surprising patience.

'Tarquin is right,' Quinlan agreed. 'The briefcase is just as much a part of our uniform as the blazer. I cannot just give it away.'

'Yes, well, you wouldn't be giving them away,' the headmaster explained, rather more courteously than was his custom. 'We would obviously look after your briefcases. We would keep them safe.'

'But Winston has got a briefcase,' Tarquin said, pointing at it.

'He does,' I said, 'but he can get away with it.'

'Because he is the rugby captain?' Quinlan guessed.

'No! He just can.' I looked to Winston for clarification.

Winston shrugged. It's just the way it was.

'If he can have a briefcase, I can have mine,' Tarquin stated categorically. Josephine tried to make him understand.

'Andrew's right,' she said. 'In this school, nobody has oodles of cash. Some have got next to nothing. Your posh briefcases make it look like you're taking the piss.'

'Carter! I don't expect that kind of language in my school,' the headmaster scolded.

'Sorry, sir,' she apologised. 'It's just that waving those posh briefcases in their faces is like rubbing their noses in it. Some will take offense, and some will take a briefcase.'

'I will keep my briefcase if you don't mind,' Tarquin said, pompously. 'If Winston's briefcase has not been stolen, mine will be safe enough. I am not swapping my briefcase for a handbag.'

'They're not handbags,' Josephine explained cordially, 'they're sports bags. They're actually very fashionable.'

'Maybe here, but not at my school,' Tarquin responded snottily.

'Come on, Tarquin,' Quinlan urged. 'They are only trying to help.'

Tarquin stood firm. 'I am not giving away my briefcase.'

'It would be so much better to fit in with everyone else,' Quinlan suggested. 'There is no point standing out like a sore thumb.'

'I am sorry, Quinlan,' Tarquin said. 'I simply refuse to lower my standards to match the school.'

At that, the headmaster almost coughed out his false teeth.

'Our standards are not lower,' he stated forcibly, 'they are just... just...'

'Different?' Winston suggested, rather tentatively.

The headmaster scowled. 'Hmm, yes. Not lower... just different.'

'Well, I refuse to give away my briefcase to meet... different standards,' Tarquin stomped.

'I would be more than happy to swap my briefcase,' Quinlan offered enthusiastically, in a brave attempt to defuse the tension. 'I have never had a sports bag before. It will be quite an experience.'

'Oh, they're all the rage round here,' Josephine chirpily chipped in.

'You're nobody without a sports bag,' I said, casting a cheeky smile at Winston.

'Nobody,' Winston agreed reluctantly.

'Maybe I should get one myself,' the headmaster replied, with mock enthusiasm. 'Grahame, please take everyone to lost property.' He waved us towards the door and kept on waving. He was determined, this time, we would pass through it.

'Yes, sir. Thank you, sir. Follow me,' Winston said, encouraging us out of the door.

We all followed Winston into the general office.

'Can I help you?' Mrs Goodfellow enquired as we all crowded in.

'Er... yes, thank you,' Winston agreed. 'The headmaster asked us to find a sports bag in lost property for Quinlan here.'

'I'm sure we can find something.' She looked Quinlan up and down like a shop assistant looking for the perfect accessory, then unlocked the door to the store room, dragged out a wide selection of bags and threw open her arms as if presenting the prizes in a quiz show. 'Ta-da. There you go. Choose what you want.'

'If these already belong to someone, won't they ask for their bag back, when they see Quinlan with it?' I asked, unsure whether my plan held water.

'Oh, I doubt it,' she said reassuringly. 'These bags were left over at the end of the school year. They probably belong to fifth formers who have left for good. We keep them till Christmas and then give them to a charity shop if no one claims them.'

'Have you got an Adidas bag?' I asked, looking for the three stripes.

'I don't think so,' she said. 'I think we've only got bags with the names of football clubs on the side.'

'Which team should I choose?' Quinlan hadn't got a clue.

'Well,' I said, 'I wouldn't choose Manchester United. They're loved and hated in equal measure, so the bag still stands a good chance of getting nicked. Liverpool are the same. Leeds United are okay, but who wants a white bag? Ah… here we are,' I said, dragging a bag out from the pile, 'Sheffield United. This one'll do. No one supports Sheffield United and they're always near the bottom of the league.'

'So why would I choose them?' Quinlan asked.

'They're off the radar. No one loves them, no one hates them, and anyone who knows them at all will probably look at you with sympathy. And, it's red,' I explained.

'Okay,' Quinlan said, 'Sheffield United it is.' I handed him the bag, and he started decanting the contents of his briefcase into it.

'Are you sure you've never had a sports bag?' I asked, doubtful anyone could survive without one.

'Yes. Of course. Why do you ask?' he said, stuffing a cloth, comb and mirror into the bag.

'Well, I assume you don't put your rugby kit in the briefcase,' I said.

'Oh, we do. Of course we do. There's a separate compartment for your rugby kit, which also has a small pocket for boot polish, cleaning cloth, comb and mirror.'

'Really?' I said. Well, I'd seen the comb, so I was willing to believe.

'No! Not really,' Tarquin the grump reported. 'We have a separate blue canvas bag emblazoned with the Rugby School coat of arms and motto: *Orando Laborando.*'

'*Orando Laborando!* What the hell does that mean?' Josephine said brusquely. 'It's doesn't make sense.'

'I think it's Latin,' Winston guessed.

'Of course it's Latin,' the grump continued. 'It means "Prayer and Work". Everyone knows that.'

'Latin is not one of our most popular subjects,' Winston advised. It wasn't a subject at all.

To be honest, the easiest way to check the type of school you were in was to check the motto. If it was in Latin, you were in a private school or grammar school, attending compulsory Latin classes to help you read it. If your motto was in English, you were in a secondary school, attending compulsory English lessons to help you read it.

'Sounds like a boring motto to me,' Josephine said, casually denigrating four hundred years of history. 'What's the point of that? It wouldn't encourage me.'

'Well, what is your motto then?' Tarquin sneered.

'Be good, be just, be kind,' Josephine replied proudly.

'That is rubbish,' Tarquin snorted. 'It is not even in Latin.'

'I wasn't aware that being able to read your motto made it any worse,' Josephine sniped back.

'I can read my motto… in Latin,' Tarquin jibed.

'You can make a bowl out of shit, but it's still shit,' Winston cut in.

Now I had no idea what Winston was on about, but it briefly caused enough confusion to diffuse the situation, along with Mrs Goodfellow, who added, 'Mr Grahame! Write out one hundred times, *I must not use the word shit in this office ever again*,' then winked knowingly at Winston. 'Now please take your wards and leave me in peace,' she said, and shooed us out of the room.

'What do we do now?' Josephine asked, looking around for clues.

'Go to maths, I guess,' I said. 'Room 2.03.'

'Follow me,' Winston commanded, and we set off down the corridor and up two flights of steps.

'What's with the shit thing?' I whispered to Winston en route.

'Why you ask, Glasshopper?' Winston replied in his best Chinese accent.

'What's it mean?' I asked.

'I dunno. I meant to say shit is shit whatever it's made of, but it came out kinda wrong, but maybe kinda better. Still, it did the trick, didn't it?'

'I guess,' I replied. I couldn't believe it; Winston could even turn shit into gold.

5 BITCH AND BRIEF SCARE

'Here we are,' Winston announced, opening the door to room 2.03, then showing us through with a gracious sweep of his arm.

'Where are we going to sit?' Quinlan asked.

The room layout followed the standard arrangement in all the general classrooms. Four rows of eight seats; each row consisting of a two-seater table with one end against the side walls, followed by aisles and a pair of two-seater tables in the middle. At the front, facing the unruly audience, was the teacher's desk, the bunker from which they spat salvos of knowledge that we dodged with the skill of a featherweight boxer. Behind the teacher was a blackboard with chalk. That was all; that was it: the essential teaching tools from Harrow to Barrow. So why were we so stupid? I can only assume we were allergic to chalk dust. It must clog the pores in our underdeveloped brains. There was also a board rubber, but this was generally used to demonstrate the parabolic arc of a missile as it traversed the room from teacher to the less attentive student.

Winston organised everyone. 'I reckon Tarquin and Quinlan should be in the middle at the front, with you each side.' He pointed to me and Josephine. 'You can help with any maths stuff, and I'll sit behind.'

'Doing what?' I asked.

'Crowd control,' Winston answered. 'I'm here to stop prodding, poking and paper planes.'

We dutifully filed into the middle row of tables, whilst Winston sat himself on the edge of the teacher's desk.

'What now?' Tarquin said, looking disconcerted.

'We're supposed to get to know each other,' Josephine reminded us.

'Yeah, okay. So where do you live and what do you do?' Winston said to the rich kids. Quinlan answered first.

'I live at the school.'

'You live at the school? At Rugby School? Actually, in the school?' My mind was boggled.

'Yes. It is a boarding school,' he replied.

'I know it's a boarding school, but I didn't know people lived there,' I said, horrified.

'That is what "boarding" means. A "boarding school" is where students live at the school. Everyone knows that.' Tarquin's tone was condescending. I got the impression he thought I was a complete idiot.

'Living in a school. That's cruel,' Winston said, appalled. 'If my parents did that to me, I'd hate them forever.'

'No! It is fine. Honestly,' Quinlan reassured us. 'You are not taught all the time. After lessons, you have tea, then you can… mess around… do what you want, and your friends are there all the time. You don't have to drive to their house or anything.'

'I don't have to drive to my friends' houses either,' Winston said, looking down from his perch. 'They all live on the estate. Everyone I know is within walking distance, apart from Baker. He lives in Widdleysquiddleborough.'

'Widdley what?' Quinlan asked.

'Wibberley-on-the-Wold. It's a small village, out towards Burlow.' Unlike Winston, I sort of got what Quinlan meant. If I hadn't got two brothers and a sister, I would have had no one to play with most of the time. In the village, we reckoned on needing just six people to play a good game of football, three-a-side. Me and my two brothers had to play, and we had to knock on doors and drag people out to get the rest. I was generally happy making model aeroplanes and playing with Lego, so most of the time I wasn't bothered about being alone. It would have been good to have a few more friends around now and then, but there is no way I would have given up living at home, for the benefit.

'That's miles away,' Tarquin said, as if it was at the ends of the earth.

'Yeah. It takes two buses to get home, but at least I get home. When d'you go home?' I was still struggling with the idea of living in a school.

'In school holidays,' Quinlan answered.

'Just school holidays, not at weekends?' Josephine queried.

'No. My parents live in the Sultanate of Oman. I would have to fly,' he explained.

'Where the hell is the Sultan of Oman?' I asked in wonder. It sounded exotic, like somewhere out of *The Arabian Nights*.

'Sultanate,' Quinlan corrected. 'It is in Asia. Four thousand miles away.'

'What's it like?' Josephine was intrigued. We were all intrigued.

'Hot! Really hot. Mainly desert.'

'Do you live in a tent by an oasis?' I said.

'No. I live in a house, next to the sea.'

'Have you got a camel?' Winston asked.

'No. we have a car. I have ridden a camel.'

'You've ridden a camel! Wow! That's ridiculous,' I said, astonished.

'There are loads of camels. It is a desert.' Quinlan seemed amused by our ignorance.

'Everyone has ridden a camel,' Tarquin stated rather snootily.

'That's bollocks,' I blurted out, shaking my head at the idiot down the row.

'Not everyone's been to a desert for a start,' Winston added.

'Furthest I've got is the Isle of Wight,' Josephine admitted. 'They don't have camels on the Isle of Wight.'

'Don't they? I was hoping that's where I'd get my obligatory camel ride,' I said snidely.

'Not everyone. Most people.' Tarquin was backpedalling fast, but in the wrong direction.

'Most! What planet are you living on?' Winston said, raising an eyebrow.

'Planet Pompous Prick,' I snapped. Tarquin leant across Quinlan, grabbed me by the collar and pulled me towards him. Quinlan tried to push us apart. Josephine pulled Tarquin back, and Winston pushed me back into my seat and pinned me there with angry eyes.

'Do you have to be such a twat?' he barked.

'Say sorry to Tarquin,' Josephine demanded, arms crossed. I couldn't believe it; my own friends were siding with that moron.

'Say you're sorry,' she repeated, as if she was my mother. 'We are supposed to be looking after them and all you've managed to do so far is start a fight.' She had a point, a good one, but I really, really didn't want to apologise. I'd figured out, however, I would look more of a twat if I didn't.

'Sorry, Tarquin,' I mumbled sheepishly.

'I apologise to you as well,' Tarquin replied, in his somewhat formal manner.

'Right. Kiss and make up,' Winston directed, but we both responded with a silent stare.

'Maybe just a hug then?' he added. The silence continued.

'No? Okay. So, Tarquin, if you're riding camels all the time, do you live in the Sultan of Oman as well?'

At that moment, the bell went.

'Uh-oh, we're about to be invaded,' Josephine said warily.

'We've still got a minute or two,' Winston calculated. 'It'll take them a while to get here.'

'So, *do* you live in Oman?' Josephine repeated.

'No,' Tarquin stated. 'I live in Dunchurch.'

'You can't move for camels in Dunchurch,' I mumbled. Josephine gave me a withering look. I shrugged innocently.

'That's just up the road past the high school, isn't it?' Winston said, keeping the conversation bubbling along.

'What high school?' I asked.

'The girls' grammar. My sister goes there,' Winston clarified.

'There's a girls' grammar? In Rugby?' I queried.

'There's a boys' grammar, so there has to be a girls' grammar,' Josephine advised.

'Why?' I asked.

'Because girls are brainier than boys,' Josephine claimed confidently.

'Oh no, they're not,' we counterclaimed, in unison.

'Oh yes, they are. My mum says boys have only one thing on their mind. There isn't any space for learning.'

'How would she know?' I said. 'She's not met me.'

'You're right. There's absolutely nothing on your mind,' she declared.

I looked blankly into space, confirming the diagnosis. At that moment, pupils started filing into the classroom, barging their way past on the way to a seat.

Then Mary walked in.

'Scary, you're with 4H today,' I said, trying to be helpful.

The room went deathly quiet. You could have heard a pin drop. I looked around, wondering what the hell had happened.

Then slowly, my mistake began to dawn on me. Oh shit! I was in big trouble. Scary Mary fixed me with those black rimmed eyes and twisted her blood-red lips into a sardonic smile.

'Did you call me Scary, Big Boy?'

'Er... no.'

'I think you did'

'No! I said Mary. I definitely said Mary.'

'You said *Scary*, lover boy.'

'It was an accident,' I pleaded.

'So, you think I'm Scary. Do I get your pulse racing then?'

'No... no... not at all.'

'No? Are you saying I'm ugly?'

'No... no... you're very attractive.' There were a few sniggers at that.

'Glad to hear it, Big Boy. 'Cos I'm coming for you. Are you coming for me?' She was edging slowly forward, her eyes in attack mode.

'No... no... of course not,' I stuttered.

'Leave him alone, Mary,' Winston cut in.

'Why? Do you want a piece of the action?' She slipped past Winston as if he wasn't there. I jumped out of my seat and headed to the back of the classroom. Other pupils unhelpfully blocked the rows to prevent my escape. Mary walked slowly towards me, wiggling the fingers of her upturned hand, as if she was massaging an imaginary organ. There was an eager air of anticipation in the room. I felt sick.

'Time to check on progress,' she said, moving in for the kill.

'Mary, give him a break,' Winston shouted, but this was one situation that even he did not know how to handle.

At that moment, Mr Samson, the maths teacher, walked through the door.

'Mary Tideswell! What are you doing here? You are supposed to be in class 4H,' he announced.

'Sorry, sir. Just saying goodbye to my classmates,' she said, smiling sweetly at me and whispering, 'Next time, Big Boy.' She turned back to Mr Samson. 'Where are 4H?' she asked innocently.

'1.08. Now hurry along.'

'Yes, sir. Certainly, sir.'

'Makes me glad we don't have girls,' Quinlan whispered to Josephine.

Josephine shrugged, resigned to the fact that Mary was not the best ambassador for her gender.

'Baker! Return to your seat,' the teacher instructed.

'Yes, sir.' I walked back and sat down on the chair next to Tarquin. I was still shaking.

Mr Samson observed me as if I was a curious specimen in a science experiment, the mould in the petri dish, the rat with two tails.

'Are you ill, Baker?' he asked.

'No, sir. I'm fine, sir,' I replied.

'Are you sure?'

'Yes, sir.'

'Then stop shaking and pay attention.'

'Yes, sir.'

Having established my health was in order, he turned to the blackboard and wrote an X with a little 2 against it, then returned his gaze to the audience.

'Firstly, I would like to welcome Quinlan and Tarquin to the maths lesson.' He gestured towards the two newcomers. 'Right! Today we are looking at squares... Karen!' Karen arrived late, as always, panting after climbing two flights of stairs.

'Karen's not square, sir,' Edward quipped.

'I'm not so sure,' someone whispered behind me.

'Thank you, Edward. Finally, you've learnt something in my lesson. Karen, please take your seat.' Karen plonked herself down next to Suzy.

The rest of the lesson was much like any other maths lesson. A few instructions, a load of examples and a ton of queries. Maths was my strong point. I found it easy, so I just got on with it. I never understood why some kids found it hard. You follow the rules and the answer appears. Quinlan and Tarquin also made easy going of it. Whether it was the level of teaching at Rugby School or natural ability, I didn't know, but they spent a fair time twiddling their thumbs waiting for others to finish. There were the usual reprimands for talking and throwing paper aeroplanes, but other than that, the lesson was quite uneventful.

The bell rang once more, and we were dismissed.

'Okay! Pack up and you can go.'

6 THE BOY AND NO BRIEFCASE

It was break, so there was a crazy rush to get out as quickly as possible and enjoy those few precious moments of freedom. We held back till everyone else had gone. Secondary school stairs at peak capacity are for thrill seekers only. You have to be prepared mentally and physically for the challenge. It was like waiting at the top of a ski slope, the terrifying ordeal staring you in the face, except, in this case, there were plenty of people willing to give you a push. As the grammar school had creamed off all the intellectuals, the genteel pursuits of accountancy and architecture were no longer on the prospectus and as a result, there was a surprisingly high percentage of would-be gymnasts, stuntmen and daredevils. The stairs were their training ground. Sliding down handrails, leaping over banisters, swinging on beams and jumping unfathomable numbers of steps was perfect practice for their future careers. The huge number of bodies in the way just added to the excitement. Leaving a few seconds late meant the carnage was over and we could descend in peace. We turned left at the bottom of the stairs, down the corridor, through the cloaks and out into the sunshine.

All the benches bar one had been grabbed by girls for gassing. Me and Winston raced to claim the remaining one, slamming ourselves down on each end. The rest rolled up at a leisurely pace. Tarquin plonked himself down in the middle, leaving just enough space for one more.

'You take the seat,' Quinlan said, graciously offering the remaining space to Josephine.

'Thanks,' Josephine replied, squeezing in between Winston and Tarquin.

Opposite, an unruly mob appeared to be engaged in a mass brawl. Occasionally, a human form would drag itself, exhausted, out of the entangled mess of arms and legs, dust itself off, heave a sigh of relief, then throw itself back into the fray. An explosion of expletives, curses, threats and screams was mixed, equally, with howls of laughter.

'What the hell is that all about?' Quinlan asked.

'It's the rubber game,' Winston responded, as if that answered everything.

Josephine rolled her eyes and shrugged her shoulders. She had given up trying to make sense of this insanity many moons ago.

Every school has its own unique games using stuff that just happens to be lying around. Ours was no exception. We had the rubber game, involving an eraser; the wall game, involving a wall; the rugby post game, involving rugby posts; and the word game, involving... words. Only the rugby post game did not involve violence. Rugby School probably had a similar set of games involving a croquet hoop, garters and a cravat.

The rubber game was probably the most bizarre of all. It involved throwing a rubber at the wall and catching it. So, you may ask, *How could you squeeze untold violence into that?* Well, it's easy when you know how. You see, the person catching the rubber, let's call them the "Numpty", was set upon by the remainder of the players for as long as they had the rubber in their hands. I know what you're thinking: *Why would you catch the rubber, when you are going to get badly beaten?* Well, it's a kind of macho thing; an "I'm not scared" sort of thing, and an opportunity to move up a peck in the pecking order. The older, more deranged and downright dangerous kids would catch it and hold onto it, daring anyone to come near, daring anyone to challenge their right to be the Number 1 Numpty. For us younger pupils, the aim was to throw the rubber back as quickly as possible before fists flew and the boot went in. It goes without saying that this game was not a regular attraction at the grammar school up the road, where brain cells were treated with a little more respect.

This was a boys' game. I don't remember a single girl joining in. There were some girls, however, that would have fared very well, and at least a couple that could have beaten off all opposition.

'What are they doing?' Tarquin looked bewildered.

'Fighting for the rubber,' I replied.

'Come on. Let's join in,' Winston urged.

'Okay!' I agreed.

Winston was already up and moving towards the mayhem. I got up and turned to Josephine.

'Look after the bags, will ya?'

'Sure,' she replied.

'You having a go?' I said to the rich kids.

'Not me,' Quinlan replied, looking unsettled by the insanity. 'I will keep an eye on the bags with Josephine.'

'Come on, Tarquin,' I pushed, 'or are you scared?'

'Scared? Me? Of a silly game? Of course not. Tell me the rules and I'll show you why we always win at rugby!'

Tarquin's snidey comments were grinding my gonads. It was my school, my friends, my life he was deriding. He needed to be taught a lesson. So, my instructions weren't entirely accurate.

'The rules are simple. The rubber gets thrown at the wall, it bounces back, and everyone tries to grab it. When the rubber's caught, the fighting stops, and the rubber is thrown at the wall again. It's not complicated, just a bit of fun. If you catch it, the important thing to remember is to cling onto the rubber, as hard as you can… whatever happens, do not let go.'

'Sounds easy,' Tarquin replied.

'Oh, it is,' I lied.

The seething mass of overexcited teenagers was like a pack of wild dogs; their eyes firmly fixed on the rubber; nothing else mattered; nothing else existed. They were transfixed. Once that rubber was thrown, all hell was going to break loose. We moved into the middle of the pack. A fifth former, Mad Jack McGonigle, had got the rubber. Everyone moved back, circling the mad dog in the middle, clinging to the prize with his greedy paws, whilst all around claws lunged and recoiled. The safe distance we kept between us and Mad Jack wasn't because he was bigger and stronger than other fifth formers, he was just a whole lot madder. The usual restraints that would stop you hitting your head against a brick wall more than once did not apply to Mad Jack; he would just keep at it until his head was a bloody mess or the wall fell down. He wasn't even nasty; nice as pie most of the time, he just lost control and struggled to regain it. He really should have been playing games with teddy bears in a padded room; he should not have been playing the rubber game.

Suddenly the rubber was released; it bounced unpredictably against the wall and we all grasped at the empty air. Snatch and release, and the rubber was flying once more. Again and again and again; the same pattern; snatch and release, snatch and release, snatch and release. The rubber pinged all around us, zipping this way and that, until it was snatched, and then stopped. Everyone looked to Mad Jack, but he didn't have it. Eyes flickered across the other monsters of the fifth form: Rump, Blocker and Cabbage, but they didn't have it either. Where the hell was it?

'I have got the eraser!' Tarquin announced, holding it high for all to see and admire. 'I have got it!' A smile of smug pride spread across his face.

Everyone paused briefly, shocked by the sheer audacity of the novice rubberee. To hold onto the rubber, with no training and so little experience, was courage beyond compare. There was a momentary nod of respect. Then, as expected, they all piled in. Tarquin held on tight, following my instructions. Fists flew and feet followed. Winston charged in, grabbed the rubber from the outstretched hand and threw it, then dragged Tarquin out of the mayhem.

'What the hell were you doing?' he challenged the confused and bedraggled pupil.

'I was holding onto the rubber, like Andrew told me to,' he spluttered.

'Did he?' Winston turned angrily towards me. I adopted a look of angelic innocence. He shook his head and gave me the "grow up" stare.

Quinlan sprung off the bench as soon as he saw the carnage. 'Are you all right, Tarquin?' he said anxiously.

'I'm fine, just fine.' Tarquin looked down and away, but the flush of red revealed his shame. He wasn't hurt, but his pride had taken a hell of a battering.

Josephine stood up and moved towards them. 'Is he all right?' she said, concerned.

'He's okay,' Winston assured her. 'Just needs a bit of muck brushing off those oh-so-clean clothes, and he'll be as good as new.'

We walked back to the bench and sat down, apart from Winston, who was still buzzing from the game. I was feeling a tad guilty about Tarquin's misadventure, so I tried my hand at reconciliation.

'Don't worry,' I said, 'everyone takes a beating every now and then. That's just the way it is.'

'Yeah,' Winston agreed, casting a disapproving glance my way, 'too many dodgy kids who don't play by the rules. You did well. A bit of practice and you could be one of the best,' he said, bigging up his downhearted ward.

'Yeah, sure,' Tarquin replied through clenched teeth, whilst brushing the dirt off his trousers with his hands.

'It's a stupid game anyway,' Josephine declared angrily. 'It's a game for morons.'

'Hey! It's not that bad. It's just a bit of fun,' Winston said cheerily.

'Hardly,' Josephine snapped.

'Yeah, 'tis. It's a boy thing. We're just… rutting,' Winston said, jigging around.

'Rutting? Are you sure you mean rutting?' Josephine queried, bemused.

'Yeah… rutting. You know, like stags. I'm honing my hunting skills,' he said, looking around for something to pounce on.

'Deer don't hunt,' I said.

'Yeah, they do. Stags do,' Winston asserted.

'They eat grass,' Josephine said, as if he'd lost the plot.

'Maybe they hunt for laughs. In their spare time,' Winston proposed, still looking for prey.

'They're herbivores,' Quinlan stated, 'they don't eat meat.'

'What's rutting then?' Winston asked.

'It is all about showing off to does, impressing the female deer. Establishing your right to a mate,' Quinlan explained.

'Yeah, well, I'm doing that *as well* as honing my hunting skills,' he declared, strutting around in front of Josephine as if he was queen of the catwalk.

'What are you doing?' Josephine asked, looking on with a mixture of curiosity and pity.

'I'm rutting. I'm impressing my doe,' Winston replied.

'I'm not impressed, and I'm not your doe,' Josephine stated emphatically.

'I doubt stags would do it like that anyway,' I said, 'not to impress a doe.'

Winston froze, mid-pose, aware that strutting had turned, inadvertently, to mincing, and quickly adopted a macho stance.

'Okay! Okay! I'll stick to honing the hunting skills.' Winston squatted, ready to pounce.

'Very useful,' Josephine suggested with more than a hint of sarcasm.

'Hey! It's a natural instinct. I can't help myself.'

'Natural instinct, my arse,' Josephine replied.

'It is,' I said. 'It's in the genes.'

'And so's my arse,' Josephine quipped.

'It is!' I said. 'We evolved to be hunter-gatherers. Wiggins said so in biology.'

'And why would you believe Wiggins?' Quinlan asked.

'He's the teacher,' I replied.

'Oh! I see,' Quinlan acknowledged.

'But I'm more of a hunter,' Winston said, 'and you're more of a gatherer.'

'I'd be a fantastic gatherer,' I enthused, getting up off the bench. 'Everyone would want me for picking fruit off the top of the trees.' I mimed picking fruit off the top of ridiculously tall trees and passing it down to tiny people below.

'You are freakishly tall,' Winston agreed.

'Anyway, it takes more brains to be a gatherer than a hunter,' I proposed. Winston disagreed.

'You gotta be kiddin'. Hunting uses loads more skills. One minute, I'm stalking my prey, next minute, I'm throwing spears.' Winston threw an imaginary spear. 'Gathering, you're just picking stuff off trees.'

'You've got to figure out what is and isn't poisonous,' I said, rejecting an imaginary apple by tossing it over my shoulder.

'And how would you do that?' Quinlan asked.

'I'd feed it to the hunters,' I suggested. 'They're thick as chips.'

'Yup,' Josephine agreed, looking at Winston.

'Anyway, we have evolved since we were hunter-gatherers,' Tarquin proclaimed pompously.

'No, we haven't,' I replied flatly.

'Yes, we have!' he snapped back.

Quinlan cut in before we descended into pantomime. 'Are you saying our huge brains evolved just to hunt sabre-toothed tigers and gather nuts?'

'Yup,' I confirmed.

'What we do now is far more difficult,' Tarquin proclaimed.

'No, it's not,' I sniped.

'Yes, it is,' he sneered. 'How can hunting tigers and gathering nuts be more sophisticated than Latin?'

'Hey! It's hard waking up in a cave, then figuring out how to make clothes and a spear so you can go out and kill a sabre-toothed tiger, just to get back and realise you've got nothing to cook it on. Latin is piss easy after that,' I mocked.

'You've got to agree, he does have a point,' Winston said coolly.

'No, he does not. Latin is much harder.' Tarquin was not backing down.

'How do you know?' Josephine asked. I had the answer:

'Fortunately, we keep a sabre-toothed tiger in the nature reserve, so we can compare the two. On one side of the fence, we have people reading Latin, and on the other side, people hunting sabre- toothed tigers. At the end of the day, we count how many have died on each side.'

'I reckon you'd have more deaths reading Latin,' Quinlan muttered.

Winston was clearly moving in my direction. 'So, you're saying our brains have not got any bigger since we hunted sabre-toothed tigers.'

'Yup!' I agreed.

'So, if our brains evolved to this enormous size, just to hunt sabre-toothed tigers,' Winston pointed modestly to his own head, 'the true test of genius *must* be how good you are at killing sabre-toothed tigers,' he deduced.

'Yup! That and gathering nuts,' I said, reminding him of my own speciality.

'So not being good at maths doesn't mean you've got a small brain,' Winston proposed tentatively.

'Not if you can kill a sabre-toothed tiger,' I confirmed.

'Hey! That's cool,' Winston said cheerfully. He was sure, out of everyone there, he would be the best at doing that.

A very large pale-faced lady emerged from the doorway ringing the bell.

'Thar she blows,' I said.

'Mrs Pudding is not a whale,' Josephine chided.

'Yes, she is. She's got a blowhole and everything,' I replied.

Josephine shook her head at me as if I was an A-grade idiot. I smiled innocently.

'Come on, it's time for class,' Winston said, urging everyone up off the bench.

'Goodbye,' Josephine said with an expression of deep, deep sorrow, 'time for me to go and play with the girls.'

'What? Where?' Quinlan said.

'Home economics. No boys allowed,' she said cheerfully.

Home economics? Do you mean… cooking?' Tarquin asked.

'Cooking, sewing, and all you need to be a good wife and mother,' she said playfully.

'And boys cannot cook?' Quinlan inquired.

'You're right,' she confirmed. 'Boys cannot cook. It's a well-known fact.'

'I'd make a good cook,' I said confidently.

'And a good wife and mother,' Winston added. I sidled up

next to him and batted my eyelashes. He bent double holding his stomach, pretending to vomit. I was outraged, of course.

'If you've got home economics,' Tarquin said, 'what have we got?'

'We've got lessons in how to be a good husband and father,' I replied.

'What's that?' Tarquin asked.

'Metalwork,' I replied. 'Welcome to the factory floor.'

'See you later then,' Josephine said, waving goodbye.

'Okay! See you at lunchtime,' we replied.

We all picked up our bags, apart from Tarquin.

'Where is it?' he called out, looking round.

'Where's what?' I sniped, assuming Tarquin was just being a jerk.

'My briefcase. Where is my briefcase?' he said, panic written across his face.

'I don't know. It must be under the bench,' I said.

'No, it is not! It has gone! My briefcase has gone!' he announced anxiously.

We all checked around and under the bench, as if his eyesight was too poor to spot a briefcase from a few feet.

'It can't have gone,' Winston said. 'Josephine and Quinlan were watching the bags all the time.'

'Yeah, we were,' Josephine agreed.

'Not when Tarquin was injured,' Quinlan pointed out. 'We got off the bench and walked towards them then.'

'Oh yeah! I guess we did,' Josephine accepted.

We all looked around, hoping to spot the briefcase amongst the diminishing number of people in the playground. To no avail.

'What're we gonna do?' I wondered out loud.

'We will go to the headmaster and get him to carry out a search,' Tarquin demanded, angrily wagging a finger at us.

'We can't do that. It's not a prison camp,' Winston said.

'Then we will just have to carry out a search ourselves,' Tarquin commanded, stepping aggressively towards Winston, pushing him back with the palm of his hand. Winston didn't flinch.

'We can't just pop into classrooms and say "Don't mind us, we're just searching for a briefcase,"' Winston protested. 'They'd lock us up.'

'Well, you might be too scared, but I am searching for it now,' Tarquin stated, and spun round to march off.

'You won't find it,' Josephine shouted. 'No one's going to leave it knocking around. Come back, come back here. We'll sort it out,' she pleaded. Tarquin paused and reluctantly turned round.

'What are you going to do about it then?' he demanded.

'I don't know. I just know we do have to get to lessons,' Winston said calmly. 'We'll think of something.'

'We'll figure it out at lunchtime,' Josephine promised, 'when we've got more time.'

Tarquin was still laying out his demands. 'Okay! We meet here after dinner, and we sort it out.'

'Agreed!' We all nodded and headed towards the door. Josephine joined a group of girls and headed off in a different direction.

'Hi, Karen,' I said, catching up with the inevitable straggler. 'Have you seen anyone with a briefcase?'

'Apart from Winston?' she said.

'Apart from Winston,' I agreed.

'Ooh, I'm not sure,' she pondered. 'I'll let you know.'

'Thanks,' I said.

We made our way inside, leaving Karen outside. She racked her brain, rerunning pictures of playtime through her mind, slowing the slides as she caught a glimpse of something interesting, and pausing the picture as it came into view. A group of girls and boys stood with their back to her. Poking out from between a pair of legs, the edge of a black leather briefcase. She honed in on the legs. There was plenty to see. The skirt was hitched up high, revealing long, strong, female legs terminating in tartan socks and a pair of black Doc Martins.

She ran inside. 'Andrew,' she shouted down the corridor, 'I think I know who it is. The person with the briefcase. I think I know her.'

'Her? Who?' I asked.

'It might not be. I could have made a mistake. I probably made a mistake,' she spluttered.

'Who is it?' I asked again.

'I can't be sure,' she said nervously.

'Who is it?' I pressed.

'You can never be sure,' she dithered.

'Karen.' Winston drew her attention and spoke slowly, calmly, reassuringly. 'We know you can't be sure, but who the hell do you think it *might* be?'

Karen blurted it out: 'Scary. I think Scary's got it.' Then she turned and scuttled off to her lesson.

'Oh shit!' I said, with plenty of feeling. 'We've got trouble. Lots of trouble.'

'Come on!' Tarquin spun round to head back up the corridor. 'We are going to tell the headmaster, and we are going to tell him now, so he can reprimand her and return my briefcase.'

'It's not that simple,' Winston replied, grabbing him by the shoulder.

'Yes, it is,' Tarquin snapped, brushing away the hand. 'We go and find the headmaster, and we go now.'

Winston rushed round in front, with his hands held out as if trying to halt a raging bull. Tarquin stopped but was looking for a gap, ready to make a dash.

'Tarquin, stop!' Winston urged. 'There's no point going to the headmaster. He won't do anything.'

'Let me through,' Tarquin demanded.

Winston attempted to explain the difficulty whilst keeping the bull under control. 'If we go to the headmaster and say Mary has got your briefcase, he will ask for the evidence. The only evidence we have is that Karen saw her with it, but if he asks her, Karen will deny it because it will put her on Scary's hit list.'

'Scary's hit list? How can you be afraid of just one girl?' Tarquin taunted us, still looking for a way through.

'Scary's not a girl, she's a monster,' I said, with certainty.

'But just one girl?' Quinlan probed. 'One girl? How can she be that bad?'

'She's not one girl, she's an army,' I stressed.

'An army? Really?' Tarquin dismissed the notion as tosh and nonsense.

'Well, not an army exactly, but she has a lot of very weird, very unpleasant friends,' Winston clarified.

Tarquin stopped jigging around and looking for a way past and started to listen.

'She's got a gang. She hangs out with a bunch of deranged fifth formers,' I explained.

Winston painted a picture of insanity. 'In a cannibal kingdom, they'd be the ones stirring the pot, gleefully pushing bobbing heads back under the water with a large wooden spoon, and...' as if that wasn't enough... 'throwing in babies by the dozen from a big bucket by the pot.'

'Oh, come on! They can't be that bad,' Tarquin said doubtfully.

'They are!' I said, uncertain as to whether anybody was really that bad.

'Okay. If we are not going to the headmaster, how are we going to get my briefcase back?' Tarquin pressed. Winston lowered his hands, relaxed his shoulders and spoke calmly.

'Like I said, we'll think of a plan at lunchtime, a good plan, over dinner, when we've got time. We've got to get to class.' Tarquin nodded slowly, resigned to the approach. We all turned round and marched off down the corridor to the workshops.

7 BRIEF CASE OF BEATING METAL

When the grand masters of educational policy created grammar schools and secondary schools, they had a definite view of future job prospects. Secondary schools were provided with superb workshops, full of the finest machines for turning, cutting and carving metal and wood. Many even had car maintenance bays. Art was the missed opportunity. Being academic drop-outs, we all needed every leg up into employment available, so instead of painting pictures of Constable's countryside, we should have been painting and decorating instead. The school could have been repainted every year for free. Grammar schools, on the other hand, consisted almost entirely of ivory towers where students learnt Latin and Greek philosophy; the perfect grounding for accountancy and law. Nobody wants a grammar school student to get their hands dirty, apart from when it comes to tax evasion and cooking the books.

The sign on the door read *Danger, Men at Work.* We entered in.

'Hurry up, gentlemen, you're late.' Mr Trent stood at a heavy workbench at the front of the class.

'We've been showing Tarquin and Quinlan round, sir,' I said, hanging my blazer up on a set of pegs by the door, and dumping my bag on the floor. Winston, Quinlan and Tarquin followed suit, although Tarquin was obviously missing a bag.

'That's no excuse, Baker. I'm sure they don't tolerate tardiness at Rugby School,' Mr Trent said sternly. He grabbed four coarse white cotton aprons from the pegs at the front and passed them out to each of us.

'No, sir,' I acknowledged, looping the neck strap over my head and tying it at the waist.

'What's tardiness, sir?' Stewart asked from the back of the class.

Mr Trent ignored the question. 'You're on those workbenches over there,' he said to us, pointing. We followed his finger to a couple of heavy wooden benches with wind-out vices mounted on each side.

'What's tardiness, sir?' Stewart asked again.

There was silence as everyone turned to Stewart. He eventually raised his hand.

'Yes, Stewart,' Mr Trent said, well aware of the question that was about to arrive.

'What's tardiness, sir?'

'Tardiness, Higgins, is the art of being late, and, along with interrupting, it is one of the few skills you have truly mastered in my class.'

'Thank you, sir,' Stewart said earnestly, pleased he'd mastered anything. Mr Trent decided to leave the pupil happy in his delusion.

We stood around the workbenches. Mr Trent handed round a piece of paper with the day's instructions on it. At the top, it read, *How to make a poker.*

'What's a poker, sir?' came the query from the back of the class. Followed once again by silence. Finally, the arm went up once more.

'Yes, Higgins?'

'What's a poker, sir?'

'It's a pointed metal pole you use to rearrange the coals in the fire,' Mr Trent explained.

'Sir?'

'Yes, Higgins?'

'We've got radiators, sir.'

'Then make it a present for someone who has got a fire.'

'Yes, sir. I will, sir. Thank you, sir.'

We were each handed a narrow section square rod about 3 feet long. We would be heating this in the forge to beat the end into a point, create some decorative twists along its length and to form a handle. Quinlan was looking round, impressed by the machinery and tools, when his eye landed on a welded metal frame, loosely fashioned into the shape of a car.

'What is that?' he said, pointing to the framework.

'*That* is why Mr Trent has a strange hold over us. *That* is why we work so hard and *that* is the frame for a 250cc racing go-kart,' I explained.

'A go-kart? What is a go-kart doing in here?' Quinlan asked.

'Inspiration, motivation and hope,' Winston said. 'It inspires courage: "I too can build a car." It motivates us: "I too will work my butt off to build a car," and hope: "Hopefully, I won't f**k it up."' He took a bow as if he had just completed his one-man show. 'Thank you, thank you.' He took the applause from an imaginary audience.

I clapped politely. He responded emotionally.

'It's a gift, a gift! I just can't help myself.'

'But really,' Quinlan said, 'Why?'

'It's the fifth-form exam piece,' I explained. 'If we behave, we build a go-kart. Well, between six of us, which you race, on the track, outside.' I pointed through the window.

'What track?' Quinlan and Tarquin asked, scanning the sea of macadam stretching out from the window.

'It's out there, you just can't see it,' Winston explained mysteriously.

'A sort of Emperor's New Racetrack,' Quinlan quipped.

'No! It's real all right,' I said enthusiastically. 'They make it after school with tyres and barriers and stuff. It's fantastic. Honest.'

'It's on after school tonight,' Winston said. 'We're both in the Karting Club, so we'll be going.'

'You might get a chance to have a go. We can ask Mr Trent,' I offered.

'Is it dangerous?' Tarquin asked, a little uncertain.

'Yeah! Really dangerous,' I replied. 'They're really fast. I almost shat myself first time I had a go.'

'Okay, you four, bring your rods over to the forge,' Mr Trent instructed, beckoning us over. He passed us some extra heavy aprons and gloves, which we put on.

Mr Trent supervised our efforts at heating and working the metal, until eventually, something vaguely resembling a poker emerged.

There are few things better than beating the hell out of hot metal with a big hammer. It makes you understand what it is to be a man. Finally, we know what all that testosterone and truculence is for. Men have clearly evolved to beat metal. If we could all be blacksmiths, the world would be a happier place. After a gruelling day pounding iron in the fierce heat of a blazing forge, every ounce of aggression would be slaked and we would return home calm, caring and full of compassion; ready to cuddle the kids, caress the wife and cry over the sheer loveliness of it all. It's a real shame there just aren't enough shire horses needing a shoe to go round.

Although our school was short of master mathematicians, we had plenty who excelled in woodwork and metalwork; practical folk whose genius lay in their hands. Our school may not have furnished the law courts of England with barristers and judges, but it probably supplied the plumbers and electricians that built them. Unfortunately for them, practical skills were not part of the eleven-plus exam. There was no grammar school for skilled craftsmen, where they could scoff at the rejects doing Latin and Greek. Although they didn't get the respect they deserved, one day their wives would watch them plumbing a sink or wiring a circuit and think, *Thank God I didn't marry a lawyer.*

In the workshop, we put the finishing touches to our pokers, grinding off burrs and burnishing metal. We tied on name tags and stacked them on racks before brushing the chaff off the benches and hanging up our aprons.

The lunchtime bell rang loud and clear, before it was drowned out by a thousand voices clattering down the corridors. We let the others go before we grabbed our bags and made for the door.

8 BRIEFCASE AND BUNS

We sauntered along the corridor, slowly winding our way round to the back of the dinner queue. We would normally have raced round like an ostrich with its arse on fire, but we guessed running off and leaving our fledgling state schoolers to fend for themselves would probably be frowned upon. We weren't used to queuing for more than a few seconds. I was beginning to feel really hungry. Maybe it was the hunger; maybe it was bloody mindedness that made me call out to a latecomer that barged in front of us: 'Hey! You! Poo Bags! Get to the back! We were here first!'

The large fifth former turned slowly round, grabbed the lapel of my blazer, tightened his fist around the fabric and pulled me towards him, until our noses touched, his four bloodshot eyes burning into mine.

'What y'gonna do about it, dick face?' he said. Fear and anger left me shaking like a volcano that could either blow up, or fizzle out to nothing. He pushed me away slightly so he could focus on my face. 'Hey! Aren't you the kid that had his face flattened last week? Don't y' know when to shut it?'

Before the volcano could blow its top, Winston stepped in,

speaking to the kid in a conspiratorial kind of way, as if he was sharing his troubles. 'Look, you can make a bowl out of shit, but it's still shit.' He nodded to the kid as if the two of them were reconciled to some inevitable truth. The kid nodded back, probably embarrassed that he had no idea what Winston was on about, and made his way to the back of the queue.

'Was that witchcraft?' Quinlan asked, astounded.

'No,' I replied. 'Winston thinks he's found a universal saying that resolves all conflicts and brings peace to the world.'

Winston shrugged and grinned. 'It worked, didn't it? Anyway, maybe it does have magic powers. Maybe if someone had said that to Hitler, there wouldn't have been a second world war.'

'Maybe that's how it all started in the first place,' I suggested.

'What?' Tarquin was looking pretty confused by now.

'The Second World War. Maybe Hitler pushed in front of someone in the dinner queue and it all got out of hand,' I explained.

'If only I'd been there.' Winston shook his head as if the missed opportunity cut him deeply.

'I don't think saying, "You can make a bowl out of shit, but it's still shit," would have stopped the Second World War,' Tarquin said, dismissing it all as nonsense.

'How do you know?' Quinlan joined in. 'There is the Butterfly Effect.'

'I don't think butterflies would have stopped the Second World War either,' Tarquin said, rejecting the notion out of hand.

'Unless they were armed with machine guns and grenades,' Winston pointed out.

'Obviously,' I agreed.

'No! The Butterfly Effect is where a butterfly's wing can cause a hurricane on the other side of the world,' Quinlan explained.

'How big is this butterfly?' I said, assuming an enormous beast of a butterfly.

'It is an ordinary size butterfly,' Quinlan advised.

'Does it have special powers?' Winston asked.

'No!'

'Does it have a massive fan or something?' I queried.

'No! It is just an ordinary butterfly with no fan, no special powers and no butterfly god it prays to. It is just an ordinary f**king butterfly,' Quinlan answered, exasperated.

'Did you swear?' Winston scolded.

Quinlan shook his golden mane in frustration. He had given up trying to explain. It was clear we were going to have to wheedle it out of him.

'Well, how does it cause this hurricane then?' I asked.

Quinlan paused to clear his thoughts. 'It is just an idea, that something tiny on one side of the world can tip the balance to cause a chain reaction leading to a hurricane on the other side of the world. Small things can have a huge effect.'

'Oh! I get it.' It seemed to have clicked with Winston. 'You're saying a butterfly in Britain could cause a hurricane in Germany, stopping the Second World War.'

'No! No! Forget it!' We had pushed poor Quinlan too far. We attempted some form of reconciliation.

'We do understand. Honest,' I said. 'We're just taking the piss.'

'Yeah. We get the gist,' Winston confirmed. To prove it, he tried to explain his grasp of the theory.

'You're saying, if someone had said, "You can make a bowl out of shit, but it's still shit," to Hitler in the dinner queue, he might have got confused, stumbled over his words in his next big speech and the crowd might have gone, "You know, I think I preferred the other guy, the one that likes puppies and flower arranging," he gets elected, and instead of a world war, there is an epidemic of rabies and hay fever.'

'Correct!' Quinlan agreed.

'Can we get back to my briefcase?' Tarquin had been silent up to that point, pondering his own concerns, but now he wanted solutions. 'How are you going to get it back?'

'We'll talk about it while we eat,' Winston proposed. 'We're nearly at the counter.'

'All right, but it needs sorting,' Tarquin grumbled.

As we approached the counter, we each picked up a brown melamine tray and slid it onto the runners.

'What's on the menu?' I asked.

'I think it's meat in gravy, but it's hard to tell,' Winston replied, a little louder than he should have so close to the kitchen. A dinner lady raised her enormous ladle and threatened to dispatch Winston with one blow.

'You won't be getting seconds, young man,' she said, as if the threat was something we should fret over. Personally, I wasn't sure I could get through firsts.

'Sorry,' Winston apologised. 'It looks lovely. I just wasn't sure if it was beef or lamb.'

'Okay, my love. I'll let you off this once. Beef, lamb, they're so alike,' she said, accepting the apology.

'Which is it?' I queried.

'Chicken!' she replied, with a face full of thunder.

'What is for dessert?' Quinlan asked politely.

'Manchester tart,' the dinner lady replied.

'What is Manchester tart?' Quinlan asked again.

'Tart… from Manchester,' was the response. We hadn't had many conversations with the dinner ladies before, and I was beginning to see that as a blessing. We continued silently down the servery as mashed potato and stewed vegetables were heaped onto plates, plus extra gravy, and finally, on separate plates, the Manchester tart.

We made our way to a table in the corner with enough space for all of us and sat down. Tarquin and Quinlan inspected the contents of their plates, moving it around with their knives, as if carrying out a forensic examination of the ghastly remains of some unfortunate creature. Tarquin was the first to raise his head. He looked at the two of us, then looked back down at the plate, then he looked up again. His face was a mixture of pity and regret.

'Now I know why our school fees are worthwhile. I feel sorry for you,' Tarquin said, with uncharacteristic compassion.

We laughed out loud.

'That's the funniest thing you've said all day,' Winston said with a smile.

Tarquin stiffened, then relaxed, and laughed a little. 'What are we going to do about my briefcase?' he asked, but in a less demanding tone than usual.

'We need a plan,' I said.

'Let's get Josephine over here,' said Winston. 'She seemed to have a good head for this kind of thing.'

We looked around. She was on table four, a few rows away, chatting to a group of girls. 'I'll go,' I said. It wasn't until I was approaching the table that I remembered just how attractive she was; how confident she was; how impressive she was; and then I realised how many boys were watching me. I felt sick again, I began to sweat, my hands quivered, and my face turned red. I looked down. 'Er, Josephine. We'd... like you to er... join us... if that's okay?' I added.

The other girls looked me up and down as if scoring me out of ten as a possible suitor. I don't think I fared very well, as they soon turned back to each other and continued chatting.

'No problem,' Josephine agreed cheerfully. She said goodbye to her friends and followed me to our table and sat down in the empty seat.

'Hi,' she said. 'So, what's up?'

'We need a plan,' Winston said. 'A plan to get the briefcase back. Any ideas?'

'Do you know who's got it?' she asked, taking a seat.

'Scary Mary,' I said.

'It's easy then,' Josephine replied. 'Andy asks Scary Mary to give it back.'

'Me! You've got to be kidding. She's a f**kin lunatic,' I asserted.

'Did you swear in the presence of a lady?' Winston asked imperiously.

'Of course I f**kin swore,' I swore, even louder. 'I can't ask Scary. Not me. You know what she's like. She goes for me every time. She'll rip me balls off.'

'She's only a girl,' Josephine reminded me, but I knew different.

'She's not a f**kin girl, she's a f**kin psychopath,' I declared.

'Keep your f**kin voice down,' Winston instructed. 'Unless, of course, you want Scary to hear everything you're saying.'

I looked around anxiously. I couldn't see her. I sighed and sank down into my chair.

'She's just a girl,' Josephine repeated.

'She is not a girl,' I stated, somewhat quieter than before.

'Look, all you've got to do is ask for the briefcase back. How bad can it be?' Quinlan asked.

'How bad?! How bad! You've seen her, Winston. She's a nutter, isn't she?' I pleaded desperately.

'She's not that bad,' Winston suggested.

'Not that bad! She's like a rabid dog. She goes for me… she… she… grabs me… bits,' I spluttered.

'Don't worry. We've got your back,' Winston said calmly.

'It's not my back I'm worried about,' I said.

'She cannot do anything. This is a school. There are teachers around,' Quinlan suggested. I don't think he could believe the fuss I was making.

'Why can't Tarquin do it? It's his briefcase,' I said pointedly.

'We can't ask Tarquin. He's… a… guest,' Winston explained.

'Why not Josephine? You're a girl. She won't go for you,' I said, abandoning any semblance of chivalry.

'She doesn't want me. She wants you. We have to give her what she wants,' Josephine said matter-of-factly.

'Why?' I demanded. It was all so unfair.

'Because,' Josephine explained, 'she won't give me the briefcase… but she just might give it to you.'

'After she's stripped me naked and wired me bits to a 12-volt battery,' I winced.

'Twelve volts is not that bad,' Quinlan said.

'Oh, she's already done it to you, has she?' I sniped.

'No, just saying,' Quinlan replied apologetically.

'Why can't we all go? Why can't we all ask her?' I said, in desperation.

''Cos that's aggressive. She'll just say "No!"' Josephine explained.

'She wants to be on top,' Winston suggested.

'I don't want her on top,' I stated emphatically.

'She wants control. She wants power. So you have to be vulnerable,' Josephine advised.

'I am vulnerable,' I confirmed.

'Well, it might just work then,' Josephine said, upbeat.

'But why should I? Why should I do it?' I squeaked, my pitch rising with anxiety.

'You're the reason she's got the briefcase,' Josephine said.

'No, I'm not. You were watching the bags,' I said defensively.

'Yes, you are. You know you are. You told Tarquin the wrong rules for the rubber game,' she said coolly.

'So what?' I replied, as if that shouldn't make any difference.

Josephine tidily wrapped up the case for the prosecution:

'If he hadn't got attacked, we wouldn't have been distracted, and the briefcase wouldn't have been stolen. That's the truth. You're responsible.'

'You told me the wrong rules for the rubber game?' Tarquin said angrily.

'Oh, for God's sake!' I didn't want a fight with Tarquin as well. 'All right. All right, I'll do it. But stay nearby, so you can rescue me,' I pleaded.

'Of course we will, you'll be all right,' Winston said, trying to calm my anxiety.

'There's nothing to be afraid of, honest,' Josephine said, in the same tone my mum used before I had a tooth extracted.

'We'll do it straight after lunch,' Winston proposed.

'You mean, I'll do it straight after lunch,' I replied despondently.

'Yeah. You'll do it straight after lunch,' Winston agreed.

'Better sooner than later,' Quinlan joined in chirpily.

'Okay! Okay! I said I'll do it, so I'll do it.' The plan was set; my fate was sealed. Everyone, apart from me, heaved a huge sigh of relief and started to work their way through the agglomerate of objects that was the main course. Gradually, the plates emptied, and attention turned to dessert.

'Is Manchester tart a real thing?' Quinlan asked.

'Of course it is a real thing. It is there, on the plate, in front of you,' Tarquin replied, looking at Quinlan somewhat bewildered.

'I know it is there, on the plate. But does it exist outside this school?' Quinlan clarified.

'It won't explode if you take it outside the gates,' I said, nonplussed.

'How do you know? Have you tried?' Winston enquired.

'I mean, outside this school, would anyone recognise a Manchester tart?' Quinlan asked.

'Ask the people of Manchester,' Winston said.

'Ask a tart,' I chipped in, unfortunately whilst looking at Josephine.

'Ask a twat,' Josephine said, looking at me.

'You know what I mean, like a Bakewell tart, or a Chelsea bun,' Quinlan explained further.

'Or an Eccles cake,' Tarquin added.

'Or a Rugby bun,' I proposed.

'Rugby buns are not a thing,' Winston said.

'Yes, they are,' I stated.

'No, they are not,' Tarquin replied.

'You buy 'em at the baker's in the centre,' I said. 'They've got a rugby ball on the top.'

'That is the game not the town,' Quinlan said.

'Oh, we're doing towns, are we?' I asked.

'Yes, we're doing towns,' Quinlan confirmed.

'So, Eccles is a town?' I enquired.

'Of course it's a town. What did you think it was?' Winston said.

'I thought eccles were small freckles,' I said honestly.

'Small freckles? Why small freckles?' Quinlan asked.

'You know... icky bicky freckles... eccles,' I explained. 'The currants are like little freckles.'

'You're nuts. You don't get buns named after mad things,' Josephine stated.

'What about Bath buns?' Winston said.

'What about them?' Quinlan asked.

'They're named after a bath,' Winston said smugly.

'No, they're not,' Tarquin said.

'They're just a bun made in a bath, aren't they?' I queried.

'Why the hell would you make a bun in a bath?' Josephine said.

'No mixing bowls? I dunno,' I said, shrugging.

'A Bath bun is a bun, made in a place called Bath,' Quinlan stated.

'There's a place called Bath?' I asked.

'Yeah,' Tarquin advised.

'Weird,' I replied.

'Anyway, I was just saying, this school is the only place in the whole wide world I have ever seen a Manchester tart,' Quinlan proclaimed.

'Have you ever been to Manchester?' Winston asked.

'No,' Quinlan admitted.

'Maybe that's where you should look first,' Winston suggested sensibly.

'Is this it?' Josephine asked.

'What?' I said.

'Is this what I've been missing?' she asked.

'What do you mean?' I asked, dumbfounded.

'Is this what boys talk about?' she said, looking sorry for us.

'Cake? Yeah, mostly,' I confessed.

'Cake and ponies and knitting and dollies and make-up,' Winston added.

'And the latest fashions,' I chipped in on theme.

'Latest fashions? Really? And where's the evidence?' she responded sharply.

'Here, darling. I am fashion. I ooze fashion. This blazer's Dior,' I said.

'But your jumpers are pink,' she revealed.

'Even the girls,' I said, realising news of my fashion *faux pas* had reached every corner of the school.

'You wear pink jumpers?' Quinlan asked, somewhat surprised.

'I did once,' I said, 'but never again.'

'He still bears the scars.' Winston nodded sympathetically.

'Emotional?' Quinlan asked.

'Always, darling,' Winston replied.

'Emotional scars, moron,' Josephine said, glaring at Winston.

'More physical really.' I grimaced at the memory.

'Pink brings out the brute in some boys,' Winston said.

'I took a bit of a beating,' I admitted.

'Why? I mean, it was a truly horrible jumper, but it didn't deserve a beating,' Josephine said with a degree of compassion.

'I became a legitimate target,' I said, shrugging as though it was inevitable.

'I didn't know boys had such a passion for fashion,' Josephine said.

'They chased me round the playing field shouting "Gay boy, gay boy," then jumped on me,' I explained.

'Are you gay?' Quinlan asked, intrigued.

'No!' I said emphatically.

'It wasn't nasty,' Winston explained, 'it was just a game, a bit of fun.'

'Did you join in?' Josephine asked.

'Yeah, but just for the chase,' Winston said.

'Thanks!' I said sarcastically.

'Hey, I did stop Gus Drayton punching your lights out,' Winston said in his defence.

'True. He went berserk,' I said, recalling the hate in his eyes.

'What did you do?' Tarquin asked.

'I took the f**kin' jumper off. I don't want people thinking I'm gay,' I said.

'Why?' Quinlan asked.

'Because they'll beat me up, that's why,' I said, as if stating the obvious.

'It must be hard for gay kids,' Quinlan said.

'Are there any gay kids?' I asked.

'There must be gay kids if there are gay men,' Quinlan asserted.

'People might become gay when they're older,' I said.

'Gay kids know they're gay when straight kids know they're straight,' Quinlan said, matter-of-factly.

'How do you know?' I asked.

'I read it in the newspaper.'

'Why aren't there any here then?' I looked around.

'There will be,' Quinlan said.

'I've not met any,' I argued.

'How d'y'know?' Winston asked. 'You can't be sure.'

'I'd know.'

'They don't all wear pink jumpers,' Quinlan said.

'They're not going to let anyone know, are they?' Winston added.

'Why?' I asked

'They'd get beaten up,' Winston reminded me.

'I guess so,' I said uncertainly.

'They thought you looked gay and you got beaten up. Think what would happen if they *knew* you were gay,' Quinlan said.

I paused for thought. Wearing the pink jumper had been scary. Never being able to take it off would have been a nightmare. I felt strangely sick.

'I don't suppose you could tell… anyone,' I murmured.

'Not even your best friend,' Winston said.

'You'd have to be really, really careful,' Josephine said, nodding slowly.

'I'm useless at keeping secrets,' I said. 'I wouldn't last a day.'

'You might do if you were scared enough,' Quinlan suggested.

'Hmm, yeah, maybe,' I mumbled. Then my grasshopper mind jumped to something else. 'Hey! It'd be weird in the changing room. It'd be like me getting changed in the girls' changing room.'

'No, it wouldn't. You'd stick out in a girls' changing room,' Josephine said.

'In more ways than one,' I quipped, but Josephine was not amused.

'No one would know if there was a gay kid in the boys' changing room,' Winston said.

'They might fancy me when I'm naked,' I said.

'With that body?' Josephine looked doubtful.

I curled my biceps like a bodybuilder and attempted the "majestic" look but got the "oh really" look in return.

'Gay kids are not going to be staring at naked boys,' Quinlan said dismissively.

'Why not? If I was in the girls' changing room, I'd stare at naked girls,' I said.

'Oh no, you wouldn't. We would make absolutely sure you didn't. You'd be lucky to leave with everything still attached,' Josephine threatened.

Quinlan made the case. 'They would not be staring at boys because, A, they have to get changed, B, they do not want to be found out, and C, it is probably the worst place in the world to be a gay kid.'

'Why?' I asked.

'Because,' Winston said, 'if you get found out, you get beaten up, and in the changing room, no one can hear you scream.'

'Apart from the other people in the changing room,' I pointed out.

'Apart from them, but they aren't gonna help you,' Winston said confidently, 'they'd be too busy joining in.'

'Okay, yeah, I guess it would be a pretty bad place to be gay,' I acknowledged.

'Is there a good place to be gay?' Quinlan asked.

'Well, I like it,' Tarquin stated categorically.

'What?' we responded in unison.

'The Manchester tart. I think it is… tasty.' Tarquin licked his lips to make the point.

'The tart! You like the tart!' I replied, with double helpings of incredulity.

'Food poisoning. Must be.' Winston looked concerned.

'Addled his brain,' Josephine added.

We waited for Tarquin to finish off his last piece of tart.

'Time to play Hunt the Scary,' Winston said.

'Can we use a harpoon?' I asked, not expecting a response, and not getting one.

We got up, pushing back our chairs, which screeched as they scraped across the lino tiles. We left the pile of empty plates on the table and wiggled around the table maze to the door. We made our way down the corridor, our conversations encrypted by echoes. I turned to Winston.

'Hey, Winston, we could be the only straight kids in the school. How would we know otherwise?'

'Funny,' Winston replied, 'I thought we were the only gay kids.'

I tried to decipher Winston's expression, but his features gave nothing away. *I guess we don't know anything,* I thought, *and I guess it doesn't matter.* We walked past the trophy cabinet, through the cloakroom, and out into the sunlight once more.

9 THE BRIEFCASE AND THE BITCH

We looked out across the east playground from the top of the steps. There were no signs of Scary or her friends. We walked down the wide path running in front of the main façade, the wall of glass glinting in the sunlight. Opposite, the playing fields stretched out in front of us. Two rugby pitches took pride of place, the huge posts an impressive landmark.

Kids were already playing the rugby post game. Two teams either side of the posts, throwing a tennis ball at the crossbar, in the hope it would hit and return to be caught for a point, instead of passing to the other side. I desperately wanted to join them, but I was on a mission, a mission I couldn't avoid. We looked out over the playing fields, shielding our eyes from the sun, scanning the horizon for a specific silhouette. There were kids chatting and chasing, the odd scuffle, and even an impromptu cricket match, but no sign of Scary. We walked to the very end of the path where it reached the car park and the games court. A few loners wandered aimlessly, lost in their own thoughts, but still no sign of Scary.

'Nobody here,' I said. 'Maybe she's gone home. Maybe she goes home for lunch.'

'No, she doesn't,' Winston said. 'We've seen her before in the dining room. She'll be round the other side. Come on.'

We turned back and made our way round to the north playground. This was where the go-karting would take place after school. To the left, at the end of the tarmac, a tall blue wall enclosed the outdoor swimming pool, behind which was the nature reserve. It was an extremely chilly October and we had been excused the excruciating torture of diving into an unheated open-air pool. Even Mr Rubble, the PE teacher, a man with few feelings in general, and none when it came to the cold, didn't fancy breaking the ice before taking a dip. So, the covers were on, the gates were locked, and this little enclave, forlorn and forgotten, was left abandoned, waiting for the onset of spring.

A motley crew of miscreants slouched against the turquoise blue, a pose intended to convey arrogance, contempt and scorn. Straggly hair, nicotine-stained fingers and Doc Martin boots shouted 'rebel!' but whispered neglect. Four boys and three girls dictating their terms to a world unwilling to listen. This was performance art and they had mastered their style. It would've been magnificent; it would've been fine, if they weren't such an unrelenting bunch of bastards.

The boys weren't obviously aggressive. They didn't shake with rage, eyes ablaze, baying for blood. They weren't werewolves. They were more like hyenas waiting for the weak to separate from the herd; the child left behind in the playground, the last kid in the cloaks, or the lone boy in the toilet block. Kids were pushed down muddy banks and dragged through puddles. Heads were pushed down toilets, bags torn open, clothes ripped and holes burnt through anoraks with cigarettes. And then there were the fights; the scars on their faces and the scabs on their knuckles bore testament to those.

Fighting wasn't all bad, and it wasn't just for dropouts, ne'er-do-wells, and good-for-nothing evil scum. Everyone, well, all the boys, would have a scrap at some time, and many were serial scrappers. There was nothing wrong with that. Fighting was a sport. It had rules; it had arrangements; it had honour. A fight was considered the most respectable way of resolving a dispute. Participants would meet after school in a prescribed place; seconders would hold the combatant's blazer, and a watchful crowd would ensure rules were obeyed. When someone gave in and surrendered, the fight would stop. Apart from the few who didn't know when to walk away, nobody was beaten to a pulp. The principle injury was fatal embarrassment; having to face your mates the next day, knowing you had been humiliated in the ring; that heart-sinking feeling when your head is in your hands, your pride is in your boots and dignity is down the drain. There were no knives, just bare knuckles, boots and the occasional head butt. Biting, scratching and hair pulling were off limits; they were strictly for the girls. The world, with all its little imperfections, worked perfectly well, because we all knew the rules, and we all abided by them.

Apart from the boys by the wall. That's what made them scary. You didn't know where you stood, you didn't know what rules applied, and you didn't know what they were going to do. The fights didn't even start in the time-honoured way. There was no dispute, no prescribed place, no seconder, no watchful crowd, and when you fell, there was no safety net. After school, they lurked in the alleyways and ginnels that filtered through the housing estates, looking for their next victim.

Dangerous though they were, during a period of inactivity, they didn't do much more than slouch. There was the occasional utterance, obscene gesture or gobbing, but apart from that, there was very little to entertain the casual observer.

Queen Mary and her crones were a different kettle of fish. They were artistes and we were the audience. All they needed was a little illicit accompaniment. Mary removed a portable radio from her blazer pocket and tuned the dial to a crackling AM radio station playing the latest sounds. Over the fizzing interference, you could just make out the slow, steady beat of a bass guitar and sweeping chords of a synthesiser. They were entranced by the sound, dancing around, slow and slinky, twirling their arms as they slithered and swayed, like a praying mantis enchanting its prey. The Queen in the middle, a powerful muscular figure, ruling over her slender soulmates, who danced for her delight and purred in her presence.

Their look was carefully crafted. The enormous Windsor knot hung loose around the neck, leaving a short, stubby spike, sneering contempt for the tie that should have been. The half-unbuttoned blouse gaped open, allowing a sly glimpse of a black bra beneath. Big socks, bovver boots and a short, short skirt completed the outfit. Hair was meticulously tousled to appear unruly and wild. Thick black eyeliner, ruby red lips and rouged cheeks emphasised their exaggerated expressions. Two tattoos of big lips with a long, extended tongue, high up on the inner thigh of each leg, licked each other as they danced around. At a time when tattoos only adorned sailors and cell mates, this was art intended to shock, and it did. They were the quintessential vamp; exotic, erotic and cruel; a cross between the mad witches of *Macbeth* and Morticia Addams.

This was my destiny; this was my fate. It was time to be a man, but I was only a child.

'I can't, I can't. No! Look! I mean I can't, can I?' I turned quickly and bumped into Winston.

'Yes! You can! Go. On.' He span me round and nudged me back in destiny's direction.

'They're only human,' Quinlan cried, geeing me on.

'No, they're not! Look at 'em!' I directed their gaze to the weird creatures by the wall. 'They're not human, They're f**kin' aliens. They'll take me to their mother ship, rip out my innards and replace me with a robot.'

'Don't be ridiculous,' Josephine snapped.

'I'll be an automaton walking round with straight arms, glazed eyes, going beep every five seconds.' I made like a robot to illustrate the point.

'Yeah, but how will we spot the difference?' Winston joked.

'Come on, it'll only take seconds,' Josephine urged.

'It only takes vampires a second to suck your blood,' I replied.

'I thought they were aliens,' Quinlan mentioned.

'Alien vampires. They turn you into a mechanical bat,' I explained.

'A mechanical bat? Why a mechanical bat?' Josephine asked, briefly drawn in by the distraction.

'I'd need an aerial to connect with the mother ship,' I said, as if the answer was obvious.

'Could be a cyborg bat,' Quinlan suggested.

'True!' I responded, nodding appreciatively.

'Or, a biological bat using telepathy,' Winston added.

'Good point,' I agreed.

'No, it's not!' Josephine cut through my carefully crafted delaying tactics. 'Look, I'm not spending the next half hour debating the difference between cyborg bats, mechanical bats, or any other kind of bat. The bell'll be going any minute. Go and get that briefcase. Now!'

If I'd been ordered by anyone else, I would have told them to get lost, but it was Josephine, and I knew if I didn't do this, I wouldn't be able to face her ever again. I couldn't let that happen. It had to be done, and I knew it had to be done now.

'Okay, okay. But stay nearby. Grab my feet if they beam me up,' I said, girding my loins.

'Sure,' Josephine said, playing along half-heartedly.

'Go on,' Winston prodded.

'Okay, I'm going,' I said, uncertain my feet would do the walking. I slowly meandered towards the menacing menagerie.

'Hello, Dick!' Mary said.

'I'm not Dick,' I replied nervously, glancing round to see if there was anyone else she could have been referring to.

'Funny, you look like a dick from where I'm standing,' she sneered, her witches dancing around, dark smiles upon their lips.

'Er, no, I'm A... Andrew,' I stuttered. I felt like a lamb to the slaughter, and she was the butcher.

'Hmm. So, *Andrew*, the boy has become a man at last. Your balls have finally dropped, and you've come to have them weighed.' Her voice was slow and sinister, and all the time she fixed me with those evil eyes.

'Er... no, no! I came about the briefcase... just the briefcase,' I spluttered. I got the feeling this was not going well.

'What briefcase?' she asked knowingly.

'Tarquin's briefcase. The black one with the clip on the top.'

'The rich kid?' she asked, stroking her neck.

'Yes! The rich kid,' I agreed, nodding.

'Has he lost his briefcase?' she said innocently.

'You know he's lost his briefcase.' I was a mouse in the grip of a playful cat.

'Why would I?' she teased.

'Someone saw you with it.'

'Oh really? And who was that?' Her unblinking eyes demanded an answer.

'I can't say.' I wasn't serving Karen to this psychopath. The secret would go with me to the grave.

'Oh yes, you can. Help me out and I will help you,' she advised forcefully, whilst her underlings danced around, casting their spells.

'I don't know,' I pleaded.

'I'm sure the boys will help you remember,' she said, looking over at the muscle by the wall.

'Winston told me,' I blurted.

'Oh!' She held no sway over Winston. She knew she would get no further with him. The conversation turned.

'Well, I don't know where your briefcase is,' she said dismissively.

'But I have to get it back… I have to.'

'Why?' she probed.

'I just do. It's important. Please give it to me. Please,' I begged. I was close to tears; I could feel my eyes welling up.

'Aw, look at him, he's going to cry,' she said to her weird sisters.

'Poor little baby,' they cried.

'So sweet! You want to lick him all over,' she said, whilst the vamps licked the air in anticipation.

'Well, I have to help little babies, don't I?' she said.

'Poor little baby,' the weird sisters chorused.

'It's my maternal instinct,' she said, hands on heart.

'Y… y… you will give me the briefcase?' I asked hopefully.

'I will do what I can to get the briefcase, but you'll have to meet me after school, half past four with the rich kid,' she instructed.

'Which rich kid?'

'The one that owns the briefcase.'

'But he can't. He'll be going back to Rugby School,' I explained.

'Oh no, he won't,' Mary asserted, wagging her finger at me.

'He will,' I squeaked.

'He won't, 'cos he won't get his briefcase if he's not here, will he?' she explained coolly.

'But where? Where will we meet?' I asked.

'Back gate to the swimming pool,' she said.

'Why can't it be somewhere else?' I asked desperately. The back gate was well hidden from the rest of the school.

'It just can't,' she said. 'Half past four, back gate to the pool, if you want the briefcase.'

'Okay. I'll find a way,' I said. I was eager to make a move. The muscle was beginning to take an interest in me, and I didn't want to be on their radar.

'Say thank you,' she instructed, reminding me of my manners.

'Thank you,' I said, keen to get away.

'Thank you... *Mary*,' she instructed firmly.

'Thank you, Mary,' I repeated.

'Good boy. Now run along.'

I could hear them laughing loudly behind my back as I ran back to my friends.

'So, where's the briefcase?' Tarquin asked, looking at the empty space under my right hand.

'She wouldn't give it to me,' I answered gloomily.

'So what are we going to do now?' Tarquin demanded.

'She won't give it to me now,' I said, 'but she will give it to me later, half past four, after school.'

'That's all right. That'll be fine. What's the problem with that?' Winston asked, wondering why I looked so glum.

'She wants Tarquin there too,' I explained.

'But I'm going back at four,' Tarquin said hotly.

'I know,' I said. 'But she won't give it back to me any earlier. She said half past four.'

'You'll have to go back and tell her four o'clock,' Tarquin instructed.

'She won't change her mind,' I said, shrugging my shoulders.

'He's right,' Josephine advised. 'She won't negotiate. It's a take-it-or-leave-it offer.'

'So what now?' Tarquin asked.

'I could disguise myself as Tarquin,' Winston suggested half-heartedly.

'I don't think so,' Josephine said. 'I'd have a better chance of fooling her than you.'

'I wasn't really serious,' Winston confessed.

'Tarquin will just have to be here at half past four,' Quinlan stated. 'There's no other choice.'

'What're we gonna do? Break you out of Rugby School?' Winston said, baffled.

'No. We just need a good reason to stay here.' Tarquin pointed at Quinlan and himself. 'If we have a good reason, we can ring the housemaster and he will pick us up later.'

'Yeah, but what could possibly be the reason?' Winston asked. We all stood in silence, pondering possible excuses for hanging around after school. Nothing came to mind.

'Go-karts!' Quinlan cried all of a sudden. 'The go-karts! We say we have been asked to attend the go-karts. He won't refuse if he thinks we have been asked.'

'Okay,' Tarquin said, 'but what time do the go-karts finish?'

'Half past five,' I said.

'Perfect,' Quinlan said encouragingly. 'The housemaster picks us up at half past five and takes us back for tea at six.'

'We'll have to speak to Mr Trent,' I said, working out the implications.

'Yeah, but he'll be all right. He loves showing off his fancy cars,' Winston advised.

Ring! Ring! Mrs Pudding waddled round the corner, bell in hand, waving it up and down with considerable force. Ring! Ring!

'C'mon, we've got to see Mr Trent before he starts teaching.'

We ran back in through the cloaks, down the corridor to the workshops, and piled in through the door.

'Damn, he's not here,' I said, disappointed.

A voice came from the workshop stores.

'You are supposed to wait outside until I call you in. Now go back out until I'm ready.'

'Mr Trent, sir,' Winston called out.

'Out! Now!' Mr Trent ordered.

'Mr Trent, sir, we need to speak to you, sir,' Winston called again.

A head popped round the corner of the door.

'Grahame and Baker? What are you doing here? You haven't got a lesson with me now.'

'I know, sir. We wanted to check with you, sir. Would it be all right for Tarquin and Quinlan to join the go-kart club tonight, sir? They're really keen.'

'We were so impressed that you made your own go-karts,' Quinlan explained. 'We do not do anything like that at Rugby School. It is amazing.'

'Well, it is a little amazing, I have to admit,' Mr Trent said, grabbing a cloth rag off a workbench. 'They are fantastic machines. Top quality.'

'How did you manage to design them?' Quinlan asked, sounding impressed.

'I used to be in automotive engineering,' Mr Trent replied, wiping oil off his hands with the rag. 'Piece of cake really, when you know what you're doing.'

'Would it be okay for them to join us, sir?' I asked hopefully.

'Well, there are normally subs and things, but provided Rugby School think it's okay, then I'm sure it would be okay for them to join us next week.'

'Next week!' I exclaimed.

'It has to be tonight, sir,' Winston said, a little more calmly.

'And why is that?' Mr Trent asked, intrigued by the urgency.

'They're... they're... they're practising medieval Latin chants next week, and the week after,' I said, assuming that was what they did in all private schools.

'Medieval chants?' Mr Trent reeled back in horror. 'Rather you than me,' he said, dropping the oily rag into a bin by the bench.

'So, would tonight be possible?' Quinlan asked politely. 'It's our only chance.'

'If you can get permission from Rugby School,' Mr Trent conceded.

'We've already spoken to the head, and he contacted Rugby School to check. They said it was okay,' Winston lied, convincingly.

'Our housemaster is picking us up at half past five,' Quinlan embellished.

'Well, it's a bit presumptuous.' Mr Trent folded his arms and looked up at the ceiling, nodding as he thought through any implications. 'But... yes... I think we can fit you in.'

'Thanks, Mr Trent. That's fantastic,' I replied gleefully.

'See you at four o'clock down by the track,' he said.

'We'll be there,' Winston confirmed.

'Now you'd better head off to your next lesson,' Mr Trent said, smiling, clearly delighted by our enthusiasm for his Karting Club.

'Yes, sir, thank you, sir,' we choroused.

We darted out of the room and back up the corridor, away from the ears of the awaiting kids.

'Medieval f**kin chants! Are you out of your mind?' Winston exclaimed.

'I panicked and said the first thing that came into my head,' I said honestly.

'You could have left us to fill in the detail,' Tarquin suggested.

'I panicked. It worked, didn't it?' I said in justification.

'I know, but medieval chants!' Tarquin said, shaking his head.

'Well... er... actually, Andrew does have a point,' Quinlan said. 'The Latin Psalms in choir are probably medieval.'

'Aha! Not so stupid,' I said smugly.

'No! Choir is on a Friday,' Tarquin said, as if that made all the difference. It was time for me to shake my head.

'Right, what do we do now?' Quinlan asked.

'We've got to get to the admin office, and quick,' Winston replied.

THE BRIEFCASE AND THE BITCH

We walked down the corridor. Running was strictly forbidden, but our legs were moving so quickly it made very little difference. We turned the corner into the staff corridor and marched on up to the office. Winston knocked on the door. It was opened by Mrs Goodfellow.

'Can I help you?' she said, smiling.

'Quinlan turned on the charm. 'Yes, thank you. Mr Trent kindly offered us the opportunity to join his go-karting club tonight. We are very keen to go. It is such a wonderful club. But we need to check with our housemaster first. You see, he will have to pick us up later than was originally intended. I hope you don't mind, but could we use the phone?'

'Do you know the number?' she asked.

'Yes. I have it written on a piece of paper.' Quinlan drew a neatly folded piece of paper out of his back pocket and handed it to Mrs Goodfellow.

'Yes, that will be fine. Come in, all of you. You're blocking the corridor.'

We all crammed into the admin office whilst Quinlan made the all-important call.

'Hello. Can I speak to Mr Pickering, please...? It is Quinlan... Quinlan Weston-Smythe... Hello, sir... We have been asked to attend a go-kart club this evening... I know, sir, it is short notice, but our new friends are in the go-kart club, sir, and they are keen for us to join them... Yes, Tarquin has also made friends, sir... Thank you, sir... That is very kind, sir... Half past five, sir... In the staff car park... Where you dropped us off... Thank you... Yes, we will... Goodbye.'

'Well? What did he say?' Tarquin asked, as if he hadn't overheard.

'He said it was okay. He's picking us up at half past five,' Quinlan replied.

'Fantastic!' Tarquin proclaimed.

Mrs Goodfellow ushered us towards the door. 'Come on, there's no time to celebrate. You should be in your next lesson.'

'Thank you, Mrs Goodfellow. Thank you,' we responded cheerily.

'That's fine, now run along.'

10 BAD LANGUAGE

We headed off down to the English faculty, room 1.06. We spotted Karen entering the class as we turned the corner. We were the last to arrive, but students were still getting out their exercise books, waiting for instruction from Mrs Penn.

'Miss,' I said, 'would it be possible to move some people around? We have been asked to sit next to Tarquin and Quinlan.'

Mrs Penn ordered some reluctant students to move to the back of the room, and we occupied the tables to the front. She laid out our instructions:

'Today, we are carrying on with reading comprehension. For the benefit of our new students, Quinlan and Tarquin, I will run through the process once again. Everyone in turn come to the front and I will give you a colour. Select a card of that colour from the box on my desk. Write the number of the card and the colour at the top of the page in your exercise book. The card includes a short text from a newspaper, magazine or book, followed by a series of questions. Read the text, and then answer the questions. At the end of the lesson, hand in your exercise books for me to mark. Any questions?'

'How will you know what card is right for us?' Tarquin asked rather nervously.

'Don't worry, I've spoken to your English teacher, Mr Quill, and he has helped me select something suitable.'

'Oh, thank you,' Tarquin replied.

'No problem. Now, back row, can you line up first, please.'

When the student reached the desk, the teacher handed them a coloured piece of paper which the student took to the box. All the cards in the box were sorted into rows by colour, and in front of each row was a space for the student to place their coloured paper. When they had selected a card, they returned to their seat to begin the exercise.

'Next row,' the teacher shouted, and the process was repeated.

'Second row.' The routine was repeated once again.

'Front row. Time for you to come up.' The teacher beckoned to Tarquin and Quinlan. We lined up at the desk, received our colours and went to the box. Mrs Penn handed Tarquin and Quinlan their cards and an exercise book in which to complete their answers.

We weren't streamed in English. We weren't streamed in any class. This system was Mrs Penn's attempt to teach to our ability. The colours avoided an obvious 1 to 5 or A to E grading. One of the great things about secondary school was the belief we were all equal; equally stupid maybe, but equal nevertheless. There was no underclass, because we were all underclass. There was no intellectual snobbery at our school.

Mrs Penn's class, however, was the only time I got a sense of the vast range of academic ability being taught. One week, I had been happily reading and answering questions on *Watership Down*, but the next week, I accidently picked up the wrong colour card. The writing was big, but the words were small. There was virtually nothing on the card. I was lucky. I found reading easy, and assumed everybody else did too. I was kind of shocked and surprised at the time. I never mentioned it to anyone. I didn't know what colour they were on.

I looked across the desk. Quinlan was green, same as me. Tarquin was blue. Blue was middle ability. Middle for our school but presumably way down the list for Rugby School. I didn't get it. Tarquin could read Latin, or so he said, but struggled with English. How did that work? I wondered whether it was better to be at the top of a secondary school, the bottom of a grammar school, or the middle of a comprehensive. Where was the best place to be?

'We need to figure out what we are going to do,' I whispered to Winston.

'What do you mean?' he whispered back.

'How to make sure me and Tarquin don't get beaten up by a bunch of homicidal nutters.' I thought it was obvious to everyone. It was to me.

'You'll be all right,' Winston said confidently.

'How do you know? Look what happened to George, they broke his f**kin nose,' I mentioned, with more than a hint of anxiety.

'We don't know it was them. George doesn't know it was them,' Winston said dismissively.

'He won't say, but he knows all right,' I assured him.

Winston tried to look comforting. 'We'll make sure you're sorted. Don't you worry.'

'I'm scared,' I confessed.

'Baker, are you whispering?' Mrs Penn asked, though it wasn't really a question.

'No, miss,' I lied.

'Are you telling me it was just the wind?' Her expression suggested she knew better.

'From your arse' came the whispered comment from behind, combined with a pencil point in the back.

'Oh! Now the wind seems to be blowing from a different direction… George?' The shift of attention was worth the pencil in the back.

'Yes, miss?'

'Please share your thoughts with the rest of the class,' Mrs Penn said patiently.

'I've not had any thoughts, miss.'

'Quite, and, as you have no thoughts, there is no point talking, as only rubbish is coming out. Is that right?' The question did not allow for dissent.

'Yes, miss.'

'Good. Now please get on with your work.' George put his head down to avoid the teacher's attentive gaze.

'Break, in the library,' Winston whispered, not turning his head.

'Okay!' I whispered back, and focused on my work.

I enjoyed English. I liked the work. It was a pleasant distraction from what lay ahead, so the end of the lesson came all too soon.

Brrrrrrr.

The bell rang once more.

'Please hand in your exercise books. Tarquin, Quinlan, make sure your names are written on the front of your books. Thank you everyone. Once your book is on my desk you may go.'

We headed out into the hustle and bustle of the corridor. A voice cried out from behind us.

'Hey! Andrex.' Aaron (pronounced air-on, though we pronounced it hair-on) Mycock had a tendency to turn everyone's name into something else. I think it was some kind of revenge for having the worst name in the world. We just called him Ron, on the basis that he had already suffered enough, and, to be honest, there wasn't anything worse we could change his name into. In my case, the name Aaron had chosen for me was a well-known brand of toilet paper which fairly closely matched my first name. Andrew became "Andrex" and would eventually morph into "Bog Roll", the name that would plague my final year.

'What?' I replied.

'Are you in the super maths set?' We all stopped and turned around.

'What super maths set?' I asked.

'I heard Willy W**ks and Todger Rubs talking about it at lunch,' Aaron said.

'Let me guess. Mr Banks?' I queried.

'Yup,' he nodded.

'Is he called William then?' I looked at Winston.

Winston nodded. 'I think so.'

'Makes sense,' I said, acknowledging the name change was within credible limits. 'And Mr... Stubs... maybe?'

'Uh-huh,' Aaron nodded in agreement.

'Is he called Roger?' I asked.

'He's called Danny, isn't he?' Josephine said.

'Danny! Damn! I was sure it was Roger,' Aaron cursed.

'It's definitely Danny,' Winston confirmed.

'Needs work,' I said, referring to the name change. 'Todger won't cut it, I'm afraid.'

'Yup, Todger's out and tossed away,' Ron said, accompanied by a tossing action.

'Anyway, what about the maths set?' I was intrigued.

'Oh yeah. They were on the next table to us at lunch. I heard 'W**ks say they need a maths set for highfliers, an O-level set.'

'O-level. No way?' I called out.

This was a big surprise. O-levels were for grammar school kids; we were strictly CSE, a second-level, second-class qualification for secondary schools. CSEs were graded 1 to 7, whereas O-levels were graded A to E. In theory, a grade 1 CSE was equivalent to a grade C O-level. C was the all-important "pass grade" you needed to do A-levels. A secondary school kid needed four grade 1 CSEs to get into a grammar school to do A-levels. A big ask, and even if achieved, they would be thrown into a new school with a different culture, and none of their existing school friends. It was a tricky cliff to climb, but university was waiting at the top.

'Yeah. O-level. You're bound to be in it,' he said.

'Hope so. Thanks, Ron,' I said appreciatively.

'No problem,' he replied.

'Hey, Ron, what're yer names for Quinlan and Tarquin?' Winston asked.

'Hmm, let me see.' Ron looked them up and down as if he was a tailor, fitting them for the perfect suit. 'Well... for Quinlan... I think... Tin Man, and for Tarquin...' he looked him up and down a few more times, 'I think... Dorothy.'

'Dorothy!' Tarquin looked somewhat disappointed.

'Tin Man is a friend of Dorothy, everyone knows that. You need to read up on your *Wizard of Oz*. I was so sure you would know the classics.' Feigning disgust, Ron turned and left.

'I bet he's praying for a Mr Hunt,' Josephine said.

'Or a Mr Magina,' Winston proposed.

'Or Mr Parsole,' Tarquin added.

'Parsole?' I asked.

'Parsole – Arsehole,' Tarquin explained.

'You've still got a lot to learn,' I said.

'What is wrong with Parsole?' Tarquin demanded.

'It's obvious, isn't it?' Winston suggested.

'No!' Tarquin stated emphatically.

'Well if you can't see the issue, I'm not sure we can help you,' I said, with apparent regret.

Me and Winston shrugged a smug, shrug of intellectual superiority and turned away. It was utter nonsense of course, but watching Tarquin tie himself in knots trying to figure out a set of rules, that did not exist, was well worth the effort.

We had resumed our journey to the next lesson when Ron shouted to us down the corridor.

'Hey, Andrex, I've got it. William Banks and Danny Rubs... Willy W**ks and Fanny Rubs. Whadaya think?'

A booming voice responded.

'I think, Mr Mycock, you should report to my study at once. Now!'

'F**k! Shit! Sorry! Shit! Sorry!' Ron looked around quickly, as if seeking an escape route.

'Mycock! My study,' the voice boomed once more.

'Yes, sir. Yes, sir. Right away, sir.' He sped up the corridor mumbling 'f**k shit, f**k shit, f**k shit' under his breath, as he went.

We almost peed ourselves laughing as we climbed the stairs. We laughed so much we forgot to warn Quinlan and Tarquin about what was in store. We were going to French. These lessons weren't like any other.

We paused outside the door to room 2.03 to regain our composure. Winston was about to explain to our guests when we heard the call.

11 LE GARÇON ET LA MALLETTE

'Entrez! Entrez! Bonjour, bonjour. Aah, les nouveaux enfants. Venez vers moi et asseyez-vous.'

We followed the teacher's gestures and instructions and occupied the seats on the front row. During our distraction, Karen snook in and slipped into a space at the back. Madame Oublions, the French teacher, was without doubt one of the more colourful characters in the staff room. She was the epitome of all things French, or so we thought.

She was young and shapely, with tight-fitting clothes that clung to her ample curves. Her long, straight black hair flowed down over her shoulders and out around her bosom. Cut to a fringe, it framed her friendly face with its small upturned nose, long eyelashes, hazel eyes and full, deep red lips. Her body was as expressive as her words. She shrugged uncertainty, shook with anger, embraced friendliness, frowned sadness and smiled happiness. Whilst most people were shades of grey, she was full blown Technicolor. She was lively, joyous, and just a little bit barmy. Anyone this open and emotional should have been torn apart by a classroom of kids, but we liked her. She was fun, and lots of it.

She addressed the newcomers in turn.

'*Comment t'appelles-tu?*'

'*Je m'appelle Quinlan.*'

'*Bon! Merci. Et tu? Comment t'appelles-tu?*'

'*Je m'appelle Tarquin.*'

'*Très bien! Très bien! Bonjour, Tarquin. Bonjour, Quinlan.*' After welcoming the newcomers, she turned to the rest of the class.

'*Bonjour, tout le monde.*'

'*Bonjour, Madame Oublions,*' we all replied.

The flamboyant French teacher started by painting a picture with words:

'Do you know that France is so close, if we were standing on the top of the White Cliffs of Dover, on a clear day, looking out over the sea, across the waves, beyond the tankers, the trawlers, the liners and pleasure boats, past the porpoises, the seals and the flippy, flappy fish, on the horizon, you could just make out the French coast? With binoculars, you can see the fishermen in their stripy jumpers playing boules on the beach, and the stylish French ladies striding along the promenade in their silky chemises and swishing culottes. Concentrate that little bit harder and amongst the umbrellas in the street cafés you can hear the swing and sway of the accordion, the laughter at the tables, the glug of wine, the ting of glass and the clack of crockery. You can even taste that famous French food; you can taste *les escargots et grenouilles.*'

'Miss! What is less cargo and green wee?'

'Snails and frogs' legs, Roger.'

'I think I'd prefer green wee, miss.'

'These are delicacies, Roger, the *crème de la crème* of French cuisine. You can have *pommes frites* or chips if you wish.'

'Can I have both?' She rolled her eyes and dismissed the suggestion with a wave of her hand.

'As I was saying, France is just a stone's throw away. But have any of you been to France?'

Only Quinlan and Tarquin raised their hands.

'It's nice to know that some people appreciate the fine things France has to offer,' she said graciously.

'That's not fair, miss. Only rich kids go to France.'

Roger was right. No one went abroad from our school. Everyone went to the beach, a British beach, and stayed in a caravan or a tent nearby. Kids played in the sand and swam in the cold, cold sea. For a treat, they might play on the slot machines, or occasionally take a trip to a theme park. It was cheap entertainment and good wholesome family fun. The most expensive thing on the menu was fish and chips, and for Dad, a pint of beer in the pub. No one ever went abroad. Madame Oublions, however, had other ideas.

'That is where you are wrong, Roger. Today, we are all going to France. All of us, including you. With a little imagination, we are going to walk the streets, eat the food and drink the wine.'

'But how are we going to get there?'

'Roger, we will be travelling in the mind.' She tapped the side of her head to make the point. 'You may not have noticed, but this is not a classroom, it is the deck of a cross-channel ferry. Josephine here is the captain steering a course for Calais.' She saluted Josephine, who returned the favour. 'I am your tour guide. I am here to tell you all about the beautiful buildings, the incredible art, the fabulous food and the wonderful wine. Julian, what is that over there in the water?' She pointed with one hand whilst shielding her eyes with the other, as she scanned the vast ocean.

'A boat?' he guessed.

'In French, Julian, *en français, s'il te plaît.*'

'*Un bateau?*'

'*Bon!* Macy, *que vois-tu?*' She tapped the side of her eye and then swept the horizon to reveal the view.

'*Un pissoir.*' There were a few sniggers from those in the know.

'Hmm… Macy, does this *pissoir* have fins and a flappy tail?'
'*Oui.*'

'I think, Macy, that may be a *poisson*. Henri, what do you see out there?'

'*Un éléphant.*' Henry's knowledge of animals was limited.

'*Un éléphant? Mon dieu, c'est un catastrophe.* Noah's Ark has capsized. We must save *les pauvre animaux.* What else can you all see?' This was the clue for us all to chip in.

'*Une vache.*'

'*Aah oui. Je la vois.* Throw it a line, someone. Bonjour, *Madame Vache.* Welcome aboard. Oh, *ce n'est rien.* Happy to help.'

As well as the elephant and the cow, we managed to save *un chat, un chien, un cheval, un poulet, un lapin, un cochon, un mouton* and *un lion.* The rest, that we didn't know the French for, had to fend for themselves.

'Aah, there it is. The port of Calais. France at last. Josephine, steer us in.'

'*Oui, madame.*'

Josephine successfully steered us into the docks, carefully drawing us into the quayside.

'Jude, throw the dockworker a rope. George, lower the gangplank. Careful with that lion. Oh dear, it's eaten the mayor. Everyone off.' By now, we were really into it, doing all the actions.

'How fortunate, the train station – *la gare est à côté du quai* – is by the quay. Everyone on board. This is the super-fast train to Paris.'

We all climbed on board and set off, arriving a few seconds later.

'*Nous sommes arrivés.* Paris, Gare du Nord. Follow me.'

We followed Madame Oublions past the Sacré-Coeur and through the busy streets of Montmartre with its artists and vendors. Jo had her portrait painted, but Madame Oublions refused to pay because, she claimed, it looked nothing like her.

Eventually, we arrived at the Champs-Elysées. There she selected the most expensive restaurant with the best view of the Arc de Triomphe and we all sat outside soaking up the sun. She hailed the waiter and ordered d*es escargots, des grenouilles, des cervelles d'agneau, des moules marinières* and *des animelles.*

'Madame Oublions.'

'*Oui*, Henri.'

'We know about green wee and snails. But what about servo de ag new and animal?'

'*Cervelles d'agneau* is a speciality I have ordered specifically for you, Henri, because you have such a big one.'

'*Oh là là.*'

'Thank you, Stacy, for keeping it French. However, from the two small white lumpy balls on the plate, I think you can see these are brains, sheep's brains as a matter of fact.'

'Sheep's brains, sheep's brains, yeuch.' Henri spat out the offending offal.

'*Mais non.*' She put her hand over her eyes as if a tragedy had befallen us. '*Je suis désolée. Tu ne les aimes pas.*'

'Yeah, *je n'aime pas*,' Henri confirmed.

'Never mind, you can swap with me. Here, have the *animelles.*'

'And what is the "animal"?' Henri asked, looking concerned.

'Well, from the size of the balls on your plate, Henri, I think you can see, these are bull's testicles.'

'Is that because he's got such a big one, miss?' Caroline asked, but was studiously ignored amidst the general sound of revulsion mixed with laughter.

Madame Oublions patted the laughter down until it was suitably quiet, then asked the question.

'Is that okay for you, Henri?'

'Ugh! Yeuch. That is the most disgusting thing I have never eaten.' Henri spat out his imaginary meal. 'I am never ever going to France again,' he said.

'You are quite right, Henri. This food, *c'est horrible! Garçon! Ici*. Take away this weird-looking French food and bring us *pommes frites avec sauce tomate. Vite!*'

The waiter scurried off and soon came back with plates of chips covered in tomato sauce.

'*Mesdames et messieurs*. I have a special treat for you now. Waiter, please bring a selection of the best French wines. *Merci*, Jean Claude. *Excusez-moi. Q'est-ce que c'est?* Blue Nun! Blue Nun! This is the horrible sweet German wine you get in Britain. Take it away. My guests are far too sophisticated to drink this German rubbish. Bring the French wine *immédiatement... Merci.*'

From behind the desk she brought out a series of empty wine bottles and placed them on the top.

'Here we have a selection of typical French wine. In France, at the evening meal, young boys and girls will drink wine with the family. Unfortunately, in Britain, if I serve you wine, they will lock me up and throw away the key.' She mimed turning a big key in a lock, then tossing it carelessly over her shoulder.

We all booed in unison.

'So once again you will have to use your imagination. You all have an imaginary wine glass in front of you. Winston, that's a beer glass. George, that's for brandy and, Pierre, that is a sherry glass. Please swap them for the right one. *Merci*. Karen, is that a bucket? How much are you going to drink?'

'It's to be sick in, *madame*,' Karen replied.

'Very wise, Karen.'

'Winston. What makes a good wine?'

'I dunno, miss.'

'Is it the grape?'

'I guess so.'

'*Non, non, non! Ce n'est pas le raisin.* But, is it the soil?'

'I suppose it must be.'

'*Bien sûr que non.*' She hit her head with the heel of her hand, as if trying to knock some sense into this conversation. '*Pas du tout.* Not at all, Winston. Think carefully, one last chance, is it the weather?'

'Yes?' he asked hopefully.

'Well… actually… *c'est tout ça et rien de tout ça.* It is all of these, and none of these.'

By now, we were all scratching our heads.

'What makes French wine the finest wine in all of the world is not the grapes, they have grapes in Germany; it is not the soil, they have soil in Germany; and it is not the weather, they have weather in Germany. They have all these things in Germany, but they make terrible wine. What makes French wine the finest wine in all the world is… the French. To be precise, *les vignerons*, the wine makers. For hundreds and hundreds of years, they have developed the skills and techniques, passing their secrets down from father to son until the wine is perfect. They are farmer, craftsman, scientist and sorcerer. They conjure up wines for every occasion. You name a meal, a mood, a moment, and there is a wine to suit, which is why I have to have so many. So, what are the different types of wine? What is *vin rouge*… Suzy?'

'Red wine, miss.'

'*Oui. Très bien. Mon favourite. Et vin blanc*? Peter.'

'White wine?'

'*Parfait. Vin doux* is sweet wine, and *vin sec*, dry wine, which just means it isn't sweet. Are you ready to try your first French wine?'

'Yes!' we cried.

'Our first wine is: …Côtes du Rhône.'

She went round the class pouring imaginary wine into imaginary glasses.

'Now, please take a sip. Mandy, what did you notice?'

'It is warm and smooth and heady.' She threw back the remainder of her glass and collapsed on the table as if drunk.

'*Les jeunes!*' she said, rolling her eyes in exasperation. 'If you weren't so drunk, you would also notice it is fruity, lively, red, dry and, as you have shown, very, very easy to drink.'

We worked our way through Bordeaux, Burgundy, Alsace, and finally we came to Champagne. This was the only bottle that still had its cork intact, along with four wires straining to keep it in place.

'This is Champagne, the queen of all wines. This is a sparkling wine. If I undid this wire here, there would be an explosion of bubbles and the cork would fly off, probably killing someone in the front row. So, I cannot open it, as I would be in prison for murder and serving alcohol. But I will be opening it later on, as I have brought a lot of bottles back with me from France, and the staff are having a wine tasting session straight after school. But maybe, just maybe, we can open it now.' She held the bottle out in front of her and pretended to unscrew the wire holding the cork then shouted, 'POP!'

Everyone in the front row ducked as an imaginary cork flew across the room. George on the back row gasped, clutched his chest and dropped dead on the desk as the bullet passed straight through him and embedded itself in the wall.

'*Quel horreur.* I will be tried for murder; they have the bullet. I am doomed,' Madame Oublions cried in desperation.

Peter looked down at George and then at the wall. With his fingertips, he prised the cork out and held it aloft. He looked at Madame Oublions, shrugged, placed the cork in his mouth and swallowed hard, washing it down with what was left of his wine.

'*Merci*, Pierre. *Tu es mon hèro.*' She put her hands on her heart then blew him a kiss. He blushed red and looked down to hide his embarrassment. She looked at her watch. '*Vite!* We must return *immédiatement. Garçon! Téléphone, s'il vous plaît.*' The waiter handed her a phone, which she dialled round and back to call the number. 'Is that the pilot of my private jet? *Bon!* Please land it on the Champs-Elysées. I know it's a road, but it's a very wide road. No! there aren't any cars, well, not many. *Vite.* Ah, here he is. Quick, everyone, climb on board. Take one of these parachutes.'

'Are we flying back?'

'It is a plane, Evy,' Madame Oublions said, pointing to the invisible aircraft.

Evy hunched her shoulders and giggled with embarrassment.

'Okay! Everyone, we are on our way. *Monsieur Pilote,* please circle over the school, will you. We are going to have to parachute straight down that chimney into room 1.03.'

'It's too small for Winston, miss,' Peter cried out.

'Quick, Winston, cover yourself in butter and remember to go in headfirst.' Madame Oublions passed him a knife and the butter, which he dutifully spread all over.

'Breathe in, Winston. You will be okay,' Madame Oublions reassured him.

We all parachuted down one at a time and landed in our seats as the bell started ringing.

'*Bravo, tout le monde. A la semaine prochaine.* See you next week. Don't forget to bring your swimming costume. We are going to the beach.'

We all piled out of the room and followed the crowds down the stairs.

'What the hell was that?' Tarquin had clearly never experienced anything like it before.

'That was Madame Oublions,' I said, as if that explained everything.

'She is as mad as a box of frogs,' Quinlan decided, but Winston disagreed.

'A box of tap-dancing frogs,' he said, upping the insanity level by one.

'A box of yodelling, tap-dancing frogs,' I said, upping one more.

'Well, there are plenty of frogs who would say she's madder,' Josephine declared, topping out.

'You do realise she is probably clinically insane,' Tarquin advised with caution.

'Did we actually learn any French in there?' Quinlan asked uncertainly.

'Do we care?' Winston replied as we reached the bottom of the stairs and stepped out of the surging crowd into the relative calm of the hall foyer.

'We must have learnt something,' Josephine asserted. 'You can't go through all of that and learn nothing.'

I started to reel off the things we had learnt. 'Well, there was the name of all the animals. We went through those at the beginning. We learnt green wee is frog's legs and less cargo are snails.'

'We learnt they eat bull's testicles,' Winston recalled, looking green.

'And, the kids are drunk on wine half the time,' Tarquin mentioned.

'And champagne is the queen of wine,' Josephine said, regally sipping a sparkling glassful.

'As well as a dangerous weapon,' Winston said, firing an imaginary bullet and blowing the smoke off his fingertips.

'And we learnt what a great place Paris is,' I said. 'To be honest, I reckon we learn more from the Mad Dame than we learn from anyone else.'

'I am certainly a better sea captain,' Josephine informed us.

Quinlan thought it over. 'Yes. O.K. We did learn a lot. Maybe she is not mad, maybe she is a genius.'

We all turned this over in our minds and came to the same conclusion, at the same time.

'Nope, she's mad.'

'She doesn't like Germans though, does she?' Josephine said, as if she might have a darker side.

'She doesn't like German wine. She might be passionate about Germans,' Quinlan said in Madame Oublions' defence.

'She likes German cars,' I pointed out.

'How do you know?' Winston looked doubtful.

'She drives that pink Volkswagen Beetle,' I said, pointing through the glazed screen to the car park beyond.

'The one with the flowers on the bonnet and the eyes on the lights?' Josephine queried.

'Yup!' I confirmed.

'It looks like Herbie's joined a hippy colony,' Winston said, looking at the absurd vehicle rather dubiously.

'That is a terrible car,' Tarquin said.

'It is a good car,' Quinlan countered.

'Ah, but what makes *le* good car,' I said in my best French accent. 'Is it *le* wheels?'

'Yes!' Winston stated emphatically.

'*Non! Dummkopf,*' I replied.

'That's German,' Josephine said.

'It's a German car,' I pointed out.

'French teacher.'

'Okay! "*Le Dummkopf*" then,' I said.

'Putting "*le*" in front doesn't make it French,' Quinlan said.

'*Le* f**kin' does,' Winston declared.

'*Le merci, le Dummkopf,*' I said. 'So, is it *le* wing mirror that makes it a good car?'

'Yes!'

'*Non! Le Dummkopf,*' I said. 'Is it *le* seat?'

'Yes!'

'*Non*! *Le* French cars have *le* wheels, *le* wing mirror and *le* seat, and they make *le* shit cars.'

'So what does make a good car?' Tarquin asked.

'*Le* walnut dashboard. Hmm, lovely.' Winston stroked an imaginary dashboard and moaned with ecstasy. 'All the best cars have a walnut dash: Rolls-Royce, Jaguar...'

'Allegro Vanden Plas,' I said, moaning in harmony.

'Okay, maybe not the Allegro Vanden Plas,' Winston admitted.

'My mum's car is an Allegro Vanden Plas,' Tarquin said.

'You've got a second car?' I clutched my hands together and looked to heaven as if "only in dreams".

'You've got a mum?' Winston said, adopting a similar pose.

Tarquin, Josephine and Quinlan folded their arms and scowled in silence.

'Have you quite finished?' Josephine said. It wasn't a question.

'What is wrong with an Allegro Vanden Plas anyway?' Tarquin asked sincerely.

Me and Winston shrugged, then looked at each other... and burst into fits of laughter.

This resulted in more folded arms and scowling. Eventually, Josephine decided words were not enough and slapped me round the chops.

'F**kin' hell. That hurt,' I said, holding the side of my face.

'You deserve it,' Josephine said, without any obvious sign of remorse.

'No, I don't,' I said, rubbing my cheek. 'The Allegro Vanden Plas is the world's funniest car. Everyone knows that.'

'Cars are not funny,' Josephine stated categorically.

'They've taken a Rolls-Royce grille and stuck it on the front of a Mini. It's a joke.' I could see Tarquin flicking through mental images of his mother's car, then nodding and smiling, as if he'd just grasped the punchline.

'So then,' Quinlan said, 'if the Vanden Plas is the funniest car, what is the best?'

'The best are still British,' I said. 'We make loads of great cars. There's Rolls-Royce, which must be the best car in the world, Range Rover, Bentley, Jaguar XJS, Aston Martin Lagonda, Lotus

THE BOY AND THE BRIEFCASE... AND THE MOOSE

Esprit, Jensen Interceptor, Reliant Scimitar, Mini, Ford Capri and Triumph Stag, to name but a few.'

'How come you know so many cars?' Tarquin asked.

'My dad gets a motor magazine. He lets me read it,' I said.

'So, you *can* read magazines and *not* just look at the pictures,' Josephine said snidely.

'The inner workings of a car are very interesting,' I said.

'And the inner workings of a woman aren't?' Josephine replied caustically.

'Those mags aren't gonna help me figure out how women think,' I said. 'They're more... er... more... y'know?' My nervous fingers wiggled back and forth. They seemed to be signing what I struggled to say.

'More what?' Josephine said, glaring.

'They're more... more... y'know?' I was pleading for her to say 'Yes' so I could drag myself out of this hole.

'No!' The hole was bottomless, and I was in free fall.

'More women's... women's... bits and pieces rather than their brains,' I said, my hands inadvertently pointing to the bits and pieces in question.

'You are truly the most disgusting person I have ever met,' Josephine said, batting my hands away.

'Just saying. I don't read 'em. I don't even look at the pictures.' I clenched my hands to stop them embarrassing themselves any further.

'How do you know then?' she said.

'Someone had one in the cloaks. They showed me.'

'And you looked!' she snapped.

'I'm curious,' I said.

'Oh yeah!' She leant in, scowling.

'Yeah. If your friends had a mag of naked men, you'd have a look,' I said, edging backwards.

'No, I wouldn't!'

'Yes, you would,' I said, easing further away.

'No, I wouldn't.' She spat a salvo of spite in my direction. 'Those magazines turn women into sluts. They make it look like we are only here to entertain your desires. We are stupid, emotionless sex slaves. Any boy gets a dick out, we can't help ourselves, we have to jump on it!'

I reeled backwards as she moved forward.

'And you buy them!' She pushed me back with her fingertips. It was hardly a push really, but just when I expected the wall to come to my rescue, I stepped back against the doors to the hall and they parted. I vaguely remember looking back on a row of open mouths and reaching hands as I fell through, landing with a crash.

'Who is that!' the deputy head roared.

I got up as quickly as I could. 'Sorry,' I said, 'lost my balance.'

'You shouldn't be inside anyway,' she said, moving quickly towards me from the other end of the hall. 'You should be outside with everybody else. Get out, now!'

'Yes, miss. Sorry, miss,' I grovelled, quickly reversing back through the doors, which closed around me.

'We've got to go,' I announced, 'Garland's on the prowl.'

'Follow me.' Winston beckoned, darting down the staff corridor.

'Where are we going?' Quinlan asked, nipping along behind.

'To the library,' Winston directed, arm up like a tour leader.

'But only fifth formers can go in the library during afternoon break,' Josephine pointed out.

'We're showing Tarquin and Quinlan round. They'll let us in,' Winston said confidently.

'Why don't we just go out into the playground?' Josephine asked, annoyed at being bossed about.

'We need to be away from Mary and her crew of psychopaths,' I explained, rushing along.

'The library will give us a quiet place to figure out what to do next. A place to plan how to get a briefcase back,' Winston said.

We all followed Winston up the stairs to the first floor. We paused briefly outside the big glass doors, in order to catch our breath. Winston waltzed in and walked up to the counter.

12 ARSE IN THE LIBRARY

'Now, now, young man, you know full well, only fifth formers studying for exams are allowed in the library during afternoon break. I am afraid I will have to ask you to leave,' the librarian said, looking over her half-moon reading spectacles at Winston, who adopted his most charming smile.

'I do apologise, Mrs Wilderbeast, but the headmaster asked us to show Tarquin and Quinlan from Rugby School the most important places in the school, and the library was top of the list.'

'Well, yes. Of course. You must show them the library. It is after all the most important repository of knowledge in the whole school. You may not know this, children, but we have an exceptional collection of books here. Lady Elder donated a huge sum to stock it. We have all the classics, ancient and modern. I chose them all myself. Let me give you a guided tour.'

'I'm sure that won't be necessary,' Winston replied.

'No, no, I insist. I can talk you through the card index, the Dewey decimal system, and show you some of our most prized possessions. We should get through all that in the afternoon break.'

THE BOY AND THE BRIEFCASE... AND THE MOOSE

'Don't worry, Mrs Wilder. I can take them round.' Karen emerged from round the corner of the office, carrying a stack of books.

'Oh, oh... er, yes. Thank you, Karen. I suppose it will leave me time to catalogue our recent additions. Yes, please show them round. I might catch up with you later.'

Karen dumped her books on a reading table and led us further into the library, out of earshot of the librarian.

'What the hell are you doing here?' Winston asked.

'What the hell are you doing calling Mrs Wilder, Mrs Wilderbeast?' Karen replied, waving a finger at Winston.

'I didn't... did I?' Winston asked anxiously.

'Oh yes, you did,' Karen replied, nodding.

'I thought it was a weird name,' Quinlan confessed.

'Is that not her real name?' Tarquin asked.

'No, you numpty,' Josephine chided. 'Have you ever met anyone called Wilderbeast?'

'No, but I've not met anyone called Wilder either,' Tarquin said in his defence.

'But what are *you* doing here?' I asked.

'I volunteer to help in the library,' Karen said with a smile, looking around as if she owned the place.

'Why?' I asked.

'I like books, and while you are outside in the freezing cold, I am in here in the warmth, listening to Mrs Wilderbeast's stories of her time at the British Library. Seems like a good deal to me. Anyway, why are you here?' she said, looking curiously at the five of us.

'We are trying to figure out how to get Tarquin's briefcase back from Scary Mary,' I said. 'We need space to plan.'

'Okay, I see. So, you probably want a quiet spot out of the way.' We nodded in agreement. She looked around for the perfect hideaway. 'I know, you can have Conrad Clarke's place. He's not in today. It's tucked around the corner at the end, between the big bookshelves. No one can see you there,' she said, beckoning us to follow her.

'Wow! Conrad Clarke's place. Awesome,' I said.

Conrad Clarke was the intellectual god in the school. There was every chance he would achieve the four grade 1 CSEs necessary to get to the grammar school to study A-levels. He was also head boy, and captain of the year 5 rugby team. He and Janet Johnson were like school superheroes, with unnatural ability no one else could match. Clearly, we would all prefer invisibility, or being able to fly, but we would have settled for a Conrad/Janet combination of talents. Conrad's godlike status meant he had his own special place in the library. His chair was left vacant just in case he graced the library with his presence, but today, I was sitting in it.

'Y'know, I reckon this chair is the source of Conrad Clarke's special powers. I can feel all the knowledge in the universe crashing into my mind. My brain is expanding, my head is going to explode, aaaaahh.'

'Shut up, Andy, we need to get on with the plan,' Winston said curtly.

'Sorry,' I apologised, embarrassed.

'What about the Wilderbeast? She could turn up any moment,' Josephine said, looking around nervously.

'Don't worry about her,' Karen said. 'I have a plan. She reached up to the top shelves and selected an old leather-bound volume with gold writing running down its spine, and an intricate pattern embossed upon the cover. We watched mesmerised as she flicked it open and leafed through to the middle of the book, and then, tore out the centre pages.

'What have you done, you maniac?' Winston looked dumbfounded.

'Mrs Wilderbeast was a book binder at the British Library. I will claim someone tore the pages out of this book. We will spend the next quarter of an hour talking about this outrage, and then, she will take it home and lovingly restore it. Over the next few weeks, she'll tell me exactly how she did it. She won't bother you, and I'll learn the art of book binding. Enjoy your peace and quiet.' Karen walked back to the librarian, book in one hand and the torn-out page in the other, a look of outrage on her face.

'She... is amazing,' I said, watching her leave.

'Yeah, sure. What's the plan then?' Winston said, dragging attention back to the matter in hand.

'I thought you had a plan,' I said.

'If I had a plan, we wouldn't need to come here to work out a plan, would we?' Winston said, looking at me as if I was a tad simple. 'So, what are the problems?'

Quinlan raised the issue I was most concerned about. 'If Tarquin and Andrew have to be at the back gate to the swimming pool at half past four, how are we going to keep an eye on them?'

'We've got to figure out how they get to the gate first,' Winston said. 'We are all supposed to be at the karting when you two...' he pointed to me and Tarquin, '...have to be at the gate. So, you will need a good excuse to leave the club.'

'I could say that I need to show Tarquin where the toilets are,' I said. 'They're a fair way away, back inside the school, so Mr Trent would expect us to be away for some time.'

'Yeah, that would work,' Winston agreed. 'Me and Quinlan will hang around the karting, as close to the pool as possible to keep an eye and ear out for trouble.'

'What about Josephine? She's not in the Karting Club,' I said.

'We've got netball practice tonight after school,' Josephine said, 'so I'll be around.'

'Yeah, but you won't be able to help, will you?' I said, assuming they'd be too far away.

'Yes, we can,' she replied. 'You can see down the other side of the swimming pool from the games court. I know it's across the car park, but we should be able to see who is coming and going.'

It was Tarquin who spotted the obvious problem with Josephine's plan. 'Presumably there will be a teacher with you,' he said. 'Surely they will wonder why you are looking at the pool all the time.'

'Mrs Stubbs. Hmm, yeah, we need a reason to get her out of the way.' Josephine rested her chin on her hand as if the weight of the problem was too much without the prop.

'Could one of you feign an injury so she has to take them inside?' Tarquin asked hopefully.

'Hmm, don't think so. She's not very sympathetic when it comes to injuries. I reckon if your leg dropped off, she'd make you hop around the court,' Josephine said, pouring cold water on that idea.

'What can we do then?' I asked, looking around for answers.

'Well, she does like a drink. When we go to a match, she always has a drink or two afterwards,' Josephine pondered, trying to work through a solution.

'From the size of her, I'd've thought ten,' Winston said, indicating a huge waist between outspread arms.

'I know. She's massive,' Josephine said, 'but it's amazing how she gets around the court.'

'How's the drinking going to help?' Quinlan asked, dragging us back to the matter in hand.

'What about Madame Oublions' wine tasting?' I said. 'Could you get her to go to that?'

'Could I? I don't think she'd be able to resist,' Josephine said with confidence.

'How're you gonna get her to go?' Winston asked.

'She'll know about it anyway,' Josephine assured us. 'She'll probably be pissed off that she can't go because of netball. I'll mention that Madame Oublions talked about the wine tasting in the French lesson, that she described all the different wines and how nice they taste and everything. I'll tell her about the sparkling champagne, that it's just waiting for her to take a sip.' She mimed gently sipping the sparkling liquid, then throwing it back, as she anticipated Mrs Stubbs would do. 'She'll be desperate to go. I'll tell her I can run the training session for once and that she can go and have a good time. And she will.'

'D'y'think it'll work?' I asked, doubtful it could be so easy.

'Yeah. Pretty sure,' Josephine said, nodding. 'She loves her drink.'

'Okay! It's sorted then,' Winston said. 'If any of us see or hear anything, we run over to help. Simple.'

'Sounds okay,' I said despondently.

'How do we let you know we need your help?' Tarquin asked.

'Just shout and wave your arms around or something. We'll come running,' Winston said, as if it was going to be a breeze.

'I'll let the rest of the netball team know what's going on,' Josephine said. 'We'll all keep an eye out.'

'What are you most worried about?' Winston said to Tarquin, who still looked uncertain.

'Not getting my briefcase back,' Tarquin replied, matter-of-factly.

'I'm more worried about getting beaten to a pulp by that bunch of morons,' I said, feeling uneasy about the whole adventure.

'If they fought fair, we could have settled it with a fight,' Winston said. It was the first time I'd heard Winston mention fighting. I'd assumed he wouldn't fight anyone, for any reason.

'You might have been able to,' I said, looking at him and then at myself, 'but I reckon I would come off somewhat worse.'

'Are you always fighting at this school?' Quinlan asked.

'There does seem to be a fight most weeks,' Josephine replied. 'Boys! They're crazy.'

'Do you have fights at Rugby School?' Winston asked.

'Yes. It happens,' Quinlan answered, 'but not a lot.'

'But you can't fight after school 'cos you're at school all the time, aren't ya?' I said.

'Yes,' Quinlan replied.

'So, when do you have fights?' Winston asked, intrigued.

'We do have free time,' Tarquin said. 'We're not being taught all the time.'

'Do you fight outside the school then?' I asked.

'No. You would get into loads of trouble if you got caught. It would ruin the school's reputation,' Tarquin said. The school's reputation was clearly something that could never be tarnished.

'So, you fight inside school then?' Winston queried.

'Yes. There are places away from prying eyes,' Quinlan advised.

'It is all arranged. There are strict rules, and the rules have to be obeyed,' Tarquin explained.

'A bit like here then,' I said.

'Sort of,' Quinlan half agreed. 'I think we are a bit more formal at Rugby School. Both parties wear sports kit, there is a referee, and we even have a first aid kit.'

'But what about the bullies? There must be fights that aren't arranged,' I said.

'You can't afford to be bullied in a boarding school,' Quinlan advised. 'You are there twenty-four seven. You would never escape. You'd be living in fear all the time. It would mess with your mind. It would screw you up completely. Forever.'

'But you must have bullies,' I stated. A school without bullies seemed impossible.

'Yes, we have bullies, but we don't allow them to bully. At a boarding school, we stick together. We stop the bullies ourselves. They cannot fight an army,' Quinlan explained.

'So, whadaya do?' Winston asked, keen to understand the solution. Quinlan explained the process.

'Firstly, we shun them. They suddenly find they don't have the friends they thought they did. Then we follow them. We follow them wherever they go. Everywhere. At least two of us watching them at all times. There is no place they can go where they will not be seen.'

'Whenever they push someone, they are pushed back harder. Whenever they kick someone, they are kicked back harder. Whenever they taunt someone, they are ridiculed,' Tarquin added.

'It wears them down. In the end, they give in and they stop bullying. It is a bit like training a dog. You stick to it, time after time, until they do what you want them to do, no matter how long it takes.' From the steely determination in Quinlan's voice, I guessed he had either been a victim or a trainer.

'God! It's brutal,' Josephine said. 'Doesn't it drive them mad? Don't they go off the rails and murder everyone in the dorm?'

'When we have broken them, we let them back in and we make friends with them. They are not ostracised forever,' Quinlan said, with a little more compassion than before.

'And it does not last years or anything. It normally only takes a day or two, before everything returns to normal,' Tarquin suggested. 'We get along most of the time. We just want to have fun. Have a bit of a laugh. Bullies are boring. They get in the way of a good time.'

'It normally works, doesn't it, Tarquin?' Quinlan's tone suggested a shared experience.

'Yes, it works. I can vouch for that.' I couldn't help feeling Tarquin had probably been a recipient of the anti-bullying regime. There was a hard edge to his personality. You could imagine him as a bully, given the wrong environment or the wrong friends.

Winston was curious. He listened intently, mulling things over in his mind.

'We've got to do that here,' he said at last.
'Whadaya mean?' I asked uncertainly.

'We've got to get our own bullies under control. There's just too many at the moment. They're making everyone's lives a misery. We've got to break up the gangs,' he said, determined.

'But everyone rushes off at four o'clock,' I pointed out. 'It's not like Rugby School where you're there all the time.'

'I know, but it's got out of hand. There's George and the broken nose, Eggy's blazer torn in half, and you've had cigarette holes burnt into your anorak. We've got to do something. It's got to stop. We're gonna make a stand.' He nodded gently, but there was steel in his eyes.

'But that's… like… massive,' I said, arms outstretched to emphasise just how big. 'How're you gonna get everyone involved? We'd need to work together from year one to year five. You'd need a system, with rules and stuff. You've gotta figure out who the bullies are and then you've gotta follow them round. How're you gonna organise that?' My tone implied it was simply impossible. Winston wasn't giving up that easily.

'We'll set up a club, a union or something. We'll do it through the teams. We all talk to each other,' he said, as if it was a piece of cake. Josephine was happy to take a bite.

'There's netball and hockey teams as well as the rugby. I could get the word out through them,' she said enthusiastically.

'We need a place to meet, but where?' Winston said, nibbling his thinking finger.

'First, we've gotta decide who needs to meet,' I said. The whole idea was mad, but Winston was on a roll.

'I reckon we start with the captains. They have players they can use as enforcers, all of which are bigger and stronger than most of the other kids. I don't think there are bullies in the teams, but the captains will know if there are.'

'Every captain needs a deputy,' Josephine said, thinking of the to-do list. 'Someone who can stand in for them. Someone who is good at organisation, writing lists and rules and stuff.'

'Andy, I nominate you as my deputy,' Winston said, as if a great honour was bestowed on me. I was doubtful of both the honour and my ability to fulfil the requirements, but someone had to do it.

'Okay, I'll do it,' I said reluctantly.

'I reckon Karen would be a good deputy for me,' Josephine said. 'She worked out how to handle the Wilderbeast pretty well. Maybe she could sort it so that we met in the library. Maybe we could claim we're a book club.' The library was certainly comfortable and warm. I wasn't so sure.

'I don't think so. Wilderbeast would want to give us a talk on book binding and weird writers like Shakespeare and Agatha Christie.'

'Agatha Christie is not weird,' Quinlan said.

'She's old though, isn't she?' I said. Old, by definition, was weird.

'Not really old,' Quinlan said. 'Not dead yet. At least I don't think so. She writes those detective stories. You know… Hercule Poirot and Miss Marple.'

'Did she do those?' I asked, interested.

'Yeah. I've read a few. They're really good,' Quinlan said. 'There are lots of clues. You have to guess the murderer.'

'I've read one,' I replied chattily. 'I think it was called *Murder on the Orient Express*. They all did it in that one.'

'Yeah, that's a good one. I could lend you one if you want,' Quinlan said generously.

'I could probably get one from in here. We are in a library,' I said, looking round. 'Look, there's shelf C over there. We could have a look, see what they've got.'

'Can you just shut up!' Winston cried. A few fifth formers looked round, scowling. We all mouthed sorry and made apologetic jazz hands.

'Please can we get back to bully club?' Winston pleaded.

'Sorry,' we mouthed again, looking suitably chastised.

'Thank you,' Winston said. 'So, whadaya think?' he said enthusiastically.

'About what?' I asked, nonplussed.

'The... bully... club.' Josephine spoke slowly, as if talking to a moron.

'Oh that! Yeah! It's good. Don't know if it'll work. It's a bit mad, but it's worth a go,' I said happily.

'You cannot call it bully club though,' Quinlan suggested. 'It sounds like you are encouraging it, not fighting it.'

'You need an acronym,' Tarquin suggested, 'like NASA or RAC.'

'How about, Anti-Rough Stuff Establishment?' I proposed.

'We're not calling it ARSE,' Josephine said, quick on the uptake.

'You could call it ABC: Anti-Bully Campaign,' Quinlan suggested.

Surprisingly, Winston agreed with me. 'No! I reckon ARSE is good. People will remember it. The slogan can be: *Nobody Kicks ARSE.*'

'Or... *ARSE, We Give a Shit!*' I proposed, looking for approval.

'You're a pain in the ARSE.' Josephine's eyes flashed a warning that became more and more threatening with every idiotic saying I reeled off.

'What about, *The ARSE that Covers Your Back?*'

'Or... *The ARSE at Your Elbow?*'

'*The ARSE on Your Side?*'

'*ARSE About Face?*'

'*Your ARSE is a...* ' I looked at Josephine, whose eyes had just threatened murder.

'Are you going to kill him or shall I?' she said to Winston, but before he could answer, I trotted out one final suggestion:

'How about, *Join ARSE... Become a Ringleader?*'

I burst into laughter, whilst Winston grabbed me in a headlock.

'Shut up or I'll kill you,' he promised, but I was in a bit of a laughing frenzy and couldn't stop.

'Shut up, you moron,' Josephine instructed with a strangled shout. 'You'll get us all kicked out.'

There was a lot of shushing and evil stares from all sides. Karen poked her nose round the corner, shushing angrily with a finger over her lips. She pointed at me and mouthed 'Shut up' whilst trying to pat the noise down with her hands. I managed to cut the laughter down to a few splutters and a grunt, then silence. Karen shook her head and gave me an *Are you insane?* kind of look. She wagged her finger at me, censuring my stupidity, then turned and left.

I breathed a huge sigh of relief. The laughter was under control. I looked at Winston, whose eyes were saying, *Don't you dare.* I almost cracked up again but reined it in, just in time.

Everybody was being extra careful not to mention anything to do with bottoms, just in case it set me off again. Winston and Josephine said they would talk the anti-bully club through at the captains' table. Wednesday lunchtime, a dinner table was set aside for the captains of all the teams to get together and share ideas. They also got a few perks, like second helpings of Manchester tart. They needed to find out what the others thought before they pushed it any further.

'Thank God that's sorted,' Winston said, looking at me. 'You are a dipstick. For a minute, I thought we were up shit creek without a paddle.'

That was all it took. I spluttered and guffawed as Winston dived over to strangle the life out of me. Fortunately, the bell rang before a crowd of angry fifth formers could lend him a hand. I grabbed my bag, attempting to keep an arm's length away from Winston, who was still promising to prevent me laughing forever.

We weaved our way around the tables towards the door. I had just about managed to stifle the laughter to a few spluttering grunts and snorts as we walked past the counter.

Karen was still talking to the Wilderbeast about the torn-out pages as we shuffled past. She looked up and glared at me disapprovingly, then softened and smiled, before returning her gaze to the book and Mrs Wilder. There was something about that smile.

'Do you think they did it deliberately?' Karen said to Mrs Wilder, looking concerned.

'I think so. It's been torn right out. Such a clean tear as well. It's as if someone just ripped it out like this.' Mrs Wilder demonstrated the action involved.

'They've hardly damaged the page,' Karen said thankfully.

'Yes. We're very lucky. It's easy to repair. But what I don't understand is why choose *Paradise Lost*? It's such an old text. I know it's a classic, but it's not an easy read, and it's not on the syllabus.'

'I know,' Karen agreed, 'it just doesn't make sense...'

13 DON'T TELL THE TEACHERS

You may be wondering why we didn't report the bullying to staff. You forget; this was the seventies. There was no safeguarding policy, no anti-bullying policy and no child protection policy. Bullying was on the curriculum. Bullies toughened you up. Bullies turned boys into men. Anyone who reported anything to staff would be a tell-tale, a squealer and a snitch. They would be bullied all the more. A boy would never, ever claim to being bullied by a girl. They would be humiliated and ridiculed by both staff and kids. Their lives would be unbearable. A generation before, when everyone was born, raised and died in one tight-knit community, bullying was dealt with by parents. Everyone knew everyone's business, everyone knew where everyone lived, everyone knew who the bullies were, and parents would step in and stop it. The school played no part. It didn't need to. Now that people were moving around, those communities were breaking down, cohesion was ebbing away and natural safeguards were no longer there. We were on our own. It was up to us.

14 MAPS AND MANOEUVRES

We headed up the stairs to the art department on the top floor, where rooms were higher and the windows taller. The room would have been flooded with daylight if the blinds hadn't been down to counteract the glare of the sun. The big broad wooden benches and sturdy stools were covered with the paint of a thousand artists. With windows running down both sides of the room there wasn't any opportunity for paintings to be stuck to the walls, so the hand-decorated furniture and splodges on the floor were the only evidence that any art took place at all.

Mr Turner was not the most inspiring art teacher. In fact, his name was the only thing about him that seemed to have any artistic connection at all. Despite this, he had a quirky personality that appealed, particularly to us boys. He also had an authority that prevented classes disintegrating into anarchy. Most of the time, we were just given paper, paint and a random theme, and left to our own devices. However, today was unusual. Today's theme was maps, and maps were different. When it came to maps, he was enthusiastic. When it came to maps, he was obsessed, and his obsession was evident to all those who entered his classroom.

The floor was marked out with tape to make a grid. The grid was marked with letters up one side and numbers along the other. He would occasionally refer to pupils as A4 or D3, and we would have to check which square we were standing in before we responded. There was a large map of Europe pinned to the wall next to the blackboard with various lines drawn across it in red ink. We suspected he had been a navigator for the RAF in the Second World War, as he would occasionally point to something on the map and say, 'Can you imagine spotting that from 20,000 feet.'

We picked table B3 and mounted the high stools down both sides. In the centre of the table was a large piece of paper, and to one side a jar of pencils of differing hardness, some charcoal, watercolour tablets, a glass of water and a pot of long-handled paintbrushes, the bristles so worn they were more likely to scratch a hole through the paper than apply any paint.

'Today,' Mr Turner said, 'we are making maps. We are making maps because maps are beautiful, and great maps are great works of art. Van Gogh, da Vinci, Picasso; the world's finest painters, but did they ever create anything as beautiful as an Ordnance Survey Landranger Map? I think not!'

He dragged a map off the table and held it up for us all to see.

'*This* is an Ordnance Survey Landranger Map. The accuracy is astounding, the clarity incredible, and the symbolism, well, these little symbols here...' he pointed to the key '...simply divine. I never leave the house without an Ordnance Survey Landranger Map, and I never get lost.'

We glanced at each other, wondering whether Mr Turner had finally lost his marbles. I was comforted by the thought that he probably had them all located on an Ordnance Survey Landranger Map and would find them in a jiffy. In his current mood, Mr Turner sounded like a sergeant on the parade ground, and we responded accordingly.

'E5, the *Mona Lisa* may look beautiful, but will she help you navigate the North York Moors in the middle of winter?'

'No, sir!'

'A4, Van Gogh's *Sunflowers* may brighten a room, but will they help you off the top of Skiddaw in a snowstorm?'

'No, sir!'

'C6… Picasso's *Guernica* may intrigue and excite, but will it help you walk the Pennine Way? C6! C6!. Master Watts. Are you, or are you not, C6?'

'No, sir. I'm C7.'

'Master Watts. Your bag may be C7, but you… you… are most definitely C6. So then, Master Watts… will Picasso's *Guernica* help you walk the Pennine Way?'

'Sir, Picasso's hernia won't help anyone walk the Pennine Way.'

The sound of suppressed laughter spilled off the tables and slid across the floor like morning mist, then faded away into nothing. Even Evy kept her crazy laugh under control. Such was the authority of Mr Turner. Some teachers have it, and some teachers don't. Mr Turner did.

'*Guernica*! Master Watts. Picasso's *Guernica* and most definitely *not* Picasso's hernia. Picasso's *Guernica* is a painting depicting the tragedies of war. Picasso's hernia is something else entirely. Now, can anyone tell me something you find on a map?'

'Greenland,' said George from table F6.

'No! Not Greenland.'

'Yes, you do. It's on the map of the world in geography.' George was sure he was right.

'That's not what I meant,' Mr Turner advised. His expression discouraged further dissent.

'Iceland!' Peter shouted from table F2.

'No!'

'Finland.'

'No!'

'China.'

'No! No! No! No! No!' Mr Turner put a stop to the catalogue of countries. 'Not a place. What are the things you find on all maps?'

I stuck my hand up.

'Yes, Master Baker,' Mr Turner said with a sigh, as if hoping against hope for something sensible.

'A grid, a scale, a north point and a key.' I knew it wouldn't make me popular, but I thought it better to chip in with the correct answer than wait till we had circumnavigated the globe.

'Thank you,' Mr Turner said, with some relief. 'A grid, a scale, a north point and a key. Each of these things is to be included on your map. Do not forget them. Each table must agree, between all of you, the subject of your map. It can be a country, city, town, village or anything else a map would help you to navigate your way around.'

'Can I do my own map?'

'No, Jo. There is one piece of paper. There will be one map. You will work with your friends to make that one map.'

'They're no friends of mine.'

'Then, you will work with your enemies to make that one map.'

'Does it have to be real?' Simon asked.

'No. It can be imaginary, futuristic, historic, or whatever suits your mood.'

We all looked at each other and shrugged our shoulders.

'I know,' said Winston. 'Let's draw a map of the school.'

'Why the school?' I spent enough time there; I didn't fancy drawing it as well.

'So we can work out what's going on where... after school... the briefcase... remember?'

'Oh yeah. Okay,' I agreed. I was pretty good with a pencil and didn't want the others to make a complete hash of it, so I decided to take control of the sheet of paper. 'I'll rough out the shape of the building in the middle, then everyone can draw the bits around it,' I said.

'How are we going to help?' Tarquin asked. 'We hardly know the school.'

'Look out the window,' I said, pointing around. 'You can see both sides from here.'

I quickly drew the shape of the school, the three-storey block south of the courtyard, workshops to the north, halls to the west and the rest to the east. Josephine drew the games court and car park; Winston had a go at the swimming pool and nature reserve; Tarquin added the rugby pitches and I helped Quinlan with the playgrounds. It wasn't long before we had a reasonable plan on which to shape our strategy. Winston added the essential details.

'Okay. You two will be by the back gate with Scary Mary.' He drew three circles by the back gate to the pool and labelled these A, T, and SM. 'Josephine, you will be in the games court.' He added another circle labelled J along with a big circle labelled NT.'

'Netball Team?' Josephine queried.

'Uh-huh,' Winston agreed. 'Quinlan and me will be here.' He drew two circles to the edge of the north playground near the pool. 'From here we should be able to hear anything on the other side of the pool.'

'The karting will take place here.' He drew the track on the north playground.

'Where do you think the four henchmen of the apocalypse will be?' I asked, feeling a little uneasy.

'I dunno. I guess they'll probably be over here, behind the big tree.' He drew four circles and labelled them all A.

'Their names don't start with A,' I said.

'A is for Arsehole,' Winston replied. 'Well, in their case, it is.'

'That's pretty close to our club name,' I pointed out. 'Could be another slogan: *Where There's an Arsehole There's an ARSE*.'

Winston looked at me steely-eyed, daring me to laugh. I resisted the temptation.

'What about the wicked witches?' I asked.

'Do you think they will be with the four henchman?' Tarquin queried, pointing to the tree.

'Hmm, no. I reckon they'll stay closer to Mary if they can,' Josephine said. 'My guess is they'll squeeze in behind that bit that sticks out, where they store the floats and things. It should be there.' She pointed to the back wall of the pool, where the store should be.

Winston changed the line of the wall to create a recessed store to the pool and a projection outside. He drew two circles labelled WWE and WWW.

'Wicked Witch of the East and West?' I guessed.

'Well done,' Winston congratulated me.

'I've been brushing up on *The Wizard of Oz*,' I explained.

'I forgot about that bit sticking out.' Josephine looked concerned. 'We can't see the gate from the games court.'

'That's true. You will be able to see anyone coming and going,' Winston pointed out. 'It'll have to do.'

'I guess so. I think we'd be able to see the four henchmen if they moved in from the tree.' Josephine went over to the window to check the sight lines. She returned, nodding. 'I think we'd be able to see well enough.'

'How would you let us know if you saw something dodgy?' Winston asked. Communication from the games court was going to be tricky.

'We'll shout something loud. As loud as we can.' She thought for a second. 'How about FOUL?'

'Yeah, okay. When you shout FOUL, me and Quinlan will rush around here.' He drew an arrow showing the direction of movement around the north end of the pool.

'And we'll come in from here,' Josephine said, drawing a line from games court to pool gate.

'And I'll be shitting myself just here,' I said, drawing a dashed arrow emerging from my circle.

A looming figure suddenly appeared over my shoulder.

'Planning military manoeuvres, B3? Looks like a classic pincer movement to me. Are you anticipating an attack?'

'You can't be too prepared, sir,' I replied.

'Sir, how would you prevent an attack from the north-west?' Winston asked, diverting attention away from our real dilemma.

Mr Turner transformed into an officer in uniform. He stood up straight, hands clenched behind his back as he observed the plan, then leaned in, arms straight, hands flat on the table as he picked out the detail. There was a hushed silence as he surveyed the battlefield. He frowned, then nodded gently, as if he had considered, and discarded all the options apart from that one perfect solution.

'Well, chaps, you are right. Preparation is key. Firstly, I would have snipers high up, here in the three-storey block, covering all four corners. They'd also be my spotters with radio communication to the command centre here in the staff room.' He prodded the plan firmly with his index finger.

'Is that because of the view, sir?' I asked.

'Good tea-making facilities, Baker. Tea is why we won the war. The Germans: coffee; too much caffeine; overstimulated and impulsive; invasion of Russia; Hitler's downfall. The British: tea; refreshing and relaxing; cool, clear heads; El Alamein; Allied victory.

'Tea is what you need. Tea and heavy gun positions here, here, here and here. Tanks here. Holes in the pool wall to create a bunker; protect the north approach, and machine gun posts here, here and here. Medical facility in the gym; easy access; next to car park; evacuation. Hall… the hall would be my canteen. Hmm… Yes! With the right preparation, we could defend the school from an army at least three, maybe four, times the size of that garrisoned here.' At that, Mr Turner moved on to the next table.

THE BOY AND THE BRIEFCASE... AND THE MOOSE

We absorbed Mr Turner's words of wisdom in silence. I was wondering where we were going to get the tanks and machine guns. In the background, we could hear analysis of other cartographic creations:

'Table F7, your sheet is entirely yellow. Is it a map of the desert maybe?'

'No, sir! It's a world made entirely out of cheese.'

'I see. Well, that explains the giant mouse.'

'Table F3; town centre; bank highlighted in red. Can I assume you are planning a heist, and this blue car is the escape vehicle?'

'Yes, sir.'

'That's appalling, E3.'

'Sorry, sir.'

'Double yellow lines; illegal parking; out front; no escape; unavoidable incarceration. Move the car to here, Winter Lane; no restrictions; out of sight; easy escape; life of luxury... Sloppy, very sloppy, E3.'

'Yes, sir. Sorry, sir.'

'Do you think he knows what we are planning?' Quinlan asked in a hushed voice.

'Not from this plan,' Winston asserted. 'It's incomprehensible.'

'He managed to plan a battle using it,' Tarquin pointed out.

'Yeah, but he didn't know what our labels meant,' I stated confidently.

Josephine was less certain. 'I don't know,' she said. 'He's some kind of map-reading genius.'

'Don't worry,' Winston said. 'He doesn't know what's going on, and even if he did, he wouldn't do anything about it.'

To be honest, I would have quite liked Mr Turner to know about our quest. I couldn't help feeling he would be a big help in planning our strategy, or maybe as a sniper firing out of the art room window.

As we neared the end of the second period, nerves were

beginning to set in. I glanced across at Tarquin. He caught the look in my eyes and nodded in recognition. He was obviously feeling it too. Quinlan kept looking across at the two of us, checking up on us, I guess, or wondering what we would look like after our encounter. Josephine seemed preoccupied, probably working out what she was going to say to Stubbs to get her out of the picture. She also had to get the rest of the netball team on board. It was quite a task. Winston was as calm as ever. I reckon he thought we had got it sorted. I wasn't quite so sure.

We carried on refining our map in silence, adding trees and houses and anything else we could remember or observe from the windows. As time went by, my panic level rose. First, there was a hint of nausea. Then my stomach decided to work its way slowly up into my chest. There was a lump in my throat and my mouth was dry. A cold sweat appeared on my brow and my knees began to shake. I am not brave. In fact, I am something of a coward. In the past, I had got into a number of fights, but that was through utter stupidity rather than bravery, and this incident looked like it fitted the mould perfectly. However, with previous fights, I had felt there was always a chance, no matter how slim, that I could come out on top. If this turned into a fight, I was pretty sure I would be a long, long way from the top, so far from the top, in fact, that they would have to send in a team of divers to drag me out. I was bricking it. But I was responsible for this mess; I couldn't back out now. Everyone had spent the whole day planning my defence. There's no way I could let them down. I would never be able to face them again. I was screwed and I knew it. There was no escape. I wasn't just looking down the barrel of a shotgun; I was climbing into it.

'Ten minutes to go,' Mr Turner announced. 'You should now be down to the fine detail; finishing off those contours, adding cows in the fields, fish in the sea and leaves on the trees.'

'Sir! Did you—'

'No, Macy, I didn't really want you to add cows in fields, fish in the sea and leaves on the trees. I was being ridiculous to make you think of the detail you could add. That is what is known as exaggeration for effect. Does anyone know the word that means exaggeration for effect?' George put his hand up.

'Yes, G2?'

'It's ENORMOUS,' George said, looking down at his nether regions with a look of amazement on his face.

We started to laugh. I'm sure we started to laugh, but it stopped as soon as it started. I think Mr Turner actually sucked all the laughter out of the air. He certainly seemed to expand, and it would be fair to say George appeared to shrink at the same time.

'No, George, it is known as hyperbole. What is it known as?'

'Hyperbole, sir.'

'Yes, George. And as you have shown such a keen interest in literary terms, I am inviting you to stay behind so we can also discuss metaphor, allusion, juxtaposition and antithesis. Would you care to join me? It should only take an hour or two.'

'I... I'd rather not, sir, if... er... you don't mind, sir.'

There was a moment's silence during which Mr Turner burnt holes through George's soul with his laser vision.

'Maybe next time, George.'

'Yes, sir. Thank you, sir. Sorry, sir.'

Mr Turner turned his attention to the rest of the class.

'So... whilst some are adding the fine detail, others should be adding the four essentials of all maps, which are... A4?' Silence filled the room.

'A4... A4... Master Baker!' The powerful voice dragged me out of a dismal daydream where Scary Mary had grown eight arms and a tongue the size of a snake.

'Yes, sir?' I squealed anxiously.

Mr Turner stood there, waiting patiently. 'The four essentials, Master Baker?'

'Er... A grid, a scale, a north point and a key, sir?'

'Yes! A grid, a scale, a north point and a key. Do not forget.'

We added the fine detail and the four essentials just before Mr Turner put a halt to things.

'Stop what you are doing. Collect up the pencils, charcoal and chalk and rinse your brushes out in the jars provided. Nobody leaves until everything has been tidied away.'

There were just a few minutes to go. I made my last-ditch attempt at freedom.

'Do we really have to do this?' I pleaded.

'Absolutely! Definitely! Without a doubt!' Winston replied, leaving very little room for uncertainty. 'We're gonna get that briefcase back, and if they mess with us, we're gonna make them pay.'

'We've got to get the briefcase somehow,' Tarquin stated. 'This seems like our best chance.'

'They won't have expected this level of planning, or this level of back-up,' Quinlan pointed out.

'We've got it sorted,' Josephine confirmed. 'Nothing, absolutely nothing, can go wrong.'

I wish I was that confident.

'Well done, everyone, for such a tidy studio,' Mr Turner congratulated us. 'When the bell goes, I will release you one table at a time. Do not run. If you run, your whole table will return and wait for everybody else to leave. Do I make myself clear?'

'Yes, sir!' we chimed.

The second hand on the clock above the classroom door ticked slowly round, second by second, counting down to twelve.

Bring bring. The bell rang out. Four o'clock. Home time. Freedom at last. Freedom for most. Time to find out what the Fates had in store for me.

'Table B7, take your bags and leave.' Table B7 marched out of the room like super-fast soldiers. Technically, they were walking. There was always one foot on the floor, but their legs were a blur.

'F7.' F7 followed in the same manner, as did J7, J3 and F3. The super-fast stickmen sped away, legs going like the clappers. When they reached the door, they paused for a fraction of a second, before being sucked out by a swirling vortex and flung down the stairs at breakneck speed.

'B3… B3?' That was us. We were somewhat more reluctant. We dragged ourselves off the stools, slung our bags over our shoulders and trudged wearily towards the door. Mr Turner observed us with keen interest as we passed by, as if assessing the ability of troops on the way to the battlefield. I wondered if he thought we made the grade, whether we cut the mustard. As we left, I caught sight of the military mastermind looking down over the swimming pool, deep in thought. Perhaps he had managed to decipher our scribbles after all. I hoped he had a gun.

15 HEROES AND LEGENDS

By the time we left, evacuation was almost complete. If there was ever a fire in our school, I reckon everyone would be out in ten seconds flat, apart from those trampled to death in the rush, of course. As far as I could see, this time everyone made it out alive. The rattle and hum was gradually fading away, and the walls echoed with the sad, hollow silence of an empty school.

We plodded down the steps, each of us wondering what on earth the next hour would bring.

'I've got to go,' Josephine said as we reached the bottom. 'Good luck. You'll be okay.' She smiled warmly.

'Thanks,' I replied. 'I hope Stubbsy likes her wine. We're banking on it.'

'Oh, she definitely does,' Josephine said confidently, and headed off to the changing rooms. We wandered down the corridor in the opposite direction, hands in pockets and heads down, apart from Winston, who was his usual ebullient self. He seemed to be enjoying everything.

'Come on, guys. It's an adventure. It's exciting. We're superheroes on a mission,' he said proudly.

'I don't remember Batman's briefcase adventure,' I replied, a little more restrained.

'Exactly. Even Batman never dared to do this,' Winston said, disappointed we didn't share his enthusiasm.

'This doesn't make us superheroes. This doesn't make us Batman. This just makes us shit-scared,' I said nervously.

'Batman was never at a secondary school in Rugby. Batman never knew real fear,' Quinlan professed.

'You are right. This is real courage,' Tarquin said, all fired up. 'Fortune favours the brave!'

It was bravado; it was bollocks; but it worked. We were all feeling that little bit braver, a little bit stronger and a touch more confident. We were going to do this; we were going to get through it, and we were going to come out heroes.

'All for one, and one for all,' Tarquin shouted. It clearly wasn't right; more "Three Musketeers" than *Marvel* or DC, but it would do for now. The most unlikely set of superheroes the world has ever seen was battle ready. Heads high and shoulders wide, we strode proudly round to the north playground.

Final touches to the karting circuit were being made by a combination of parent enthusiasts and eager pupils. Tyres were stacked up around the corners and heavy timber kerbs or hay bales marked the straights. It was a big playground, and it was a big course. There were plenty of twists, turns and chicanes to slow the drivers right down. Mr Trent was orchestrating activities, issuing instructions via a team of student runners. A large gridded sheet pinned to a stand contained a list of drivers for the time trials, with a space beside each name to record their achievement.

Four go-karts were being wheeled out of a concrete garage at the edge of the playground and lined up in a row next to the track. Teams of wannabe mechanics swarmed over the carts, running through checklists of checks; tyre pressure, oil, steering and suspension, and finally filling the tanks with petrol from a large circular metal can. A trolley with helmets of different sizes was wheeled out next to the entrance to the circuit.

Mr Trent called us over. 'Welcome, gentlemen,' he said with a smile. 'I've added your names to the list. Note your place in the order. One of the senior carters will run through the controls with you before you go onto the track. Be warned, these carts are not toys. They are proper racing go-karts, and they go like sh... they go very, very fast. The aim is not to get round the track as fast as you can; the aim is just to get round the track. So, take care and don't do anything stupid, leave that to *Messieurs* Baker and Grahame. Okay?'

Tarquin and Quinlan nodded their agreement.

'Right, check your times.' He pointed to the board. 'Be back here five minutes beforehand. There's a clock next to the list if you haven't got a watch.'

They had watches; they had the rare digital watches just coming into fashion, and time was ticking by. We wandered over to the board. First trials were at 4.30pm, the exact same time as our briefcase encounter. Me and Tarquin were down for 5.00pm and Quinlan for ten past. Winston was down for 4.45pm, which was a bit early if we were delayed, but we were confident it would give us enough time to pick up the briefcase and get back. It was now 4.20pm; time for me and Tarquin to make our excuses and head off to the pool.

'Where are you going?' Mr Trent said as we passed by.

'I'm just showing Tarquin the way back to the toilets,' I said.

'Surely he knows his own way by now,' Mr Trent said. 'He's been here a day. Can't he go on his own?'

'I do find it difficult to find my way around. It is a mental thing. My brain does not work quite right. I get lost easily. I probably will not know where anything is until the end of the week,' Tarquin said convincingly.

'Okay, but don't take too long.'

This was where the adventure really began. We headed back the way we came, walking quickly through the cloaks down to the workshops. I could feel my pulse accelerating as we went. Ears and eyes were on red alert, seeking out any signs of staff. We turned the corner and strode quickly past the workshops, just the changing—

''Ere, you!' We stopped abruptly and turned around. A fierce-looking cleaner stood in the doorway we had just passed, mop and bucket in hand. 'Where do you think you're goin'? Bringing your dirty feet into the corridor I just cleaned.'

'I'm sorry, miss,' I said. 'We've got a message for Mrs Stubbs, the PE teacher.'

She frowned and shook her head. There was no way she was believing that. 'And what message would two young boys 'ave for the girls' PE teacher?' I extracted a ready-made excuse from our carefully constructed plan.

'Madame Oublions has got some wine tasting thing going on in the staff room. She wondered if Mrs Stubbs would like to attend. She forgot to say. She knew Mrs Stubbs had netball training and asked if we could pass on the message.'

'Wine tasting, eh? I 'eard somethin' wa' goin' on. Dem staff 'avin' a whale of a time, not inviting us low life. Us oo do all the 'ard work round 'ere,' she claimed.

'She did say if we saw any cleaning staff to say you were welcome to pop up afterwards,' I lied.

'Well, well! Ood a believed it? She did, did she? Maybe she not a stuck-up... er... maybe she not so bad after all. Okay, you can go, but no messin' around, and no messin' me floor,' she stressed.

'Thanks, miss,' I said, somewhat relieved.

'Mrs, if y' don' mind,' she said firmly.

'Sorry, mrs,' I corrected apologetically.

We carried on down past the changing rooms.

'Why the hell did you say that?' Tarquin asked.

'I don't know. I kinda panicked,' I replied.

'Surely they will ask questions in the staff room when she gets there.' He mimicked the teachers: 'Who told you? Two boys? I wonder what those two boys are doing down there.'

'She won't be there till later,' I said. 'Hopefully, they'll all be drunk by then.'

We reached the rear entrance and peaked outside. Mrs Stubbs was standing outside with the netball team. A massive net of balls, coloured discs and bits and pieces was slung over her shoulder. She was talking to Josephine. We could make out Mrs Stubbs' booming voice through the gap in the door. We couldn't hear Josephine's soft tones at all, but we got the gist from Mrs Stubbs' replies.

'I know she's having a wine tasting session, but I've got to run the training session. We won't win the league if we don't practise, will we?'

'Oh, I don't think I could leave a student in charge. It wouldn't be right, would it?'

'I'm sure you are quite capable, but you haven't got my years of coaching experience, have you?'

'Yes, you could rerun my training session from two weeks ago. It was good, wasn't it?'

'Yes, all the kit is here. I haven't got the ropes, but you could use the lines, couldn't you?'

'I would like to go. All that French wine. And Madame Oublions, she's great fun, isn't she?'

'Okay. I'll head off then. I'll be back at quarter past. You'll need me to help pack away, won't you?'

'I suppose you could put it all in the net and leave it in the changing room. Yes, do that! That would work, wouldn't it?'

'Okay, see you tomorrow. Have a good time. Work them hard, Josephine.' She dropped the bag on the floor and headed back towards our entrance.

'Shit! What are we going to do now?' Tarquin asked.

'Quick. In here.' I barged the door to the sports hall, but the door barged back. 'Shit, it's locked.'

'What can we do? We can't go back.'

'Stand to the side of the door and hope she doesn't see us.' We stood flat against the walls either side of the double door, our heads turned to the side so she wouldn't smash our noses in when she barged through the door. Brunhilda Battle-Axe couldn't have been more brutal than Mrs Stubbs. She crashed through the door like a stampeding rhino and charged down the corridor. She didn't even glance behind her as the doors swung back to reveal two battered figures squashed flat against the walls. We peeled ourselves off and nipped through the doors before they closed again.

Josephine and the team were holding back before heading around the car park to the games court. We waved across to her. The whole team waved back.

'Good luck,' she said. 'We're keeping an eye out for you. We'll stay here for as long as we can. We'll be over in an instant if you need us.'

'Great,' I said. Everything was sorted. What could possibly go wrong now?

Crash! Bang! Brunhilda Stubbs burst out through the doors into the sunshine. Her few dazed seconds gave us time to dodge behind a bush.

'Have you seen two boys around here?' she said.

'No! No one's come out this way since you left,' Josephine lied.

'The cleaner said they were heading this way with a message for me.'

'No! We've not seen anyone.'

'Oh, okay. Shouldn't you be heading over to the courts by now?' she asked, curious about the delay.

'Maureen's just tying her shoelace,' Josephine said. Maureen quickly bent down to make it look convincing.

'For God's sake, Maureen. Buy some self-tying shoes, will you? People can't spend all day waiting for you. Come on now, off you go.'

Josephine's eyes said sorry to Maureen, before they traipsed around the car park to the games court on the opposite side, all under the watchful gaze of Mrs Stubbs. It was going to be somewhat harder to see us from there, and just as hard to get over and help us. When they got to the court, Stubbs turned around, smiled a sly smile, rubbed her hands together then punched the air with excitement, before running back into the school. The wine was calling, and she was going to wallow in it.

We dragged ourselves out from behind the bush, brushed ourselves off and heaved a sigh of relief. That had to be the last obstacle. Tarquin looked at his watch. It was 4.30pm.

'Come on, time to go,' he said.

'Time to face our demons,' I said with determination.

We were only a few yards from the back of the pool building. The short wall sticking out around the float store concealed the entrance. We couldn't see if Mary was or wasn't there. At least we could be sure the wicked witches weren't hiding on this side. We waded through the long grass of the nature reserve and stopped when we got to the store. This was it. The last opportunity to turn chicken and run. It was, after all, just a bag made of leather; just a bag with a fancy handle; just a briefcase. There is no way I would have gone through all of this for a sports bag, even a Sheffield United sports bag. But we had come so far, been through so much and planned so carefully, it couldn't… we couldn't… have done all that for nothing.

We nodded at each other. This was it. We were going in.

16 BITCH AND BOYS IN BRIEFS

We walked round to the gate. Mary stood there, the usual slippery smile on her face, but no briefcase.

'Well, well. Braver than I thought. Maybe your balls have dropped after all,' she said to me.

'Where is my briefcase?' Tarquin asked forcefully. Mary looked at him through cold, uncaring eyes.

'It's in here,' Mary said, pushing the gate to the pool open. 'Come on in, my lover,' she said, staring me in the eye.

'Why can't you give it to us here?' I asked nervously.

'Now, where's the fun in that?' she said. 'Come on. Come in.' She beckoned us forward like the Pied Piper luring children to their doom.

We followed her through into the pool enclosure. The witches were inside, smiling their manic smiles. The cover had been dragged off the pool and dragged up onto the walkway at the side. If I'd thought about, I might have twigged it was too heavy for the three girls to remove the cover on their own. They had needed help, so there must be others around as well. But this little detail passed me by. As far as I could see, it was just us, Mary, and the mad witches. The odds didn't seem so bad. The briefcase was there, at the far end of the pool, in the centre, waiting to be retrieved.

So why wait? I sprang into action, dashing off down one side. Tarquin dashed off down the other. Fuelled by adrenalin, we tore along the walkways, hearts racing, muscles pumping, eyes on the prize. We were going to sweep it up, throw it over the wall and fling ourselves over with it, until... SMACK, we hit two immoveable objects. Two of Mary's henchmen had jumped out from behind the changing rooms and charged into us. We went from sprint to stop in an instant. They grabbed our blazers by the neckline and yanked us up close. Their breath stank of stale cigarettes, as did their clothes and hands. Unfortunately, smoke and tar were yet to smother their lungs, cripple their strength and turn them into coughing hacks. That was yet to come. For now, they were big, ugly and menacing. Like a couple of orcs. They pushed us backwards then pushed us again.

'Help!' I screamed. 'Help! Help!' At that same moment, four 250cc petrol engines with no silencers roared into life. The sound was deafening outside the pool. Even shielded within the blue block walls, it was ridiculously loud. There was no chance anyone would ever hear us over that. 'HELP!' I shouted again. 'HELP! HELP! HELP!' Tarquin chorused in desperation. Nobody heard. Nobody came.

What we didn't know was that Winston was in one of those noisy go-karts. A driver in the first set of trials hadn't turned up, so Mr Trent had called Winston forward to take his place. Winston had suggested he wasn't ready, but Mr Trent would have none of it. He handed Winston a helmet and told him to take the end cart. The go-karts entered the circuit and lined up one behind the other. They would be released in ten-second intervals. To get the biggest length of track, the organisers had sacrificed the width. No one would overtake. If someone caught up with someone else, next time, they would be at the front of the grid. Winston was at the back. It wasn't that he was bad. On the contrary, he was one of the best of the fourth form, but this was an elite group of battle-hardened fifth formers. Winston didn't mind being at the back. It would be easier to keep an eye on the pool; not that he could do much from inside a go-kart.

Quinlan had gradually eased his way over towards the pool and was leaning against the blue wall, trying to figure out what was going on round the other side. He had been urged back once by one of the supervisors, who didn't want students too close to the track, but he had quietly eased his way back again, as close to the end as he dared to go, without looking like he was wandering off. He was listening as intently as he could, but as soon as the engines started up, he knew there was no way he was going to hear anything going on round the back. He moved a little further so that he could occasionally glimpse round the corner, but there was nobody there. *Where are they?* he thought. *Maybe they've got delayed by a member of staff.* He kept looking round the corner, in case something turned up.

Inside the pool enclosure, we were scared. We were outnumbered, outgunned, and we had no idea how we were going to get out of this alive.

The orcs smiled, enjoying our anxiety.

'Look! We just want the briefcase. Let us have the briefcase,' Tarquin implored.

'You can't use it. It's got his initials on it,' I pointed out, and pointed to Tarquin.

The big orc shrugged his heavy shoulders. 'We could burn it,' he said.

'Why?' I yelled, bewildered.

''Cos it burns,' he said, as if that was a perfectly rational answer to the question.

'Back!' grunted orc number two.

We traipsed back to Scary and her vamps: "Sick" was doing her weird dance moves and "Twisted" just stared and licked her lips. Every now and then, a poke in the back would encourage us to move a little quicker. Two more orcs had emerged from the float store and were guarding the exit gate. We weren't going to get out, unless someone else got in to save us.

'Oh dear, there's nobody coming,' Mary said in a sinister tone. 'You're just going to have to get the briefcase on your own.'

'But how can we? You won't let us,' I said anxiously, looking over at Tarquin, who was equally confused.

'You're not going to walk round and get it,' she said. 'You're going to swim.'

'You've gotta be kiddin'!' I shouted. 'It's f**kin' freezing. We'd freeze to death.'

'I am not swimming in there,' Tarquin said. 'You can keep the briefcase.' He made his way to the exit, but the orcs at the gate made it clear there was no way out.

'I didn't say you had an option, did I?' Scary advised, her smile matching the menacing tone of her voice.

'We'll get soaking wet. Our clothes will be dripping!' I shouted.

'You're not going to be wearing them,' she said.

'We're not taking our clothes off. That's nuts,' I said.

'That is sexual harassment,' Tarquin said. 'My father is a lawyer. He will have you locked up.'

Mary recoiled slightly at that suggestion, then recovered her poise.

'You don't wear clothes in a swimming pool,' she said, 'but you do wear trunks. I'll let you keep your pants on.'

Strangely, despite our horrendous predicament, being able to keep your pants on was a massive relief. I could contain my fear if I could keep my pants on.

'What're we going to do?' I whispered to Tarquin.

'I do not think we have much of a choice,' Tarquin said,

THE BOY AND THE BRIEFCASE... AND THE MOOSE

looking across at the orcs. 'I would rather remove my own clothes than have somebody else remove them for me.'

'Okay,' I said. 'We'll take off our own clothes.'

'Such a shame,' Mary said with regret, 'I was hoping to remove them with my teeth.' Tarquin's response combined concern and revulsion in equal measure.

'You know, you are very weird. Don't you think you should see a psychiatrist?' he said.

Mary almost went ballistic. Only the threat of attracting hoards of go-karters stopped her screaming like an air raid siren. She opened her mouth so wide that I thought she was going to swallow him whole. She was proper mad. She was shaking. She was apoplectic.

'Get your f**kin' clothes off, tosspot,' she shrieked.

My trousers dropped in an instant. They may even have dropped on their own. I don't know. One second, they were up; the next, they were down. I was born to obey orders. It's an instinct or a compulsion. I just can't help myself. When someone says run, I run. When someone says jump, I jump. When they say drop your trousers, that is exactly what happens. I was made for the infantry, or maybe marriage. I was soon throwing aside clothing in all directions. My blazer followed my trousers in quick succession. Socks were wrenched off and cast aside. Tie was loosened, whipped over my head and discarded, like a noose. The shirt was awkward. I grabbed the tails, threw them up over my head and almost pulled my ears off as I wrenched the collar free. It was still attached to me by the cuffs. I curled my hands into tiny tubes as I yanked the rigid cuffs inside out and over them. The button scraped a groove in the skin on the way. In my enthusiasm, I grabbed my pants and was about to whip these off as well, when one of the orcs shouted out, 'Not the pants, dipstick. I don' wanna see y' todger, no matter how tiny it is.'

I was shocked. I didn't know the orcs could string sentences together. This one sounded almost human.

Whilst I had been whirling round discarding clothes like a rotary washing line in a hurricane, Tarquin had been carefully removing his and folding them neatly in a pile. The blazer was first. He slipped it back and down over his arms, then folded it neatly into thirds and placed it on the concrete flags. He sat on it to undo his laces and slip off his shoes. He took off his socks, rolled them up and inserted them deep inside the shoes. Then he placed the shoes together and put them to one side of the blazer. He undid his belt and removed it, winding it round and round into a liquorice whirl, before also placing it in one of the shoes. He dropped his trousers down over his knees before raising one foot out of one leg and then the other foot out of the other. He held the trousers up by the bottoms, until they hung flat to the creases, then he dropped the waist gently down onto the blazer followed gradually by about a third of the trousers, folding them back once, and once again. He undid all the buttons down the front of his shirt, followed by the cuffs, sliding it partway down over his arms, before taking hold of one cuff to pull out his arm and repeating on the other side. Then he folded it up, nice and neat, before placing it on top of the trousers. Everyone watched in silence. It was slow, calm and meditative, the sort of thing that would be used as a relaxation video nowadays, if it wasn't for the half-naked child, of course. Under any other circumstances, I'm sure we would have clapped, but it didn't seem like the time or the place.

I stood, in nothing but my pants, shivering. Years of holidays on the Yorkshire coast, basking in the northern sunshine, had left me pale and pasty, and when combined with my skinny legs and bony arms, I didn't look up to much. But, underneath this unassuming exterior was a second team, second row forward, house discus champion and, as it happens, a pretty good swimmer. I knew I was up to the challenge.

If my exterior was considered unassuming, then Tarquin's was probably assuming. He sported a fairly muscular physique and an olive complexion that can only be achieved by spending several weeks every summer sunning yourself on a beach in the South of France. He looked like he was genetically engineered to be a future James Bond. His steely eyes and sturdy jaw certainly suited the role. It would be fair to say, even without his clothes, he looked like he didn't belong in our school. He did, however, look like he too was ready to face whatever came next.

One orc shook off his hazy stupor and gave directions.

'Stand by the pool, tossers,' he said in his gruff orcish tone. Mary decided it was time for her to regain control.

'To make this whole thing a little bit more exciting,' she said, 'we're making it a race.'

'I'm racing Tarquin?' I said, mildly excited by the prospect.

'No, lover boy,' she said.

'Are we racing you?' I said, confused.

'No! Y'moron!' she said, as if the idea was preposterous.

'Are we racing the Or... Or... orthers?' I asked. There wasn't anyone else.

'No, lover boy. You're racing time. If you can get to the end in twenty seconds, you get the briefcase and walk free. Any longer and we keep the briefcase.' She smiled smugly as if we didn't stand a chance.

'Okay!' I said, happy with the proposal.

'How do we know when to go?' Tarquin asked.

'I say, ready, steady, go.' Mary said, as if it was obvious.

'Okay!' Tarquin replied.

I knew I could easily manage a length of the pool in twenty seconds, and Tarquin looked pretty fit, I reckoned he probably could as well. We stepped up to the edge of the pool, curling our toes over the rounded coping. We bent down, arms back, eyes focused ahead.

'Ready!'

Weight shifted onto the balls of our feet.

'Steady!'

Rolling slowly forward to the point of no return.

'Go!'

BAM! The spring uncoiled. I sprung from the ledge, arms thrown forward, flying through the air, stretching out, reaching for the water and slicing through it like a knife. A single stroke then up into front crawl; fingers dip in, pull round, push, flick, reach and repeat. Head turning every third stroke to gasp for breath whilst legs thrashed around behind. I was powering along, out to set a record. I sensed movement in the periphery of my vision. I turned further and glanced a figure making for the end of the pool. The bastards were going to cheat. They were going to grab the briefcase. I pulled harder and thrashed quicker, almost there. I grabbed for the end of the pool, but the briefcase was gone.

Tarquin hit the end at about the same time.

'They've got it,' I shouted across to him. 'They've got the briefcase.'

An orc was racing back down the pool, briefcase in hand, heading for the gate.

'See y' suckers,' Mary shouted. She had a pile of clothes in her hands, our clothes. Mary, orcs and witches all headed out of the gate.

We jumped out of the pool and ran back down each side.

We charged out of the gate. Mary was heading across the grass to the car park entrance. The orcs and briefcase were heading north-west towards the top corner of the nature reserve, as far from prying eyes as possible.

I yelled at Tarquin, 'You get the briefcase. I'll get the clothes.' Okay!' he shouted back, and set off after the orcs.

Quinlan had been studiously checking round the corner of the pool every few minutes. He saw the orcs as soon as they left, followed by Tarquin chasing behind. He waved frantically at Winston and pointed round the corner. Winston was approaching the far end of the track. Taking the tight corner, he caught sight of the figures running across the nature reserve, Tarquin in nothing but his underpants. That was when Winston did something that would have been deemed insane and irresponsible in the eyes of the authorities, but truly heroic in the eyes of everyone else. He turned his steering wheel sharply to the right, swerved, and jumped the timber kerb. He was outside the track, unconstrained and heading for the nature reserve. He hit the long grass at full pelt, cutting a wide swathe straight through it. Sitting so low in the go-kart, he was almost invisible to onlookers. Just the roar of the engine, the flattened grass and his head floating over the seed heads showed he was there.

The orcs had made quick progress across the nature reserve, but Winston was catching up fast. He overtook Tarquin in no time at all and was soon chasing down the rear two orcs. He made straight for them. They dived out of the way. Winston followed, snapping at their heels. They raced to the northern boundary. If Winston had caught them, he would have run straight over them. They were running for their lives. They tore through the bushes along the boundary and jumped the fence into gardens beyond. Winston swerved back in pursuit of the remaining two. They had the briefcase. He skirted around and came at them from the side. One peeled off and scarpered towards the north-west boundary, jumping over into a dead-end street. He could be seen limping frantically away through the chain link fence. Just the one orc left. Winston spun around and chased him back away from the boundary, straight into Tarquin, who tackled him, rugby style, to the ground. Winston jumped out of the kart. The orc threw Tarquin off and jumped to his feet, but Winston was on him in a second. The orc swung a flailing haymaker at Winston, who dodged it and hit him, once in the stomach and once on the chin. That was all it took. He was out of it. Tarquin grabbed the briefcase and quickly opened it to remove a bicycle spanner. Winston looked shocked. 'Are y' gonna beat his brains in?' he questioned anxiously.

'No, I'm sorting out your alibi.' Tarquin quickly undid the nut holding the steering pin and yanked it free. 'You were out of control,' he said, and shot off in the direction of his clothes.

Winston pinned the orc to the ground as he regained his senses.

'Listen, dickface,' he said, 'if you and your flea-bitten bunch of morons do anything to anyone, anymore, we will hunt you down and destroy you.

'If you so much as touch someone, we will hunt you down and destroy you.

'If you speak to anyone in a way we don't like, we will hunt you down and destroy you.

'If you and your morons are seen together again, we will hunt you down and destroy you.

'We will make your lives hell. I have already spoken to the rugby captains,' he lied. 'They are all on board, as are the teams. Let's face it, there is nothing they like more than mindless violence. Get the message out to your mates, and let them know, they're not your mates anymore.

'Now f**k off.'

The kid scrambled to his feet and raced off.

Winston cut the engine on his cart. He could hear the crowd of teachers and kids racing down the track he had cut through the long grass. Mr Trent arrived, panting like a loon. He put his hands on his hips and tried to regain control of his breathing.

'What the hell are you doing? You could have killed someone.' Winston pointed to the steering column. The pin was gone. The steering mechanism separated from the wheels.

'It was out of control,' Winston said.

'Why the hell didn't you stop then? You've got brakes,' Mr Trent argued.

'I don't know. I panicked. I thought the accelerator was the brake and pushed harder. I was trying to avoid the trees. I wasn't thinking straight. I was scared to death.'

Winston burst into tears. Whether it was the adrenalin cutting out, the relief it was all over, or the best acting the school has ever seen, we don't know. Winston never said, but it certainly did the trick. Suddenly everyone was consoling him, saying 'It wasn't your fault,' and 'These things happen,' as if they did.

Tarquin and Winston's antics were told to me after the event. They are pieced together from their own accounts, and also from Quinlan, who had been one of the chasing crowd. Whilst they were having their adventure, I was having mine.

When Tarquin went one way at the gate to the pool, I went the other. Mary and the witches were making for the car park and the exit beyond. Although the distance was somewhat shorter than the route the orcs had taken, it was hampered by tangled undergrowth. Their feet got caught up in a mess of brambles, honeysuckle and a myriad of other stringy plants. I was catching up, and I was catching up fast. There was no way they would reach the gate before I did.

Smack, bang, I tripped over and came crashing down. I heard a voice behind me. 'What the f**k?' I turned around. I had tripped over Mandy Aicart and John Hollocks writhing around in the undergrowth.

'You t**ts, you f**kin' t**ts, I've f**kin' lost them,' I screamed. By now, my normal restraint had evaporated. It had all got too much. They probably thought I was a lunatic, standing there naked, apart from a baggy pair of Y-fronts, screaming at them at the top of my voice. They certainly got up and scarpered quick enough. 'I've f**kin' lost them.' I burst into floods of tears. It had all been too much. Josephine slapped me across the face.

'What?' It had shocked me back to reality, which I hope was the intention.

'Which of these are yours?' she demanded.

I looked down. She had in her hands both sets of clothes.

'Quick, we've got to get the others to Tarquin.'

I grabbed my garments and stood there holding them. I had stopped functioning clearly and my head was in a bit of a muddle.

'Where's Tarquin?' she demanded forcibly.

'He chased after the orcs to get his briefcase back,' I said.

'After who?' she urged. I was a little unresponsive by this time.

'Her henchmen, the orcs. They went over to the north boundary,' I said slowly. Josephine was in leader mode.

'Kate, Georgy and Anne, tabards off and give them to Karen. Karen, you stay here and look after Andy. Use the tabards to dry him. Shit! He's looking a bit blue. Get him inside quick. Dry him there.'

'Okay,' they agreed.

'The rest of you, find Tarquin. Here, take these,' she said to Anne, passing her the clothes. 'Make sure he's all right. I've got a few words to say to Mary.'

Karen grabbed me by the hand.

'Come on. We're getting inside, quick.'

I ran with her to the sports hall exit. Once inside, she handed me a tabard to dry myself off, then she swapped it for a dry one. She dried me off at the same time, rubbing violently to warm me up.

'You're dry enough now,' she said, 'you'd better get your clothes on before anyone comes.' She passed me the trousers, which I dragged up as quickly as possible over my damp legs. Then she gave me my shirt. I pushed my arms through before pulling it down over my head. Then, I put my blazer on, followed by socks and shoes. We heard footsteps down the corridor. 'Quick, in here,' she said, and dragged me into the woodwork shop, closing the door behind us. We sat down on the floor, backs against the warm cast iron radiator. We heard Mrs Stubbs talking to the deputy head.

'My girls do not run amok. If they're not on the court, there'll be a very good reason, I can assure you.' Her words were a little slurred. Clearly, the wine tasting, or at least the wine, had gone down very well.

17 BOY AND THE BRIEF KISS

The warmth from the radiator was beginning to seep into my bones, and I was beginning to feel normal once again, normal, that is, apart from the fact there was a girl sitting next to me.

'Are you okay?' she asked warmly.

'Yeah. I think so,' I said. 'How come you're in the netball team?'

'Because I'm good at netball,' she replied, stating the obvious.

'But how can you be?' I asked.

'Because I am,' she replied, slightly indignant.

'But you're slow. You're always late for lessons. Always,' I explained.

'I don't want to get to lessons,' she said. 'Between lessons is when I do my thinking.'

'What thinking?'

'I make up stories,' she revealed. 'I want to be a writer.'

'Oh wow! A writer, that's amazing!' I said, impressed.

'Is it?' she frowned.

'It's fantastic,' I said. 'It's... special.'

She smiled. 'Do you think so?'

'Yeah. I wish I could write stories,' I said enviously.

'Anyone can be a writer,' she said. 'You just need a pen and a piece of paper.'

'I don't think I could.'

'Yeah, you could,' she said. 'You talk like a writer.'

'Whadaya mean?' It was my turn to frown.

'You make up funny stories. I've heard you in class.'

'Nah. They're just stupid,' I said dismissively.

'No, they're not, they're funny. I like them.'

'Do you? Really?' I asked.

'Yeah.' She smiled; a beautiful wide smile.

'Can I read one of your stories?' I asked.

'Why?' She looked unsure.

''Cause I think you'd write good stories,' I said honestly.

'How would you know?'

''Cause I like to listen to you in class,' I admitted. 'You're funny.'

I was beginning to get that sick feeling again. My stomach was rising into my chest. I was feeling light-headed. *No!* I said to myself. *Karen's all right. I don't need to be afraid of Karen.*

'Whadaya mean, funny?' she challenged, head on one side, looking me over.

'You say funny things. Like the bucket thing in Madame Oublions' class, when you said it was to be sick in. It made me laugh.'

'Oh yeah. That was funny,' she accepted.

'And what you did in the library… that was genius.'

'Yeah, it was, wasn't it,' she said smugly.

'I'm really glad you're looking after me,' I said, a little more seriously, a little more hopeful.

She went quiet. Then she looked right at me, right into my eyes. When Josephine did the same, earlier in the day, she had examined me as if I was an exhibit in the Natural History Museum, a stuffed animal, the "Bakerus Pupilicus". Karen didn't just look at me; she looked deep inside me. She seemed to be reading my mind. And her eyes, her eyes were so beautiful.

'I'm glad I am too,' she said.

'You're... you're... so... beautiful,' I said.

And she kissed me. She kissed me on the lips, and I kissed her back, and I kissed her again, and I put my arm round her stomach, and she kissed me again. And I kissed her back. I was awash with weird and wonderful emotions. I was almost sick with pleasure.

Voices in the corridor.

'I told her to come here.' It was Josephine's voice. 'She can't have left. Her clothes are still in the changing room.'

'Where are they then?' It was Tarquin.

Karen opened the door to the woodwork room, and we both peered out, looking more than a little sheepish.

'We were in here,' she said, 'sitting against the radiator.'

'She was warming me up,' I said.

Josephine looked at me, and then at Karen. Her eyes said, *I bet you were.*

Karen's cheeks flushed red. I was probably red all over.

'Good thinking, Karen. Are you okay?' she said, checking me over. 'You looked a bit blue out there.'

'I'm fine now,' I said.

Again, her eyes said, *I bet you are.*

'How're you?' I said to Tarquin, deflecting the conversation elsewhere.

'I am fine, thank you. A bit cold, but I am warming up gradually.'

'How did you get the briefcase?' I asked, noting it hanging by his side.

'Winston played a blinder,' he said. 'But... it is a long story. I do not know all the detail. Better to wait till everyone is around.'

'Sure,' I agreed.

'I'm going to see if I can find Winston and Quinlan,' Tarquin said. 'See you later.'

'I'll show you the way,' Georgy said, winking at Josephine as she went past.

'What happened to Scary and the crones?' I said to Josephine.

'You mean Ursula and Rain?' she replied tersely.

'Is that their names?' I asked.

'Well, they're not called "The Crones", are they.'

'What sort of name is Rain?' I queried.

'A wet one,' she replied.

'Fair enough.' I said. 'So what did happen with Scary?'

'We saw you running away from the pool. You are very white with no clothes on, y'know. You almost glowed. It was like following a ghost.'

'Thanks!' I blushed again.

'So we dashed out of the court and ran across the car park, which is when we saw Mary, Ursula and Rain ahead of you. We raced over to cut them off before they got to the gate. You must have fallen at that point. Anyway, Angela did a brilliant dive and knocked Mary clean over. Completely floored her. The other two nipped over the gate and were off down the road. We didn't go after them. No point. We could see Mary had your clothes, so we brought them back over to you then headed off to find Tarquin.'

'But what happened to Mary?' I pressed.

'Angela and Sam kept her pinned down on the ground. I gave you the clothes then went back over to her.' Josephine paused and shook her head, seemingly unsure of what she had witnessed. 'She is a bit weird, you know. She was crying like a baby. Out of control. Not the tough girl we've come to know and hate.'

'Maybe it was because she needs the witches around,' I suggested.

'They're not witches. They're people.' Josephine had clearly decided she did not like labels.

'Okay! Okay! I'm sorry,' I apologised. Josephine softened and carried on.

'Anyway, I told her to stop making everyone's life a misery. To stop being a bastard, and to stop hanging around with those tosser friends of hers, those boys.'

'They're not tossers, they're people,' I said.

'No! Those boys definitely are tossers,' she said. I shrugged. This was not an argument I was going to win. 'I asked Mary why she couldn't just be nice, but she just kept on crying, on and on. It was pathetic. It was pitiful.'

'Then what?' I asked.

'I said if she so much as laid a finger on anyone else, we'd make her suffer. Then I told her to sod off. She dragged herself to her feet, eyes dripping with that black make-up she uses, then she did the weirdest thing of all.'

'What?' I wondered if anything could be weirder.

'She said, "Sorry." I think she meant it. It was very weird. Really sad. She was completely broken. Then she went out of the gate and plodded off down the road.' I couldn't believe Josephine had any sympathy for that monster.

'She almost broke me,' I said.

'I know. I know,' she acknowledged. 'She's horrible, and I hate her. But… she's not right… she's just not right, and she's definitely not happy.'

'You can't make her happy,' I said. 'I sure as hell wouldn't want to try.' Josephine looked concerned.

'I don't know. I really don't know. I think she needs help,' she said, unsure what to do.

'You can't help Mary, she's a moron,' I declared, perplexed. 'Why should anyone want to help her?'

'She's not a moron,' Karen said. 'She's quite bright really. She's just a bastard.'

I wasn't sure if the difference between "moron" and "bastard" was enough to warrant helping her, but I got a feeling I was swimming against the tide.

'I'll speak to her,' Josephine said. 'I know it sounds stupid, but like Tarquin and Quinlan said about the bullies at Rugby School, maybe… just maybe… we need to make friends with her now this is over.' She put her hands over her face as if just the thought of it was painful.

'Rather you than me,' I said, absolutely certain I wasn't taking part.

'No! You as well,' Josephine replied.

'You've got to be kidding. She almost killed me,' I blurted out.

'You didn't see her,' Josephine said, clearly affected by the experience. 'She's a mess.'

'Oh, come on. You can't make me,' I pleaded.

'Give it a try,' she said, dragging me softly towards the tipping point.

'Go on,' Karen said, nudging me gently over.

'Okay… Okay… I'll give it a try.' To be honest, my mind was wandering back to kissing Karen, and was trying to figure out how to get back there. I nudged her and with my eyes tried to suggest maybe we go back into the woodwork room. But she gently shook her head. It was over. My first sexual encounter ended as quickly as it had begun. I know it was just a kiss, but it seemed pretty momentous to me.

'I've got to get changed,' Karen said apologetically. 'See you later.'

'Hope so,' I replied.

'By the way,' Josephine said, 'if Mrs Stubbs sees you, say there were three of them; two blokes and a woman.'

'Okay,' I said, but to what exactly, I wasn't quite sure.

The girls filed into the changing room, leaving me alone in the corridor. I knew I couldn't hang around outside the girls' changing room, so I started heading up the corridor.

At that moment, Mrs Stubbs crashed through the sports hall doors, followed by the deputy head.

'I told you there was a reason,' Stubbs said. 'They were chasing intruders off the premises.'

'We can't be sure of that,' the deputy head replied.

'Of course we can. That new boy saw them as well. Helped chase after them apparently. What's his name?'

'Quinlan?' the deputy head suggested

'No, the other one,' Stubbs blustered.

'Tarquin?' the deputy head proposed.

'Yes, Tarquin. He saw them and that girl from the fourth year, the one with black hair and big…' Mrs Stubbs indicated boobs with her hands but stopped short of saying the word.

'What? Mandy? Mandy Aicart?' the deputy head queried.

'I think that's her name,' Stubbs continued, 'and the boy from the fifth year that she hangs round with. The one with the greasy hair and the lisp.'

'John Hollocks?'

'Yes, Hollocks. That's the one. Both he and Mandy said they had no clothes on.'

'Really? No clothes? That's a bit weird, isn't it?'

'Quite! Oh, and that tall kid also saw them. The skinny one, you know, the one that won the maths prize.'

'What? Baker?' the deputy head replied.

'Yes. I've not seen Baker myself, but that's what I've been told. Look, there he is now.' I tried to look inconspicuous but failed miserably.

'Baker! What are you doing?' the deputy head called out. 'You know you shouldn't be here.'

'Sorry, miss. I was talking to Josephine about the intruders,' I said.

'Do you know who they were?' She fixed me with that terrifying stare, a stare honed by the interrogation of hundreds of hapless pupils, most of which admitted to crimes they couldn't possibly have committed. I wondered if she was in the Gestapo during the war.

'No. Just two blokes and a woman. I didn't see them clearly. Most of the girls were ahead of me. I thought they came out of the pool enclosure, but I can't be sure.'

'The pool enclosure? What were they doing... swimming?' She laughed hysterically at her own preposterous suggestion.

'Probably taking drugs, I wouldn't wonder,' Mrs Stubbs proposed. 'Youth nowadays.' She shook her head despondently.

'You do know you should never engage an intruder, Baker,' the deputy head advised, somewhat too late.

'No,' I said honestly.

'Hmm, well, you shouldn't. You're lucky they didn't have knives.' She jabbed me with her index finger to demonstrate. I recoiled, staggering back a couple of steps. My left hand automatically went to cover the imaginary wound. As I pulled it away, I was relieved to see there was no blood. I looked up, annoyed by the unnecessary attack.

'Nobody carries a knife,' I said.

'Some do,' she replied, nodding sadly, 'you hear about it on the news all the time. Next time, call a member of staff,' she said in a motherly manner.

'Yes, miss,' I agreed willingly.

'Very well. Now be off with you.' She waved me away.

I trudged down the corridor and up towards the cloaks. I wasn't sure what had just happened. I was mulling it over in my head. Not the briefcase, or the pool, or the chase; I was thinking about the kiss. It was really nice; I really liked it. I wanted to do it again. But how? How could I? I didn't think the nature reserve was an option. Karen seemed too nice for a trip to forbidden places. I didn't even know if we were "together" anyway. We'd kissed, but I'm not sure that meant she was my girlfriend.

God, this was confusing. Lost in thought, I emerged into the playground.

The last dregs of sunlight were skipping over the houses and flickering across the playing field. Winston, Tarquin and Quinlan were making their way round from the north playground. It was quarter past five. Fifteen minutes to go till Tarquin and Quinlan were being picked up by the housemaster. We sat on a bench overlooking the playing fields.

'The karting's been cancelled,' Winston called out. 'They're checking the steering columns on all the other carts. They're gonna use a locking nut or somethin' to make sure the pin can't come out again.'

We sat there for a while in silence, taking it all in, wondering if we'd ever have another day like today, wondering if we ever wanted another day like today.

'That... was absolutely amazing,' Quinlan said, in a kind of dreamy voice.

'Yeah,' Tarquin agreed, 'absolutely, incredibly amazing.'

'Absolutely, incredibly, brilliantly amazing,' I concurred.

'Can't wait till tomorrow,' Winston said. 'Can we do it all again?'

'No way. Never. Not if my life depended on it,' Quinlan replied.

'Not my life, your life, my friends' lives. Not to save the world,' Tarquin answered emphatically.

'I hope so,' I said. 'I really, really hope so.'

They all turned to look at me. Their expression was one of curiosity and concern.

'What?' I shrugged. 'It was absolutely f**kin' amazing.'

18 GOODBYE TO THE BOY AND THE BRIEFCASE

Tarquin checked the time on his digital watch.

'Five twenty-five,' he said. 'We'd better make a move.'

We wandered along the path in front of the school.

'Are you coming back?' I asked Tarquin and Quinlan. It had been a hell of a day. I wouldn't blame them if they never left the safety of Rugby School ever again.

'Yes,' Tarquin said. 'Definitely. This is a very, very weird school, but it's been good fun.'

'I will be back,' said Quinlan. 'It has been mad, completely mad, but wow, what a day.'

When we got to the car park, we stepped over the low fence and sat on the steps leading up to the main entrance. It wasn't long before a silver-grey Mercedes made its way towards us and stopped just short of the steps. We all stood up. Mr Pickering, Rugby School's housemaster, got out and walked right up to us. He smiled and stuck his hand out towards me.

'Good evening,' he said.

I sort of guessed I had to shake hands but didn't really know how. I tentatively offered my limp-wristed floppy hand towards him.

He looked at it as if it was a rotten fish, or something equally disagreeable.

'No, no, no. That won't do at all,' he said. 'Firm hand, strong wrist. Shows confidence. Try again.'

My next attempt was more karate chop than friendly greeting. He grabbed my spatula hand and gave it a friendly but firm shake.

'Much better,' he said. 'Much better. I am Mr Pickering, the housemaster.' There was an awkward pause, before he continued. 'And... you are?'

'And... I... am a child,' I said.

He roared with laughter. 'No, your name, numbskull,' he said good-heartedly.

'Oh! Andrew,' I replied.

'Hello, Andrew,' he said, shaking my hand once more.

'Hi! I'm Winston,' Winston said, grabbing his hand and shaking vigorously.

'Hello, Winston. Mr Pickering,' he repeated, wriggling his fingers to loosen them after Winston's knuckle crusher.

'Good evening, sir,' Tarquin and Quinlan cut in, each proffering a well-practised hand.

'Good evening, boys.'

'So, you two are tasked with looking after our two young ambassadors,' he said to me and Winston.

'I guess so,' Winston said, 'although they're pretty good at looking after themselves, to be honest.'

'Good to hear it,' he said cheerfully, looking across at his two wards.

'Oh and there's Josephine,' I said. 'She's also been helping out.'

'Josephine, eh? A girl showing you round. How's that been?' he asked, curious.

'She is pretty good,' Tarquin admitted.

'She has been great,' Quinlan added.

At that moment, Josephine arrived with the headmaster, who immediately engaged our visitor.

'Hello, Mr Pickering. Terribly sorry I wasn't here to welcome you. There's been a bit of an incident, I'm afraid.'

'Nothing too troublesome, I hope?' Mr Pickering enquired politely.

'Intruders, three of them. Swimming in the pool, would you believe, while the Karting Club was in full throttle.'

'Goodness. In this weather, are they mad?' Mr Pickering said.

'One of our fourth-year girls, Mandy Aicart, was attacked. She's got a huge bruise on the side of her face,' the headmaster added.

'Gosh! That's appalling.'

'She said they were…' He looked around as if checking there was anybody else listening in, and whispered, 'They were… naked.'

'Naked! Naked!' Mr Pickering exclaimed, ignoring the need for quiet confidentiality. 'But it's freezing. They must have escaped from an asylum.'

'They weren't naked,' I stated. 'They had white trunks on. One of them was very pale, so it probably looked like he was naked.'

'Oh, I see,' Mr Pickering said, 'that's a relief. Even so… Rugby… it's hardly the Seychelles now, is it?'

'The Seychelles?' I asked, turning to the headmaster.

'It's like the Isle of Wight with sunshine,' he muttered.

'And white trunks! White trunks? I didn't even know you could get white trunks.' Mr Pickering seemed shocked by the idea.

'What the hell is wrong with white trunks?' the headmaster queried, perplexed by Mr Pickering's reaction.

'You'd see through them, wouldn't you… when they're wet?' he said.

'Oh! I don't know. Maybe. Uggh.' The headmaster squirmed. I have to admit I glanced down at my underpants, now safely concealed beneath my trousers, wondering if they became see-through when wet. It was a horrible thought. The whole of the netball team saw me earlier.

'What about the woman?' Mr Pickering queried. 'What was she wearing?'

'She had a full swimming costume... in black,' Josephine added, using her hands to indicate it covered her whole torso. I think she was trying to bring a hint of respectability back to proceedings.

'Well, thank goodness for that,' said the headmaster. 'We can't have a naked woman running around on site. God preserve us!' He shuddered. The thought was obviously utterly repugnant.

'So where are the intruders now?' Mr Pickering enquired.

'Young Tarquin here chased them off. He's a bit of a hero by all accounts.'

'Really?' Mr Pickering looked at Tarquin as if seeing him afresh. 'On your own?'

'Not exactly,' Tarquin admitted. 'Me, Andrew, Josephine and the whole netball team saw them off.'

'Well, Tarquin, I can't say I'm not impressed. I will ensure tales of your daring deeds reach the ear of the headmaster. Whether they go any further is up to him.' Mr Pickering's attention turned to the girl. 'So, you must be the noble Lady Josephine,' he said, offering her his hand, somewhat more delicately than to the rest of us.

'Yes. Nice to meet you, sir,' she said, accepting the compliment as though it was inevitable. She shook his hand firmly and vigorously. He seemed disconcerted by her self-confidence and easy smile. The headmaster smirked surreptitiously. He had chosen well.

'So! You and your Amazonians repelled the invaders?' he said buoyantly.

'I guess you mean the netball team,' she replied. 'We were in the games court nearby when we saw the intruders. Right place right time.'

'How did you know they were intruders?'

'Adults; swimming costumes.'

'Oh! Yes, quite. And I guess they were running as well.' Josephine nodded in response. 'What did they look like?'

'One of the men was tall, pale and skinny, looked like he'd never seen the sun.' I rolled my eyes in the background. 'The other one was more tanned and muscular.' Tarquin smiled smugly. 'We didn't really see their faces. It all happened so quickly. They were running away.'

'What about the woman?'

'Medium height, long brown hair, tanned. Nothing distinctive.'

'Are the police informed?'

'Yes, of course,' the headmaster boomed. 'The deputy head spoke to them straight away.'

'Well, I don't rate your chances of catching them, Headmaster,' Mr Pickering confided. 'They have not got much to go on.'

'I'm rather hoping that Mandy Aicart might be able to describe them,' the headmaster informed us. 'She got the closest look.'

'I see. Well, let's hope they're soon behind bars,' Mr Pickering said buoyantly.

'Quite right! We can't have perverts and thugs outside our schools,' the headmaster decreed.

'There's already too many inside,' Winston whispered.

'I thought you needed to know, so you can take precautions. You wouldn't want something similar to happen at Rugby School, now, would you?' the headmaster advised.

'Oh, I can't imagine it would,' Mr Pickering said. 'We've not got an outside swimming pool. Ours is indoors... heated.'

'Hmm, really? How nice,' the headmaster replied sarcastically.

Mr Pickering began to round up proceedings. 'Come along, boys. Say your goodbyes. It's time we were heading back. Goodbye, Headmaster. Goodbye, children.' Mr Pickering turned and made his way back to the car, where he opened a rear door. Tarquin and Quinlan said goodbye to everyone and climbed into the back seat. Mr Pickering closed the door, got in the front, waved one last time through the windscreen, turned the car around and headed out, along the drive.

'They weren't so bad in the end,' Winston admitted.

'Almost likeable,' I agreed.

'I hope they do come back,' Josephine said. 'It's been a hell of a day. I wouldn't blame them if they didn't.'

'It's been quite a day for all of us,' the headmaster acknowledged. 'Time for you to go home.' He dragged his weary bones back inside. The day had clearly taken its toll.

'Are you going back on the bus?' I said to Josephine.

'Not today, my parents are picking me up in a minute. They could probably give you a lift.'

'No, thanks. I'm fine.' The last thing I wanted was polite conversation with grown-ups.

'See you then,' she said.

'See you,' me and Winston chorused.

We climbed back over the car park fence and wandered back down to the student entrance gate. Winston turned left into Tin Town, and I wandered off towards the bus stop.

Tin Town was called Tin Town because the first floor and roof of all the houses on the estate were made of painted corrugated iron. They were homes for heroes, constructed shortly after the Second World War. They were a bit quirky and rough-looking; they didn't exactly look like homes for heroes. However, like lots of council housing at the time, they had good gardens and decent-sized rooms. It was suggested the reason why the corrugated iron started at the first floor was because women never looked up far enough to see the grot. Why they never looked up was never explained. Maybe too many were downtrodden and depressed. Women's lib still had a long way to go at the time. Or maybe it was just a load of bollocks.

19 THE BOY AND THE BITCH ON THE BUS

I wandered around the bus stop till the next bus turned up. I was thinking, and wandering helped me think. I was thinking about Karen. Now I had kissed her, did that mean she was my girlfriend? What was a girlfriend, and did I really want one? These thoughts whirred round and round in my head. I got onto the bus in a bit of a daze, flashed my bus pass to the driver as I went past and made my way down the bus. It was rush hour and the bus was packed with men and women on the way home. The work bus was always a bit depressing. Weary faces, crammed together, silently staring into space. I drifted towards an empty seat and slid into it, oblivious to anything around me; oblivious to anyone around me; oblivious to the fact that I had sat next to my nemesis, next to Scary Mary. In defence of my oblivion, she had wiped away the thick black eyeliner that defined her, and the half-unbuttoned blouse was now firmly buttoned. She looked almost normal, almost respectable, not the same person at all.

After she had run off, she must have decided to avoid the embarrassment of waiting with a hoard of schoolkids at the school bus stop, and walked up the main road, boarding at a stop further up. I'm guessing the last person she expected or wanted to sit next to was me.

But I didn't even notice her; I was thinking about Karen. I was thinking how she had smelt when I kissed her. She smelt gorgeous. She had been playing netball, so she should have been sweaty, but she didn't smell sweaty. She smelt of fruit. Not sharp like an orange or sweet like bananas, or fresh like an apple; it was a nice combination of all of them. It was more... more... pear-like than anything else. I liked pears so that was okay. I would have preferred melon, but you can't have everything.

Whilst I mused over the musk of many fruits, I made noises; thinking noises; repetitive noises; "clicks" and "plops" with my tongue and "mops" with my lips. Mops are the sound made when you seal your lips together then open them quickly, like a fish gasping for air. I also tapped my toes, and then my heels, then various heel-toe combinations. I was a one-man band of thinking sounds. It was probably the drumming on the metal rail of the chair in front, with my fingers, that was the last straw. Mary was clearly not one for thinking noises. It seems she found them particularly annoying. She bottled it all up inside, till about halfway into town, when she couldn't contain it anymore. Through gritted teeth, she quietly said, 'Will you shut the f**k up.' I was still in a dopey state of mind so I turned towards her, slightly surprised by the outburst, but with the honest intention of apologising to the young lady for my annoying habit. That was when I recognised her and that was when I discovered that my legs have a fear response all of their own. The top half of me was stunned, as if hit by a tranquiliser dart, but my legs sprung into action, propelling me out of the seat and into the aisle.

My head landed squarely in the lap of the lady opposite. I clambered to my feet, swaying around as the bus turned a corner.

'Sorry! Sorry!' I splurted, blushing a bright red.

'Don't worry, son,' she said conspiratorially, 'that's the most action I've 'ad in weeks.'

I didn't know what she meant, and I didn't care. I was staggering back over to the other side of the bus. I threw out an arm to grab a pole but missed. The bus turned another corner and I was catapulted backwards and thrown over the two ladies that were sitting in front of my seat.

There was a lot of swearing and cursing, though not from me, as I tried to roll over onto my front to extract myself from this hellhole. I ended up partly wedged between stockinged knees and the seat in front. In my struggles, I grabbed the top rail of the seat with one hand, placed my other hand I know not where, and pushed myself up and back into the aisle, landing on my knees.

'Get off me, you dirty f**kin' bastard,' one of the women said, as if I had choreographed the whole routine. 'Find your own f**kin' woman.' It would have been fair to say, if I had been seeking out a woman of choice, they wouldn't have been top of my list.

I clambered to my feet, holding firmly onto the pole I had missed a few seconds before. Mary was laughing her head off. She was crying laughing, wiping the tears from her face with the back of her hand. She was laughing at the misfortune of others, which did fit snugly into her psychological profile, but it was joyous. I guess she had been through a hard day, maybe had to face a few of her demons, and she probably needed an emotional release. When it came, she just couldn't stop. The crazy antics, the laughing, the lack of make-up, all made her look a whole lot less threatening, less scary. I warily climbed back onto the seat next to her and nervously watched whilst she regained her composure. I noticed I had placed my hands firmly over my nether regions for self-defence.

'You really are a dipstick,' she said.

'Do you know this clown?' the woman in front said to Mary.

'Yeah,' she replied.

'I feel sorry for you,' she said. 'He's not yer boyfriend, is he?'

'No.'

'Well, I'd thank Christ for that,' she said. 'He's a f**kin' liability.'

'He's not so bad,' Mary said. 'He's got a mental disorder. I try to keep an eye out for him at school, but I can't be watchin' him all the time. You know how it is?'

'You're a f**kin' saint, love. He's a disaster area. I'd dump him and run if I were you.'

She turned back round and mumbled something to her neighbour about keeping loonies off the buses. Mary looked at me and smiled. It wasn't that weird, sly smile she normally used, the sod-off- and-die smile. It was a nice smile; a friendly smile; a happy- to-see-you smile. It wasn't a smile I could trust. Not yet anyway.

I twitched nervously. She couldn't do anything. We were on a bus. But I was still... scared. Her smile faded. She looked sorry for me instead. I wasn't expecting compassion. It threw me. Made me feel... safer. I remembered what Josephine had said: *We need to make friends with her.* It was going to be a struggle to think of stuff to say, but sitting on a bus saying nothing was worse. I didn't have any clever opening lines, so I tried the obvious:

'Can we be friends?' I asked.

The woman in front said, 'Don't make friends with a loony, love. He'll drive y' nuts. Best to leave him alone. Leave him to the authorities, eh?' She looked me up and down with disgust before returning to the conversation with her friend.

Mary looked at me like a bomb disposal expert, checking me out for any traps that might blow up in her face. She must have come to the conclusion I was completely harmless.

'Okay,' she said. 'We can be friends.'

'That's great,' I said, somewhat relieved.

'How do you know?' she said. 'We've only just met. You might not like me when you get to know me.'

'Oh. Well, you look okay,' I said.

'Looks can be deceiving,' she said with a hint of menace.

'Oh, I'm sure you're fine,' I said positively.

She looked at me intently, stroking her lip.

'So what do you see in me then?' she asked.

'Er… Well… You're attractive.'

'That's just appearance,' she said. 'What do you see in *me*?'

I couldn't believe it; she had turned our encounter into a f**kin' exam. On the positive side, I was good at exams. I hoped I could pass this one.

'You've got style. The eyeliner, the hair and everything.' I briefly glanced at her bosom. I guess I was imagining the open buttons and the black bra. I shouldn't have gone there. She scowled.

'What do you see in *me*?' she said. 'What do you like about *me*, as a person?'

This was the hardest exam I had ever sat. I think it helped that I had sat my relationship mock exams not long before with Karen. I was almost an old hand at talking to girls now.

'Well…'

'Come on.'

'Okay… So… You're clever and imaginative. You can certainly plan things. The whole swimming pool thing was the work of evil genius. How the hell did you come up with that? You should write plots for James Bond. It was brilliant. The only thing missing was 007.'

'I think Tarquin fulfilled that role,' she said.

'What about me?' I said. 'I was there as well, you know. I swam the pool faster than him.'

'Yeah, but you've got to admit he looked the part.'

'And I didn't?' I queried, disappointed.

'Skinny white kid in baggy underpants probably wouldn't cut it for James Bond,' she suggested.

I tensed my bicep. 'Feel that,' I said, 'there's surprising strength in those skinny arms.' She wrapped her hands around my arm.

'Okay,' she said, nodding as if impressed, 'maybe there is more to you than meets the eye.'

'Told you,' I said. 'Tarquin wouldn't stand a chance for the part if he was up against me.'

'I'd settle for sidekick if I were you,' she said sympathetically.

'Sidekick!' I acted devastated.

'Yeah, you know, the friendly, foolish, funny guy, the one that gets killed in the first fifteen minutes.'

'First fifteen minutes. Oh, come on. I'm better than that.'

'Okay. Twenty minutes.'

'How could you kill off a face like this in the first twenty minutes?' I said, framing my face with my hands.

'Speaking as an evil genius,' she said, 'I think I could make it in five. I was being nice when I said fifteen.'

'Five! Five!'

'I am an evil genius,' she reminded me.

'You've certainly got the evil henchmen and henchgirls,' I said.

'Oh, them. Yeah, I guess they are a bit menacing,' she accepted.

'Why do you hang around with those guys?' I asked, intrigued.

'They're easily led,' she said. 'It has its advantages.'

'But they're not nice.'

'They're okay,' she said dismissively.

'They're horrible,' I stated. 'Really horrible.'

'I'm horrible,' she admitted.

'No, you're not. Well… yes, you are,' I corrected myself.

'Thanks!'

'You act horrible… you are horrible… but underneath… deep down… deep, deep down… you could be… I mean, it's possible, isn't it… it's not impossible… that you might be…' I paused.

'What? What might I be?' She waited patiently for my verdict.

I looked at her. She didn't look nasty. She looked all right. She looked okay. Maybe she was okay.

'You might be… nice.' I was shocked by my own conclusion. It was wrapped up in a great deal of hope and maybe some delusion, but it was there. I believed it.

'So, you think the evil genius has a softer side?' she said, looking at me with those searing blue eyes.

'I don't think you're really an evil genius. You're playing a part. You're the baddy in the Bond film,' I said.

'So, earlier on, you think I was just being the baddy in a Bond film?' she said inquisitively.

'Sort of. Anyway, it couldn't have been a Bond film, because there wasn't a Bond girl,' I said, as if that put an end to that idea.

'What about me?' she said provocatively.

'You're the evil genius. You're Goldfinger… but a little more alluring,' I added quickly.

She smiled. 'An alluring Goldfinger doesn't sound too promising, does it?'

'But you can't be the evil genius and the Bond girl,' I explained.

'Fair enough. There's Josephine. She'd make a pretty good Bond girl,' Mary proposed.

'I guess so.'

'She's good-looking, intelligent, athletic, confident. She's got it all.' She sounded a little jealous.

'Yeah, she's amazing, but look at yourself.'

'What do you mean?' she asked, in her slightly menacing manner.

'Well. We've established you're clever and creative,' I said, working to the positives.

'Evil genius isn't too appealing,' Mary advised.

'That's just how you use it. You could use your powers for good as well as evil,' I pointed out.

'Okay, what else then?' A hint of menace remained.

'You're funny. I didn't know you were funny till today, but you are. You're good fun as well as terrifying.'

'You're winning me over. Anything else?'

The bus was pulling into the bus stop in the centre. Everyone was shuffling around, getting themselves ready to get off. Mary pulled her bag up off the floor and onto her knee.

'You've got style. I mean, the make-up and stuff can make you look a bit nasty at times, but you've definitely got style. You're a sort of walking work of art,' I proclaimed. Her eyes softened and her mouth relaxed. She looked friendly again.

'You are sweet,' she said, 'really sweet. Quite likeable, in fact.' Then she kissed me. She kissed me. On the lips. I'd been kissed by two different girls, on the same day, on the lips.

'Does this mean you're my girlfriend?' I said jokingly.

'Don't push it, Dipstick,' she said, nudging me towards the aisle. I stepped down into the queue and made my way down the steps and out of the door. Mary stepped out behind me. 'See ya, Mary,' I said.

'See ya, Andy,' she said back. She headed off down the high street. Then I remembered. Something I wanted to say to her. I ran after her, caught up and tapped her on the shoulder. She swung round. I thought she was going to lamp me for a moment. She steadied herself.

'What?' She had lost that friendly edge from a few moments ago.

'Josephine said she wanted to be friends,' I said.

'Did she now?'

'Yes.'

'Well, tell her, from me… she can sod off,' she said, and carried on down the street.

I wandered back to the bus stop. This is where I changed buses. From here, I caught the bus out to the villages. I'd got five minutes. I nipped across to the sweet shop and bought a bar of chocolate. It had been a busy day and my energy levels were seriously depleted. By the time I came out of the shop, the bus was waiting. I ran over, showed my pass and found a seat. The bus pulled out a few seconds later.

This time, I had a seat to myself. I sat hard up against the glass. It was getting dark. The world was sliding into slumber. Only the neon shopfronts fought against the sepia world of sodium streetlights. Lonely figures strode through the after-world, heading home. Soon they would shake off the shadows and bask in the warm glow of white-hot tungsten. The black windows of day became the beacons of night, each one a tiny picture playhouse, presenting romance, comedy, tragedy and farce; until, that is, the picture window players took their curtain call.

The passing scene was just a backdrop to the thoughts drifting through my mind. It had been a hell of a day. I had been kissed by two different girls. Two girls that smelt completely different. Karen, I'd decided, was heaven scent, in that she smelt heavenly. Mary, on the other hand, was hell scent, in that she smelt like s**t. It was all Henry Cooper's fault. The wannabe world champion boxer that once knocked down Mohammad Ali was advertising aftershave. Brut 33 became a number one best seller, finding its way into many bathroom cabinets. Girls with a passion for perfume, but no cash to buy any, dabbed a bit of their father's Brut 33 behind their ears. Mary was one of them, and it didn't suit her one bit. There were no subtle notes of aubergine and cucumber with Mary. It was all Brut.

I wondered... if I could choose between Mary and Karen, which one would it be? I ran through their strengths and weaknesses. Karen was kind, clever, funny, easy to talk to and a great kisser (based on my limited knowledge, of course). Mary was an evil psychopath that smelt of Brut. It was tricky to balance the two things up. The only thing holding me back was that Mary was undoubtedly the better looking of the two. I just wasn't sure how much that mattered. Was it okay to have an ugly girlfriend? Would all the other lads talk about me behind my back? 'Do you know Andy?' 'He's the one with the ugly girlfriend, isn't he?' 'Yeah,

Karen "Bag o' Spanners" Hannah.' 'With a face like that, I don't think she'll be tightening his nuts. Ha ha ha.' Boys can be bastards. It might be relentless. Snidey comments in the background all the time. Could I handle that?

The stupid thing was, I thought she was attractive. I liked the way she looked. It was part of her personality. I knew she wasn't going to win Miss World. She didn't look like a Barbie doll, but she still looked nice. You've only seen her through my feelings, and I liked her, so you probably like her too. You may have cast her in the image of someone you know, someone that appeals to you, someone attractive, a "looker". She was not a "looker". You really need to see her to understand my other feeling, the one I'm less proud of: my cowardice. I haven't got a picture, so words will have to do.

Karen was a carthorse. She was tall, broad and muscular. She wasn't fat, but whereas some muscular builds look athletic, she looked ponderous and heavy. Being big, she pulled in her shoulders to appear smaller and less prominent, but instead, the inevitable slouch made her look even heavier. This wasn't helped by the way she plodded so slowly around school between lessons. In short, her posture was truly dreadful. However, it is easy to put right at such a young age. A bit more confidence, a bit of advice and a little practice, and she could be as tall, regal and elegant as the cream of the catwalk. But that was for the future. At the time, she slouched.

She had long red hair that started out straight, from a central parting, then fell into ringlets around her shoulders. Like most redheads, she had pale white skin, which was similar to my own, though my hair was brown. She had a long, straight nose and big cheeks. They weren't sticky-out cheeks like a chipmunk. They were long saggy cheeks, starting high up and finishing down at her jawline. They were rosy red to match her hair, getting redder and redder when she was excited or out of breath. Her slender lips framed a pretty mouth that grew considerably in size when she laughed, to reveal a fine set of shiny white teeth, even if one or two were out of line. She couldn't be bothered plucking and pruning her eyebrows, so they were bushy and bold and natural. The thing I liked best, the thing that transformed her for me, was her eyes. They were large, brown, smiling eyes. They made you feel happy just looking at them.

As far as I was concerned, her face did not look like a bag of spanners. I wish Winston hadn't made the comparison. It was making me nervous, making me uncertain whether to ask her to be my girlfriend. I still wasn't sure I could take the crap from the other boys. I thought to myself, *What would Winston do?* I reckon if Winston wanted to go out with anyone, no matter how ugly, no matter how grotesque and disfigured, he would. If Winston wanted to go out with a giraffe, and the giraffe felt the same way, then, ignoring the cross-species issues, and legal niceties, I reckon he would. So really, if I had any bottle, if I had any balls, I should do the same. Not go out with a giraffe, of course, just go out with anyone I wanted to, provided they felt the same way.

And then it occurred to me: maybe I'm even uglier than Karen. Maybe I'd be lucky if I could get a girlfriend that ugly. Maybe she was at home right now, wondering whether she could take the crap from the girls at school if she went out with me. Maybe she was thinking, *He's a bit skinny and a bit pale. His nose is too big, his ears stick out. He walks like a moose and smells like a pig.* I checked my armpits; they smelt a bit, but not "pig" bad. I got out of my seat and walked up and down the bus a couple of times to check my action. I wasn't really sure how a moose walked, but I reckoned if they walked like me, they were probably okay. I sat back down in the aisle side of my seat and looked in the mirror window. All the features were in the right place. Eyes lined through, nose in the middle and mouth below that. I swept my hair back over the top of my ears. They didn't stick out that far. I put my hair back for a final assessment. Not bad. Pretty good, in fact. Maybe even handsome. I practised my charming face, my sexy face and my James Bond chisel-jawed hero face in the window.

'For God's sake, make sure she's got a bucket handy when you do that one,' the woman said two rows behind me (the interim row was unoccupied). I turned quickly round and faced the front. I'd forgotten there was anyone else on the bus. It was pretty empty. There were only a few people left, but still enough to witness my lunacy. I hoped none of them knew my parents.

I got back to thinking of Karen. Maybe she was weighing things up at this moment. Maybe she was pondering, *I wonder what Josephine would do?* Maybe she was thinking, *If Josephine wanted to go out with a moose, she would do, even if moose do walk funny. If Josephine will go out with a moose, I should go out with Andy.* If she really did ask Josephine, in the flesh, I reckon Josephine would say I was okay; that I might be worth a try; that she could do worse. I urgently wanted to speak to Josephine, ask her to put in a good word for me, but I wouldn't see her till tomorrow, and she might see Karen first. My stomach jumped into my chest once again and I felt slightly sick. I felt a little out of control.

The bus slowed down again and stopped. Then started up. I looked out of the window. This was my stop. I rang the bell over and over. I didn't want to end up in the next village.

'All right, all right. Keep your hair on. I get the message,' the bus driver grumbled.

I shot up off my seat as the bus slowed down, racing down to the front. I was jumping off when I realised I'd forgotten my bag. I jumped back on as the doors were closing.

'I forgot my bag,' I blurted at the bus driver as I ran back down the bus to retrieve it.

'Next time you're so late, you'll stay on,' the bus driver growled angrily as I dismounted.

'Sorry,' I shouted, and ran off up the lane.

20 THE BOY AND THE BAKERY

I soon slowed down. I still had plenty to think about and I wasn't sure my home environment was conducive to clear thinking on topics such as this. Every ounce of me wanted Karen to be my girlfriend, but what the hell did that mean? What do girlfriends do? What do boyfriends do? Could I still hang around with my mates? Would I have to bring her home? Would I have to go to her home? Do I really want a girlfriend? There were no obvious answers. I trudged on. These questions needed slow, steady thinking, and this was a good place for thinking slow.

The lane was quiet and confined, hemmed in on both sides by blank-sided barns and big brick walls. The faint glow from the infrequent, antiquated streetlights dimly marked the route but failed to light the way. There was no one around and few windows to watch over me, and where walls gave way to open fields, only the endless shadows saw me pass by. But I did not feel nervous or alone. I had played in the fields, climbed the walls and walked the lane a thousand times or more. I was on familiar ground. I felt safer than houses. I could think undisturbed. Round the corner, up a short hill, the road opened out then took a sharp turn to the left. Just before the turn, on the right, set back from the road was the grey outline of a solid, stumpy Norman church with its castellated tower. The big clock face, with its bright painted numerals, was friendly and familiar. Maybe God was keeping an eye out for me, who knows. Beyond the church was the blind wall of a barn to another farm. On the left, encircled by a low picket fence, windows all aglow, the white painted walls of our house, or the Bakery as it was known. I pushed open the gate and wandered around to the kitchen door at the back. I was home.

As soon as I entered, Mum called the rest of the rabble through for tea. I was late and they were waiting, so the stools around the kitchen table filled up fast. There were six stools and one was empty. My dad worked in Sheffield and we lived in Rugby, so he often stayed there overnight to save the journey. When he did make it back, he was generally too late for tea, so it was no surprise to see his place vacant. Two of the stools were occupied by my brothers, John and Angus, and a third by my sister, June. It is unreasonable to describe your siblings in a story when they are not there to defend themselves, but you need something to go on. So, instead I'll describe the Beatles, a popular pop combo from the 1960s, comprising John Lennon, Paul McCartney, Ringo Starr and George Harrison.

John Lennon was the oldest. A fact confounded solely by Ringo, who was born three months before. However, in every other respect, Lennon was definitely the oldest. He was after all bossy, arrogant and stubborn, but he was also clever, funny and a natural born leader. Finally, he was a man with a big nose who thought he could play the guitar. At least two of these attributes, if not all, could be applied to my older brother John "Lennon" Baker.

Ringo, the drummer, on the other hand, was the down-to-earth stable influence; the glue that bound the others together; the happy-go-lucky cheeky chappie, without a care in the world.

This was not my younger brother, Angus. At the time, he was somewhat prone to whining and moaning. He was also a terrible loser and derived considerable pleasure from winding up my older brother. On the glue scale, he was more Gloy than Araldite.

George Harrison, the lead guitarist, was the youngest, and so was my sister. Quiet and unassuming with long, wavy hair, if it wasn't for the moustache, they could easily have been swapped and no one would have noticed the difference.

I was McCartney, the bass player. I had Paul's glazed look; the one that suggested his mind was somewhere else entirely, off in a dream, drifting happily above the clouds, waiting to come down to earth. In my case, the look was all too real. I was normally somewhere on that astral plane; a superhero, strong man, or saint; rescuing folks, righting wrongs and always looking good. I didn't have to try; it was what my mind did, where my mind went, at any opportunity and for any reason. It was why I got the slipper at school.

The "slipper" was one step down from the cane. The punishment of choice for the soft-hearted disciplinarian. In this instance, I was lining up to get my homework marked, standing in the queue to the teacher's desk, exercise book in hand, eagerly anticipating an A. But, being at the end of the queue, I was too close to the window. I looked out, and there I was, flying above the clouds, off on my next mission. The teacher diligently checked the exercise books one by one as the pupils went past and returned to their desks. Not me. I was still by the window, up in the clouds, when the deputy head walked in. She quickly checked her list of offences and appropriate action. There it was, at number 34, just after "free thought" and "use of imagination", "daydreaming" was an offence requiring the slipper. So, I was dragged down to the deputy head's study and promptly received six of the best. Truth is, it wasn't that bad. It stung at the time, but it soon wore off. Once experienced, it was no longer a deterrent. That was probably why the same kids got caned over and over again; they knew what was coming and knew they could live with it.

Back to the family. If us kids were the Beatles, then Mum was George Martin, the producer; sound as a pound and could play the piano. My dad? Well, I'm not sure there is anyone else quite like my dad. He would really need a whole book to himself, so it was a good job he wasn't there at the time. However, you might glean something of his personality from his handiwork, scattered around the house. We had an old vintage Ford car in the back garden with a slide built over it, so you climbed up the bonnet onto the roof and slid down the back; a tree house that could happily contain the six of us; a zip wire; and numerous Frankenstein bikes cobbled together, following trips to the tip. We had two-seaters side by side, two-seaters one behind the other, go-karts, tractors, three-wheelers, four-wheelers and bikes with trailers. We also had the world's largest tarpaulin that at times was the world's largest paddling pool, and at others, the world's widest slide, pinned to the top of an outbuilding at one end and the ground at the other. What can I say? I had a happy childhood.

At that moment, George Martin, AKA Mum, was dragging a meat and potato pie out of the oven, dragging being the operative word. Meat and potato pies in our house were along the same lines as the cow pies of Desperate Dan stories in the *Dandy* comic. The only difference being that our pie didn't have horns sticking out the top. The enormous size, however, was just the same. It did have to feed a family of six incredibly hungry characters. The pie was heaved up, over our heads, and landed in the centre of the table, where it stood, in all its glory, daring us to eat it. If pies ever grew arms and legs and a brain to control them, this one would take over the world. Fortunately, this was not that day. The pie was dished up and we all tucked in. Dessert was home-made apple pie and custard, which was gobbled up just as quickly and washed down with oodles of orange squash.

After we'd all finished, Mum made her way into the living room to watch the news, whilst the rest of us washed the pots. We worked on a rota system. One cleared the table, one washed the pots, one dried, and one put away. The following day, we'd all move along to the next job. It was never long before it was all sorted.

That meant I could get out my Airfix kit. Battleships were my favourite, and the Scharnhorst was today's subject. I covered the Formica table in newspaper, retrieved the piece of ply I used as a cutting board and opened the box. I unfolded the instructions and found the first pieces in their plastic frame. I was just about to cut through the plastic spigots with a Stanley knife, when Mum called through from the lounge.

'Andrew, come quick. There's something about your school on the local news. It said intruders broke into the pool.'

I rushed into the lounge and threw myself onto an armchair.

'I know,' I said. 'I was there when it happened. I helped chase them off.'

'Why didn't you mention it at tea?'

'Didn't seem important.'

'You chased intruders off the school premises and you didn't think it was important?'

'Happens every day at Harribold,' John quipped.

'No, it doesn't,' I snapped.

'I know, I know. I was only joking,' he said, taken aback by my hostile response.

'Shush! It must be coming up shortly.'

We waited through the usual slow torture of local television news. A pig had escaped onto the road in Wibbly Hollow and been chased back onto the farm by a lone five-year-old girl. The farmer was mighty glad to have his pig back. He said the girl was a natural pig herder. A couple of red-faced parents spoke about 'gates ajar,' 'I only looked away for a second,' and 'she's never done it before.'

Eventually, attention turned to my school. There was a reporter standing at the gate to the car park, outlining the incident.

'This is the gate where less than three hours ago, three naked intruders, two men and a woman, were chased off the premises by the school's latest recruit, Tarquin Palaster. Tarquin is actually a student of nearby Rugby School and has been here on a novel student swap with fellow student Quinlan Weston-Smythe. The whole event was witnessed by the girls' netball team, who were training for their next match in the games court over there. We can only imagine what a shock it must have been for these innocent young girls to witness such a spectacle. Earlier, we managed to catch up with Tarquin at Rugby School following his heroic deeds.

'They didn't mention you, dear,' Mum said as they cut to a previous interview.

'That's not fair,' I said. 'I did just as much as Tarquin.'

'Shush. It's that boy from Rugby School.'

'I am sitting here with local hero Tarquin Palaster, in the sumptuous surroundings of Rugby School. Tarquin, can you recount, for our viewers, the events of a few moments ago.'

'I was watching the go-karting.'

'Yes, I believe there is a go-karting club that takes place at the school every week. Is that correct?'

'I think so.'

'And what happened?'

'I was standing near the pool wall when I saw the intruders.'

'How many?'

'Three, I think.'

'And what were they doing?'

'They were running past. I could see they were not supposed to be there, so I raced after them. It was just instinct.'

'And what happened next?'

'They ran out of the gate and down the road.'

'Is it true they had been swimming?'

'I guess so. They had no clothes on and I think they were wet.'

'That was incredibly brave, Tarquin. Incredibly brave. A marvellous testament to the incredible ethos here at Ruby School. You must be very proud of young Tarquin,' the reporter said, turning to Mr Pickering, who was sitting in another Chesterfield leather armchair.

'Of course. Courage and fortitude have always been on the curriculum, and it is incredibly rewarding when students take the skills they have learnt here at Rugby School and apply them in the world outside.'

The reporter turned back to camera. 'But Tarquin is not the only hero. There is one more remarkable story of courage and determination that we need to recount, and for that we must return to Harribold School.'

'This must be your bit, dear,' Mum said in anticipation.

The picture switched to another interview, this time in the headmaster's office at Harribold School. The camera swung around the room and landed on a lone girl sat on the headmaster's oversized oak throne. She leaned forward, hands clutching the front edge of the seat between her legs, which dangled down, her toes swinging freely above the floor. She looked small and vulnerable. It was Mandy Aicart.

'That's not Andy,' Angus said, stating the obvious.

'That's Mandy Aicart,' I shouted. 'She didn't have anything to do with it. What's she doin' there?'

'Shush. I'm listening,' Mum chided us.

The reporter gently prompted his nervous interviewee. 'So, Mandy, you've had quite an ordeal and are still bearing the scars of your encounter with this evening's intruders. Can you just move your hair out of the way so our viewers can see your injuries?' She pulled her hair to one side and turned her head to display a sizeable bruise to her cheek.

'Thank you. Now, can you explain to our viewers how you managed to get the bruise?'

'Well, I heard something over the wall in the pool. I wondered what it was, so I went around the back of the pool to have a look, and this man ran past with no clothes on, so, I tripped him up.'

'You tripped him up?' he repeated, astonished by her audacity.

'Yeah,' she agreed, nodding.

'That's incredibly brave, Mandy,' the reporter said earnestly, 'but why did you trip him?'

'To stop him,' she said.

'And what did he, the intruder, do then?' the reporter said softly.

'He got up and punched me in the face.' She winced and put her hand to her cheek, as if she had been hit all over again.

'He punched you?' The reporter sounded shocked.

Mandy just nodded, as if the memory was too painful for words.

'And what happened then?' the reporter asked, quietly cajoling the vulnerable girl.

'I fell over,' she said, looking down.

'And is that why your clothes are so dirty?' the reporter asked, whilst the camera panned to a patch of mud on her blazer.

She nodded again, the image of innocence.

'And were you shocked by the fact he was wearing no clothes?' he asked warily.

'Not really. I've seen men with no clothes before,' Mandy said, a little too comfortably.

'Have you?' the reporter asked, surprised.

'In magazines,' she said, very quickly.

'We have the *National Geographic* in the library,' the deputy head mentioned off camera. 'African tribes. You know the sort of thing.'

'Oh, I see. Did you manage to get a look at him?' the reporter probed.

'Not really. I just got a flash of this ugly face screaming at me. It happened so fast.' She covered her face with her hands and burst into tears.

I rolled my eyes.

Mum gave me that scolding look.

'What an unbelievable story. What a remarkable act of bravery. The school can truly be very proud of the resilience and fortitude of this remarkable young woman. A young girl that looked danger in the eye and did not blink.'

'She didn't do any of that,' I blurted.

'How did she get the bruise then?' Mum asked.

'She was lying down in the grass. The guy tripped over her,' I explained.

The screen returned to the reporter at the school gate.

'Shush! I want to hear what they've got to say.' Mum raised her hand like a traffic cop; the signal said stop.

'So there you have it. A story of diabolical depravity and incredible courage. We have no idea what these three people were doing behind the walls of that swimming pool. We can only guess.'

'It's a swimming pool, They were swimming,' I shouted at the television.

Mum gave me that *Oh, the sweet innocence of youth* kind of look.

The reporter continued. 'Speaking as a parent and speaking on behalf of all the other parents out there, we want these people caught. Our children will never be safe until we get these debauched individuals behind bars.'

The picture returned to the studio, where the reporter wrapped up events and moved on to the weather forecast.

'Mum, what's debauched mean?' June asked.

'It means they like swimming.'

'I thought it meant—' John was about to explain when Mum cut in very quickly.

'Well, they didn't mention you, dear.'

THE BOY AND THE BAKERY

'I was there,' I said miserably. 'I did just as much as Tarquin, but he gets all the credit. Just because he's some knob from Rugby School.'

'Language,' Mum scolded me again.

'But I did. You can ask Josephine.'

'Josephine who?' Mum queried.

'Josephine Carter,' I said.

'Josephine Carter from primary school?' Mum asked.

'Yeah, her. She's the netball captain,' I explained.

'So it was her watching from the court?' Mum questioned further.

'It wasn't just her. The whole netball team helped chased them off,' I said.

'And they were naked?' Mum queried, looking concerned.

'The netball team?' Angus asked.

'No, stupid. The intruders,' I said.

'I'm not stupid,' Angus blurted.

'Yes, you are,' I said.

Mum raised a finger and the fighting stopped.

'But it's freezing,' she said. 'They'd catch their death of cold.'

'At least there can't have been much to see,' John chipped in.

Mum's eyes told my brother to hold his tongue.

'They weren't naked, they were wearing swimming costumes,' I said.

'Oh, I see. Well, at least they were covered up, but a swimming costume's not going to keep you warm, is it?'

'They were running,' I said.

'Even so! I wouldn't want to be running around in a swimming costume in this weather.' Mum shook her head and shivered in sympathy.

'They're fine,' I said.

Mum leaned forward and looked at me intently. 'How do you know they're fine?' she said.

'Because they looked okay,' I said.

'So, you did get a good look at them?' Mum pressed.

'No!' I replied defensively.

'But you said they looked fine,' Mum noted.

'Well, they weren't blue,' I said.

'So, you did get a good look at them.'

'Not really,' I said.

'Are you telling me everything?' I got the feeling Mum did not entirely believe my account of events. She seemed to know I was hiding something.

'Yes! Honestly,' I lied.

'Andrew. Do you know who they are?' she said, probing further.

'No, No!' I shook my head earnestly.

'If you know who they are, you should tell the police,' she continued pushing me.

'I don't know who they are,' I confirmed.

'Well, can you think of anything, anything at all, that might help the police catch them?'

'No! I can't think of anything.' By now, my arms were up in the air, as if I was surrendering to the enemy.

'It's important. Very important!' Mum emphasised strongly.

That is when I made my first big mistake. I just couldn't help it. I know I shouldn't have done it, but what could I do? I was being interrogated by a master of the craft. My mum was born to wheedle. No secret was safe. No stone left unturned. I crack easily under pressure, so I was looking for a way out. I chose the wrong door. When you've chosen, you've just got to keep right on going.'

'One of them had a tattoo,' I said desperately.

'A tattoo? Where?' Mum pressed.

'On his back,' I said.

'His back? Well, what did it look like?' she asked, urging me to remember. And that was when I made my second big mistake.

'I think it was a moose,' I said.

'A moose? You got a good enough look to know it was a moose and not something else?' she said, somewhat surprised.

'Yeah. It was a moose, it was definitely a moose,' I said, nodding vigorously.

'How big was it?' she quizzed. I think a moose was so preposterous it put Mum off the scent. But, she was still sniffing. I knew it had to be big for me to determine it was a moose from a distance.

'All the way across his back,' I said.

'All the way? All the way across his back? From one side to the other?' The interrogation was ruthless. All that was missing was a bright light shining directly into my eyes.

'Yes! All the way… from one side to the other,' I lied.

'And did you tell anyone?'

'No!'

'Why?'

'It was all a bit of a shock. I forgot in the excitement. They kept talking about faces. I forgot about the moose,' I explained.

'You're sure he had the tattoo of a moose?' she asked again, giving me a strange sideways look. I think she was trying to catch me out by looking at me from a slightly different angle.

'Yes! I'm sure,' I said, with as much conviction as I could muster.

'You're not making it up?' she asked, staring me down.

'No! I am definitely, definitely not making it up,' I definitely lied.

'Right. Okay. I'll ring the police and let them know. You are sure, aren't you?'

This was it; I'd reached the end of the road and was teetering on a precipice in the last chance saloon. I could tell the truth, confess to everything and go to bed with a clear conscience or… I could take a dive into the unknown. I took the dive.

'Yes!' I said, one last time.

Mum went off into the hall to ring the police.

My brothers and sister looked at me inquisitively in silence.

'A moose?' they all said together.

I shrugged. I was too tired to explain.

For the rest of the evening I watched the TV like a zombie on Prozac. I was exhausted. I had lived a lifetime in a single day and I couldn't take much more. I dragged myself back into the kitchen, put away the model-making bits and pieces and cleaned the table. It was time for bed. I staggered up the stairs, observed the usual bedtime routine and slipped into bed. Those sheets had rarely felt so nice, and the heavy weight of blankets pinning me down so secure. As soon as my head hit the pillow, I was asleep.

21 THE MARTIAL ART OF WINDOW GAZING

There was no morning alarm. There was no need. Our bedroom had the thinnest curtains in the western world and single glazed windows on three sides. If the sun didn't wake you, the pounding of rain, bleating of sheep or chattering of birds would. Once the blankets were heaved to one side, we dashed downstairs in pyjamas for a quick play before breakfast. Only I wasn't playing; I was searching. I was hunting for a book, a picture book, any picture book… with a moose. I needed a book to take to school to show the others. I needed a picture of a moose so they could describe the tattoo if anyone asked. I was dragging books off the shelves one by one and scouring the pages for animals with antlers. Eventually, I found one: the Beasley and Webb *Book of the World*. There were deer of every kind: reindeer, red deer, mule deer, key deer, sika deer, muntiacini and elk, but no moose. I would have still taken that book if I could, but, because Beasley and Webb had included the whole world within its pages, it was the size of a small car. There was, however, an alternative; a book which did actually include the animal of choice. A book by Dr Seuss, a book called *Thidwick the Big-Hearted Moose*. This was a heartwarming tale of a kind-hearted moose that allowed every animal under the sun to build a nest in his antlers until… well, I don't want to spoil it for you. Buy the book; it's worth every penny. A witty and well-illustrated book it may be, but Dr Seuss was not known for anatomical accuracy, and the moose in question, with its big eyes, friendly smile and gracefully curving antlers was no exception. But, it was all I could find. I shoved it in my bag and restocked the bookshelf, before racing upstairs to get changed for breakfast.

I was a bit straggly when I came back down; I don't think I would've cut the mustard in a military parade. Tie off to one side, collar up and shirt hanging out; I was a bit of a mess. But fashion was not my forte, and I had more important things to worry about. I shuffled in around the table, filled my bowl with Frosties and downed them with full-fat milk from a heavy glass bottle. Toast was hitting the table thick and fast, with butter and marmalade skimming the surface at a fine rate of knots. I spent most of breakfast reading the back of cereal packets or checking out the latest cards from packets of tea. Cereal companies really made an effort. Packets aimed to entertain and inform. There were stories, quizzes, facts and figures, things to cut out, things to make and plenty of gifts to collect. The cards from packets of tea had a picture on one side and facts on the other, covering everything you could think of: household tips, incredible inventions, planes and trains, bees and trees, fashion, flowers and the famous. I learnt more at breakfast than I learnt at school.

Breakfast was soon over, and me and my older brother were heading out the door to catch the bus to school. The morning bus stop was opposite our house, on the other side of the road. We didn't need a zebra, a pelican, a puffin or a lollipop to get us across. We rarely saw a car. We would often kick a ball around in the road till the bus came. When we saw the bus, we just threw the ball back over the fence.

There were three others already waiting when we got there. Julie and Ben Stokes from the farm down the road and Rupert Wiggins from the big house across the way. Julie was my age. We'd been at primary school together and had taken the eleven-plus at the same time. The eleven-plus was well named because, if you failed, it messed up everything from your eleventh birthday onwards. Julie had managed the leap to the green pastures of grammar school, but I had tripped up and was stuck in the scrub on the other side of the fence.

Ben was a year older than me and a farmer through and through. He was tough as old boots, brusque and direct, but friendly and fun to be around. Rupert, who was two years older, was also kind of agricultural in that he was built like a barn door, and a sizeable one at that. He was often found with his dad, tinkering with old cars or involved in some madcap project. He once built an underground shelter, which was fine, till the roof fell in. Fortunately, he wasn't there at the time.

'Where's the ball?' Ben shouted.

I scooped it up off the grass and tossed it over the fence. We kicked it up and down the road and bounced it off the back of the barn. When the ball flew past the last man and rolled down the hill, one of us would chase like crazy, in case the bus turned up at that moment. Julie watched calmly from the sidelines, quietly reading her book. The bus turned up and the ball went back. We all clambered on and flashed our bus passes at the driver as we went past. After we'd taken our seats, a couple of kids returned to the front to play poker dice in the footwell.

I looked out of the window. That was what I liked to do. That was what I did best. I could happily look out of a window for hours daydreaming about this and that. I had mastered the skill over many years, and in martial arts terms, I was at least black belt, first dan. It was a shame the journey to the centre of Rugby lasted only half an hour.

To be honest, there were times when the ability to concentrate on one thing at a time might have been a better skill to master. But daydreaming definitely has its bonuses. Occasionally, you can be pleasantly surprised by a random thought that creeps into your imagination uninvited. Today, the thoughts drifting in and out of my head centred on Karen, and girlfriends.

For instance, how long can you spend with a girlfriend every day? If I only saw Karen at school, Monday to Friday, I might get ten minutes before school, twenty minutes at break, an hour at lunch and twenty minutes in the afternoon. Almost two hours, I know, but you also have to spend time with your mates. So, if I spent an hour playing games with my friends every day, then that means I'd spend less than an hour with Karen. Was it worth the investment?

Maybe I could go round to her house after school now and then. I didn't do homework, so I had plenty of time on my hands. But maybe she did do homework; maybe her parents made her do homework; maybe they didn't want any distractions. Maybe they would hate me. I somehow doubted it. After all, I was Mr 98%. With a maths score like that, I could become an accountant. I might even fall into the category of "ideal son-in-law material".

What do you do with a girlfriend? You can only spend so much time kissing, and I suspected there was a rule against that in school anyway, so I wasn't going to get much kissing done. I guessed Karen wouldn't want to play the eraser game or the wall game, although I reckoned she'd be pretty good at both. So, that just left talking and looking into her eyes. I would probably be pretty good at looking into her eyes. I was pretty good at looking out of windows, and it seemed like a similar skill set. But she might only be a white belt at window gazing. She might only last a minute. That would leave almost an hour for talking. What can you talk about for an hour? And if I went back to her house after school, it would be even longer (I guessed her parents would also have rules about kissing).

Maybe you had to do things together. Share your hobbies. Perhaps one day she could come round to my house to make Airfix Kits, and on another day I'd go round to her place to write stories. Sounded fine, I just doubted girls liked making models of battleships, and I wasn't sure Karen would want to write stories with me. How do two people write stories together anyway? It's not like duets, sitting side by side at the piano, one doing the high notes and the other doing the low notes. I could check her spelling, but surely something as painful as that was for married couples only.

There were bound to be other things we could do. Things I'd never done before; new hobbies. As I stared out of the window, I pondered a list of possible pastimes:

1. Fencing:

Fencing might be fun; twirling a skinny sword around; on guard and all that. But you wouldn't be able to see behind the mask. You could be fighting anyone. At the end of the night, you might go off with the wrong person. You get to the bus stop, they take off their mask, and it's a bloke with a beard. No! Not fencing.

2. Sewing:

I am actually pretty good at sewing. I made costumes for my sister's dollies. However, nobody, absolutely nobody was ever going to find that out. My life wouldn't be worth living. And neither was anyone going to find out I could knit.

3. Swimming:

Hmm, Karen in a swimming costume. I have to admit, I quite fancied that idea. Sounds kinda sexy. But I guess, swimming pools probably have rules against kissing. Just as well really. I mean, what would happen if… you know… you wouldn't be able to get out? You might have to stay there all night. No, no, no… swimming was out of the question.

4. Painting:

We could try painting. Easels side by side, painting still life; a bowl of fruit or a vase of flowers… or… maybe we could paint each other! She might want me to pose naked, in the nude, with nothing on. Everything hanging out. Painters do that all the time. Whadaya do then if… you know… it happens? She might paint it. It might get hung up on the wall. What would people say? There is no way on earth, heaven or hell we were going to paint.

5. Fishing:

This is not a serious proposition. Fishing has to be the world's most tedious sport. As a young kid, I had once sat by a canal, for a couple of hours, with a fishing rod we'd inherited from a dead man in the village. My guess was the poor guy had died of boredom. Sat there watching the river run by, he slipped into a coma, keeled over and drowned. If you look down the river on a sunny afternoon, you can often see fishermen gently rolling over their nets into the water. It's how they'd like to go, with the least excitement possible.

6. Football:

It would be good to kick a ball around, but girls didn't play football, so that was a non-starter.

7. Climbing:

Not many mountains in Rugby.

8. Dog walking:

We could have walked a dog, but we didn't have one and she might not either. If she did have a dog, it might be one of those horrible tiny dogs that bite your ankles, or even worse, a Great Dane that could bite your whole leg off.

9. Horse riding:

I don't think so. Where were we going to get a horse?

10. Astronomy:

The stars are always there, and so are the clouds. On that rare night, when the sky is clear, we could sit out, leaning back in deckchairs, staring up at the night sky. For excitement, it is probably on a par with fishing. To make matters worse, you have to be either a polar bear or an owl. In the winter, when it is dark early, it's freezing cold, and in the summer, when it's warm, you have to wait till the middle of the night. It's ridiculous.

So, there was no perfect pastime and no obvious hobby to cover up the uncomfortable silence when the words ran dry. Maybe you had to change girlfriends every six months, when you've used up all your anecdotes. I had a terrible memory, so for me it might be more often, maybe every three months.

I tried to work out what I could remember. Nothing before the age of six; very little from six to ten; and from ten to fourteen my life has largely been about getting on a bus to go to school. I couldn't just recount a list of the most exciting bus journeys. It looked like I'd be swapping girlfriends every week if I wasn't going to bore them to death.

But then it came to me. Maybe I don't need a memory. Maybe

I don't have to remember my past. I had been talking bollocks to Winston for three years and he didn't seem to mind. As far as I could remember, I hadn't told him a single fact in all that time. Not about me anyhow. Maybe that is what you have to do; that is how you keep talking; you just make stuff up. I reckoned I could do that. Maybe all that time talking bollocks had been good training for later life. When all the other relationships fell by the wayside, ours would still be going strong, because I had mastered the art of talking bollocks. Maybe I'd become famous. Couples in distress would come for miles just to hear me explain the art of talking bollocks. I might get a medal. I might have an institute named after me. The Baker Academy of Bollocks.

But that was all in the future; we were pulling into the high street in Rugby town centre. It was time to change. I jumped off the bus and wandered down a couple of stops to catch the bus to Harribold. The bus had already pulled in when I got there, so I got on and slung my bag on the seat next to me. Roger, an oversized fifth former, signalled with a toss of his head that I needed to move over.

Sign language was common between year groups. The year below were beneath contempt and the year above were a little bit scary. So, you would instruct earlier years with dismissive grunts and gestures, and smile and nod apologetically to the year above. I smiled and nodded, grabbed my bag and squeezed up against the window. This bit of the journey, through the centre, past the shops, was a little more entertaining, so I paid more attention to what was going on outside. In particular, I wanted to have a good look at Rugby School. For the first time in my life, I wondered what it was really like to be in a school as posh as that. What did they do in the dormitories? What was it like in a boys' school? What was it like in a school with no girls? At one time, I would have jumped at the chance to go to a boys' school. Now I wasn't so sure.

As we drove past, the shiny shoes were striding across the green and tippity-tapping up the steps before wiping off the outer world on the welcome mat. It was a palace, a castle, a fortress, a school. An impenetrable world of wealth and privilege. A world beyond my imagination. A world I wanted to understand. Maybe the next three weeks with Tarquin and Quinlan would give me a chance.

A few minutes later, we were at Harribold. Roger heaved his bulk off the seat and out of the door, and I hopped off after him. I followed the crowd down the long path that ran alongside the playing field up to the student entrance. I wandered in through the gate.

22 MOOSE TATTOO

When I arrived, Winston was in the east playground with a group of kids throwing a tennis ball, so it bounced on the floor then the wall and came back. The two bounces made it slightly less predictable, less easy for a member of your own team to catch. Winston spotted me coming through the gate, made his apologies and jogged over. He was full of excitement after yesterday's events.

'Wow, what a day that was. Unbelievable. I drove a go-kart halfway round the school, you swam the pool and ran half-naked through the nature reserve, we bashed that kid and Scary scarpered. What a day. What an amazing day.'

'Yeah, it was great,' I said without enthusiasm.

'What's up? What's up with you?' he asked cheerfully. 'It was incredible. Unbelievable.'

I didn't want to talk about what had gone on; I wanted to talk about what was playing on my mind.

'Winston?' From my tone, Winston knew a serious question was coming, so he attempted "old sage" in the tone of his response.

'Yes, Andrew?'

'Y' know girlfriends?' I said cryptically.

'Not personally.'

'In general.'

'Y…e…s…' he said, none the wiser.

'You know what they look like?'

'Long hair and breasts?'

'No!'

'They do… well… not all, but most,' Winston assured me.

'No!' I said.

'You've not been looking close enough.'

'I know they've got breasts,' I said dismissively.

'Well then?' He held out his arms palms up, expecting me to give him something, a clue as to what I was on about.

'Girls… they look nice, don't they?' I said obtusely. It didn't help.

'This isn't about the discussion at dinner time yesterday, is it?' Winston said cautiously.

'What discussion?'

Winston glanced around to check no one was listening and lowered his voice.

'You're not… gay, are you?'

'No! I'm not gay,' I said, probably too loudly, by the way Winston looked around.

'Oh! Okay. What is it then?'

'What happens when they don't look nice?' I said.

'What? You mean, ugly girls?' Winston asked.

'Yeah, ugly girls. What happens with ugly girls?'

'In what way?'

It was up to me to ask that final question, the one that had taunted me back on the bus. The question I was too embarrassed to ask. It was now or never.

'Is it okay to have an ugly girlfriend?'

'How ugly?'

'I don't know.' I shrugged. 'Medium ugly, I suppose.'

'I guess if you like someone, it doesn't matter, does it?'

'Won't the other guys get at you?' I asked.

'Yeah, of course they will.'

'Won't they make jokes about you, behind your back?'

'Yeah, but only because they haven't got a girlfriend,' Winston said.

'I guess so,' I said, still a little unsure.

'Anyway, you've got to cut your coat,' Winston suggested.

'What do you mean by that?' I asked.

'It's something me mum says. You've got to cut your coat according to your cloth.'

'But what does it mean?'

'You've got to do your best with the little you've got,' he explained.

'So?' I said, seeking a little more help.

'So, you might be ugly yourself, and maybe Miss World is out of your reach,' he advised.

'Am I ugly?' I asked.

'You're no oil painting,' Winston quipped.

'Am I ugly?' I pressed.

'You're okay, in a certain light.'

'A certain light?'

'Yeah, bright and from behind,' he joked.

'Would you have an ugly girlfriend?' I asked, ignoring the flippant remarks.

'Yeah, of course I would. If I fancied a donkey and the donkey fancied me, I'd go out with them.'

'I thought it'd be a giraffe,' I said.

'Giraffes don't do it for me.'

'But what about the jokes and stuff?' I said, referring to the jibes that were bound to follow.

'You take no notice,' Winston said, as if it was easy.

'Okay,' I said, nodding.

'Are you looking at someone in particular? It's not me, is it, 'cos A) I am good-looking, and B) I'm not being your girlfriend for love nor money, well, maybe money.'

'It's not you,' I confirmed.

'That's a relief. So, who is it?' he asked.

'Karen. I like Karen,' I admitted.

'Karen Hannah? Karen the Spanner?' Winston asked.

'Do you have to call her Spanner?' I said.

'Wow, Karen. I'd never have thought,' he said, surprised.

'I like her.'

'She's not that bad. I mean, she's not what I call beautiful, but she's not that bad,' Winston said encouragingly.

'You said she's got a face like a bag of spanners yesterday,' I said tersely.

'Well, she is different, you've got to admit.'

'What do you think?' I wanted Winston's honest opinion.

'She's good. She's a good laugh. Yeah, she's all right. Do you think you stand a chance?' he asked.

'Dunno really. Hope so.'

'When're you gonna ask?'

'Today maybe.'

'Today! Bloody hell! Amazing.' Winston looked impressed.

'If I get a chance,' I clarified.

'Karen? Wow! She's good. She's not boring. Good choice,' he said, as if reviewing something from a catalogue.

'Yeah, I think so.' I was glad I spoke to Winston. I felt more confident now and I was going to need all the confidence I could muster if I was going to ask Karen out.

'Have you heard the radio?' Winston said. 'My mum said one of the intruders had a moose tattoo on their back. A moose, for God's sake. Where the hell did that come from?'

'Er, that might have been me,' I replied.

'You? How the hell did you work that one?' he said, looking at me in disbelief.

'It was my mum,' I explained.

'What, your mum forced you to make up a story about a moose?' Winston said.

'She was interrogating me. She wouldn't get off my back. I had to give her something. I had to.'

'Give her something?' Winston asked. 'You could have said, "He might have had brown hair," or "He ran with a limp," or "He had a scar." Anything at all, apart from a tattoo of a moose. Why a moose?'

'I like the way they walk.'

'What?'

'Nothing. A moose was the first thing that came to me,' I admitted.

'A f**kin' moose?' Winston said

'Yeah, a f**kin' moose,' I confirmed.

'Josephine!' he shouted across the playground, waving her towards him. 'Come here!' She wandered over. 'Have you heard what Dipstick has done?'

'No,' she said, looking at me suspiciously.

'He told the police one of the intruders had a tattoo of a moose across his back,' he said.

'A moose? Why a moose?' she asked, hoping for a sensible answer.

'Why a tattoo?' Winston added.

'Well, a real moose would have looked stupid,' I said.

'You're an idiot. Now what're we gonna do?' Josephine clasped her hands to the side of her head, as if the insanity might cause her head to explode.

'They're bound to ask if we all saw it, what it looked like, how big it was.' Winston shook his head.

'I know,' I said.

'You know! Yet you still did it?' Josephine replied.

'I know they'll ask questions. I've got a book. A book with a moose in it,' I said apologetically.

'Karen! Karen! Come here.' She beckoned Karen over to her.

'Not Karen,' I said. 'Not Karen. I feel stupid enough as it is.'

'This goes way beyond stupid,' Winston said.

'Okay! Okay! So it was unwise,' I replied. Josephine was incensed.

'Unwise! Unwise! I can't find words to describe the depth of idiocy you have descended to. Whatever words I could find, you would be way, way below that.'

'Hi, what's the problem?' Karen asked, flashing me a big smile. I smiled back, somewhat sheepishly.

'Do you know what Lover Boy has done?' Josephine asked tersely.

'No?' she said, looking at me inquisitively.

'He told the police one of the intruders had a tattoo of a moose across his back.'

'A moose! Why a moose?' she said, looking at me as if I had become a strange unfathomable curio.

'Because I like mooses,' I said in explanation.

'I like cake, but I wouldn't have it tattooed on my back,' Karen replied.

'The teachers'll ask questions. They'll want to know what the tattoo looked like,' Josephine said.

'Can't we just say he made a mistake?' Karen suggested.

'It would call everything into doubt,' Josephine said. 'We don't want teachers asking too many questions.'

'Josephine's right,' Winston agreed. 'It would be a disaster if things began to unravel now. I drove a go-kart across the nature reserve, the whole netball team lied about it, Tarquin is the hero of Rugby School, and Quinlan has been covering for everyone else. We're too far up shit creek. If it unravelled now, we wouldn't come out smelling of roses.'

'And it's not just the teachers,' Karen added. 'It's the police as well. We must have broken a few laws last night.'

'Yeah, I guess so. I'm sure Tarquin's dad could think of a few,' I said.

'So, what are we going to do?' Josephine asked.

'We've got to make sure every witness saw the same tattoo,' Karen said. 'They've all got to describe it the same way.'

'Andy's got a book with a moose in it,' Winston said.

'Great!' Josephine enthused. 'We can just pass that around. C'mon then, show us the book.'

'It's not a great picture,' I suggested. 'Not a perfect representation.'

'Doesn't matter,' said Winston, 'it's the only thing we've got.'

'I'm not sure,' I said.

'Get the f**kin' book out,' Winston instructed.

'Okay.' I put my bag down, unzipped it and reluctantly removed the book.

'*Thidwick the Big-Hearted Moose*,' I said with an apologetic smile as I held it up.

They all looked at the book.

'You've got to be kidding,' Winston said, shaking his head.

'No!' Josephine cried.

'F**k, no!' Winston confirmed

Karen just shook her head and gave me a look of complete despair.

'I cannot, cannot, pass that book round and say a moose looks like that. I just can't,' she groaned despairingly.

'A moose. A f**kin' moose,' Winston reiterated. 'We're doomed. We're f**kin' doomed.'

'No, we're not,' Karen said, thinking quickly. 'I'll go up to the library and get a picture from there.'

'Are you sure?' I said, concerned.

She held her head in her hands then shook her head, as if one action just wasn't enough to cover a cock-up of this magnitude.

'Yeah, I'll do it,' she confirmed. 'I'm in and out all the time. It won't be a problem.'

'Thanks,' I said. 'I'm sorry. I'm really sorry.'

She looked at me, shook her head and wandered inside. I think my standing as a potential boyfriend may have diminished slightly. A little while later, she re-emerged and wandered quickly over to us.

'Did you get it?' Josephine asked.

'Yes!' She removed from her pocket a folded piece of paper and opened it out in front of us. It was a picture of a magnificent antlered animal titled "Elk".

'That's no good, it's an elk,' I said.

'An elk is a moose, dimwit,' Karen replied.

'Oh. Is it?' I asked.

'Yes!' she said.

'Oh. I could have brought a picture of an elk,' I admitted.

'Well, it's too late now, isn't it?' she said.

'I guess so,' I said apologetically.

Josephine adopted her organisational mode.

'Karen, can you pass that round the netball team as quick as you can? It's just that I'm supposed to meet Tarquin and Quinlan when they arrive.'

'I'll do my best,' Karen replied. 'See you at break.'

'See you then,' I said hopefully.

Karen darted off with the piece of paper in hand. I'd got so used to her shuffling around between lessons, I was surprised to see how quickly she could move when she wanted to.

'Let's go see if the rich kids came back,' Winston said.

'Are we supposed to sit next to them in assembly?' I asked.

'I'd've thought so,' Josephine replied.

'I wonder if Tarquin will bring his briefcase,' I said.

'I think we should all have a briefcase and sunglasses, like bodyguards,' Winston replied.

'Do bodyguards carry a briefcase?' Josephine asked, unsure.

'Yup. Because they're taught Briefcase Fu, the martial art of lethal luggage,' Winston explained.

'But, master, I have just a lowly sports bag. What can I do?' I asked.

'Aah, Glasshopper, that velly clap bag; velly, velly clap. You need bliefcase for Bliefcase Fu. Look a' quality. Leather, velly good, yes?' Winston said, in something approaching a Chinese accent.

'Master, look, blass bluckle,' I said, stroking the buckle on Winston's briefcase.

'What is a blass bluckle?' Josephine knew she shouldn't have asked, but it was too late.

'Aah, girly Glasshopper.' Winston bowed to her. 'It obvious. Blass bluckle is bluckle made of blass.'

'C'mon, tosspots. Time to go.' Josephine clearly had no time for this nonsense.

'Aah, master, girly Glasshopper know our secret identity,' I said.

'How she know? You tell her?' Winston asked, outraged.

'Do you talk rubbish all the time?' Josephine asked, somewhat irritated.

'Mostly,' I said, 'but we only do it to impress.'

'It don't impress,' Josephine said sharply.

'Not even a bit?' I asked hopefully.

'Not me, because I'm normal,' she said.

'What about other girls?' I asked.

'They're normal too,' she suggested.

'There has to be someone,' I said hopefully.

'It might impress Karen,' Josephine said.

'Is she not normal?' I asked, looking for a little more.

'She took a second glance at you, didn't she?' Josephine said.

'How you know?' I asked in a Chinese accent.

'Speak to me in that accent one more time and I'll rip your head off,' Josephine warned.

There was one of those long pauses when one person is daring the other and the other is sorely tempted. Josephine's stare won the battle of wits. The tension dropped and normality resumed.

'So you think she likes me? You think I stand a chance?' I asked, trying not to sound too eager.

'Maybe. If she ever gets over the moose thing,' she said.

'Did you have to mention the moose?' I said. It made me sick just thinking about it.

'Let's have another look at that book,' Winston said.

'Yes, let's,' Josephine agreed. They both approached me with an evil glint in their eyes.

'Not on your life,' I shouted, and grabbed my bag, wrapping my arms tightly around it to prevent any chance of wrestling it free. But I was up against the netball captain and a master of Bliefcase Fu. I didn't stand a chance. It was soon freed from my clutches, zip unzipped and *Thidwick the Big-Hearted Moose* was liberated once more.

'C'mon, let's sit on the steps and look at it while we wait,' Winston said, pushing open the big wooden doors.

23 THE BRIEFCASE AND THE BIG-HEARTED MOOSE

We sat on the steps as teachers walked past, each one looking over our shoulders, curious as to what we were up to. Each time we turned a page there'd be a laugh at the next ridiculous animal lounging in Thidwick's antlers, followed by a glance at me, a look of disbelief and a comment about my mental wellbeing. Still, it was a bit of a laugh, and it is a funny book.

'What car do you think they'll arrive in this time?' Winston asked.

'A big one,' Josephine replied.

'I thought they'd come by helicopter,' I suggested.

It wasn't long before the familiar silver Mercedes made its way down the drive and pulled up next to the steps. We stood up, as if greeting royalty. Mr Pickering lowered his window and said, 'Hello again. Day two. Let's hope it's a little less eventful than day one.'

We nodded in agreement as Tarquin and Quinlan emerged from the rear door. No sunglasses this time.

'I can't believe you brought the briefcase back,' Josephine said. 'Not after yesterday.'

Tarquin laughed. 'It's the only bag I've got.'

'No one'll try anything today,' Winston said. 'The whole place is on high alert. There's sentries at every post.' It was sort of true. There was an unusually large number of staff supervising the playgrounds.

'It's a bit like Colditz,' Quinlan said, looking around.

'What's the book?' Tarquin asked.

'Oh, you're gonna love this. Guess what the Dipstick Kid did with a moose?'

'What?'

I just rolled my eyes with that not again kind of look.

'Just guess.'

'Candlelit meal for two?' Quinlan's first was the start of a whole series of ridiculous guesses.

'Drive-in movie?'

'Why drive-in?'

'Cinema seats too cramped.'

'What about antlers in a car?'

'Sunroof.'

'Yeah, makes sense, but no.'

'Cycle ride?'

'Moose can't ride a bike.'

'Stabilisers.'

'But they can't steer.'

'Tandem.'

'Yeah, makes sense, but no.'

'Ballroom dancing?'

'Moose don't wear high-heeled shoes.'

'Andy can wear them.'

'Or a dress.'

'Andy can wear it.'

'Yeah, makes sense, but no.'

Josephine and Winston chipped in with a whole series of things I didn't do:

Shag it,

Shoot it,

Ride it,

Race it,

Kiss it,

Cook it,

Marry it,

Milk it,

And so on.

Eventually, Tarquin said, 'So, what did he do?'

Winston turned to me. 'Do you want to tell them?'

I took a deep breath and blurted it out. 'I told the police one of the intruders had a tattoo of a moose across his back.'

'You did what?' they said, incredulous.

'I told the police one of the intruders had a tattoo of a moose across his back,' I repeated.

'Why?' they both asked. Winston tried to explain.

'Apparently his mother tortured him until he said moose tattoo, and then she rang the police. So, now we're trying to make sure everyone who "saw" the intruders knows what the moose looks like.'

'So what does the moose look like?' Quinlan asked.

'Karen's got a picture she's showing to everyone. As soon as we see her, I'll get her to show you too,' Josephine proposed.

'Okay,' they agreed.

The bell was ringing by this time so we made our way into the entrance hall.

Mrs Garland, the deputy head, strode on over. 'Miss Carter, Mrs Stubbs will be coming round in periods three and four to speak to the netball team, to check what they really saw of this tattoo. Can you let them know they will have to pop out of the lesson to speak to her?'

'Yes, miss. I'll make sure everyone knows,' Josephine assured her.

'Good girl. Now run along. We've saved some seats in the front row for you.'

That was the last place we wanted to be. We wouldn't be able to chat, with the head breathing down our necks.

We were late into assembly. It was largely full by the time we got there. The headmaster was standing centre stage, waving the stragglers in as if he was directing traffic. He waved us forward and directed us to our seats at the front. A piece of paper with *Reserved* scribbled over it lay on six of the seats. I'd never had a seat reserved before and felt nervous about sitting down, just in case they were reserved for someone more important. There were also six pieces of paper and only five of us. Who could be the other person? I'd put my foot in it enough times already; I didn't want my arse to be equally disgraced. I took one last look around. Satisfied that the royal family weren't about to wander down the aisle, I plonked myself down. A few seconds later, Mandy Aicart sat in the empty space next to me.

The head directed the remaining individuals to empty seats, and then adopted the Superman pose of power. That is the pose where he stands tall, legs slightly apart with fists on hips, and normally takes place shortly before he flies off to save the world. In our case, it was the sign for silence. The rumbling of voices and scraping of chairs slowly died away. The audience was ready for the show to begin.

'I am sure you have all heard rumours about what happened last night. I have heard several myself. I can tell you now, most of these rumours are the wanton fabrications and fanciful notions of liars, gossipmongers and reporters. I don't want to hear any of you spreading such rumours throughout the neighbourhood. We are a proud Church of England school with the highest of moral values, and such rumours seek to undermine our hard-fought reputation and standing in the community. It is the truth and the truth alone that we should tell.

'I can tell you now, for the avoidance of any doubt, this school has not been the subject of naked revelry. There have not been hordes of naked men and women racing through the grounds, no one has died, no one is recovering in hospital, and our ladies' netball team have not been wholly incapacitated by a state of shock.'

There was a series of girly giggles from amongst the audience.

'The real truth is that three intruders did indeed enter our grounds last night. These vile and repugnant criminals were discovered and chased off the premises by our own students with the help of one of our new recruits. If it wasn't for the courage and resourcefulness of Tarquin Palaster from Rugby School, Mandy Aicart, Josephine Carter and the ladies' netball team, they could have vandalised our buildings, daubed graffiti on the walls and disgraced our environment. They did indeed attack one student.' Mandy smiled at me and shrugged. I had assumed she didn't know it was me that tripped over her, but I was beginning to wonder.

'Can all of the people I have just mentioned please stand up?' There was a lot of shuffling and bobbing up and down.

'Yes! Yes! Everybody in the netball team, everyone that was practising last night, can you all stand up?' Eventually, reluctant heads rose above the rabble, nervously looking around, like meerkats expecting an attack.

'I would like you all to take a good long look at these students. These are the people you should be seeking to emulate. We owe a great deal to the fortitude and bravery of these individuals. Can you please show your appreciation in the time-honoured manner?' The headmaster started clapping so we all followed suit. After a while, the headmaster's hands cut the air and the clapping petered out.

'Now if you could all join them standing for hymn number 112, *God of Truth*.'

There was the usual discordant cacophony of mumbled words, uncertain melody, intriguing harmony and syncopated rhythm. Jazz for the common man. The hymn ended and we were all dismissed.

We shuffled along slowly, squeezed together in the crowd making for the exits, before being spat out into the corridor.

'Where to now?' Quinlan asked.

'History,' Winston replied. 'C'mon, let's see if we can find Karen so that you can get a look at that picture.'

We walked quickly. Our straight legs whipping back and forth like Spotty Dog in *The Woodentops*. We caught up with Karen on the stairs.

'Hey, Karen, have you got that picture?' Winston cried.

Karen nodded. She didn't want everyone to know, and her eyes said so.

'Can we have a look?' Winston asked, somewhat quieter.

Karen carried on up to the first-floor landing where everyone was waiting outside the classroom. We crowded round her. She removed the piece of paper from her pocket and unfolded it to reveal the picture.

'Good-looking animal,' Tarquin said.

'Yeah,' Quinlan agreed. 'If I was going to have a tattoo of a moose, that would be the one I'd go for.'

'I just hope I can show everyone before the teachers ask questions,' Karen said.

Josephine outlined what she'd been told earlier. 'The deputy head said they were coming round in periods three and four. They're gonna call people out of the classroom one at a time. If we can get round everyone before then, we'll be okay.'

'I should be able to show everyone by then,' Karen reckoned.

At that moment, the door opened, and we were invited in.

24 A BRIEF HISTORY OF THE CIVIL WAR

Our first lesson of the day was history with Mr Hattersley, or the Mad Hatter as he was more commonly known. Even the teachers called him Hatter, dropping the "Mad" out of respect rather than reputation. Hatter was heavily into amateur dramatics and re-enacting ancient battles. He was often out on some forgotten field dressed as a Roman or a Roundhead, reliving the good old days of dysentery and disease.

What Hatter liked more than anything else was dressing up, and hats were his favourite accessory. 'An outfit isn't an outfit without a hat,' he'd say. His cupboard was stuffed with a whole range of bonnets and boaters, Fedora and Fez, Panamas and Peaks. It was helmets, however, that gave him the greatest pleasure. For Hatter, a helmet embodied the very essence of a period in history. He would use a helmet to introduce an era, wearing it as we entered the room and took our seats. The lesson would start with a guessing game: "Which period am I from?"

Tarquin and Quinlan were a novelty, a new audience, and Hatter was more than willing to put on a show. He had invited along two of his battle-ready chums from the Re-enactment Society. His desk had disappeared and in its place was a campfire, cooking pots and characters from the English Civil War. Obviously, the fire wasn't real, just some sticks with red and yellow paper cut into flame shapes, but we got the gist. Re-enactment is a romantic notion, and participants tend to be history geeks, bookish fellows, with pail and pasty, frail and flaky figures, rattling around in oversized armour with scrawny little legs sticking out of the bottom. They are not the gnarled, hardy, leather-skinned labourers that actually fought the battles. Not the guys that would run you through with a pitchfork as soon as look at you. It looked more like a stage set from a comic opera than gritty realism.

All the tables had been stacked up at the back of the classroom and the chairs arranged in a horseshoe around the stage. Everyone shuffled around the actors into the auditorium. Tarquin's and Quinlan's raised eyebrows asked, *What's going on?* and our shrugging shoulders replied, *Who knows?*

Hatter clapped his hands excitedly. 'Okay, girls and boys… Which period am I from?' He pointed excitedly to his helmet.

'Romans,' Jane said in her dull monotone.

'Romans! Romans! Oh, how ridiculous. Look at the helmet, look at the helmet,' he said in a flouncy, exasperated manner. 'It's not a Roman helmet, is it? So, what period am I?'

'Vikings?' said Simon hopefully.

'Vikings! Vikings! Ridiculous! Look at the helmet, the helmet.' This time, his voice had gone even higher than before. He calmed down and tried again. 'I'm not a Roman, I'm not a Viking. What am I!?'

Tarquin and Quinlan were more certain of the answer to that question and cast an *I know* glance in our direction and we nodded an *absolutely* back.

'C'mon, don't hold back. What am I?'

Winston whispered, 'If you say moose, I'll kill you.'

'Why would I do that?' I whispered back.

'I hear you crack easily under interrogation,' he replied.

'Mr Grahame, you're obviously an expert. What am I?'

'A Cavalier maybe?' he replied hopefully.

'Well done! Well done! Good work, Mr Grahame,' Hatter enthused.

Winston smiled smugly.

'But wrong,' the smile disappeared, 'but right period.' It returned.

'This is the English Civil War, but I am not a Cavalier. I am from the other side. What am I? I'll give you a clue, I'll give you a clue,' he said, as if taking part in an exciting parlour game. He took his helmet off and drew a circle around his head with his finger. 'What am I?' he repeated.

'A saint?' Macy said.

'No! I'm not a saint. I'm not drawing a halo. It's the shape, the shape, it's round… round… and around my head,' Hatter said, exasperated.

'A Roundhead?' Tarquin mashed the words together.

A choir of angels sang hallelujah, the heavens opened and a voice said, *God bless you, my son,* but here on earth, Hatter and his cohort just clapped enthusiastically.

'We are Roundheads. Well done, Mr… Mr…?'

'Palaster, sir,' Tarquin said.

'Well done, Mr Palaster,' Hatter said happily. 'We are indeed Roundheads, named after the popular pudding bowl hairstyle of its leaders. Now come on, girls and boys, you can't let these newbies beat you. This is another battle, you know: Harribold versus Rugby School. I hope you're not going to let them run away with it.'

After that, we suddenly became a whole heap more intelligent. It's amazing what a little competition can do. Kids I didn't know could speak reeled off lists of weapons and armour.

'So, who was the leader of the Roundheads?'

'Oliver Cromwell,' came a shout from the back. It was Roland Bourbon, or "Biscuit", as he was affectionately known. The room went silent. As far as we knew, Biscuit had never answered a question in his life before. He spent most lessons slumped over the desk as if he'd just been murdered. This went above and beyond the elective mutes; this was a genuine miracle. If there'd been a vicar in the room, we'd have converted then and there. After the angels stopped singing and the heavenly glow faded, our attention returned once more to the skinny man in a helmet.

'Yes! Yes! Oliver Cromwell. The great Oliver Cromwell. He is our leader.' Hatter beamed. Cromwell was clearly a favourite of his. 'I am camping with my colleagues on the edge of Marston Moor, preparing for the battle that will break the Royalist grip and lead to... the Republic.'

He paused to let this momentous notion sink in, though, to be honest, it just washed right over our heads. It would have been helpful to have had a fanfare at this point, but we were short of trumpeters, so the pause had to do. He pointed to the large woman with a cloth hat and long dress by his side.

'Mrs Bunyan here is cooking a fabulous meal.' She smiled and pretended to stir the cauldron and flip things in a giant frying pan. 'Mr Bunyan is a typical foot soldier with his pike.' Mr B stood to attention with his long pointy stick scraping the ceiling, 'whereas I am in the cavalry. We have been eating stew. Our bellies are full and we are ready to fight.' I wasn't so sure, looking at them.

'But who are we fighting?' Hatter asked.

'The Cavaliers?' Winston proclaimed, repeating his earlier guess.

'Yes, the Cavaliers, the Royalists,' Hatter agreed. 'But who are they fighting for?'

'The King?' a few kids called out.

'And what do kings and queens do?' Hatter asked.

Silence.

'C'mon. What do kings and queens do?' he asked again.

We clearly weren't getting whatever it was Hatter wanted us to get, but we certainly got it more than Beth.

'Bathe in goat's milk,' she said.

'What?' Hatter said, somewhat surprised by the answer. Beth explained.

'They bathe in goat's milk. I saw it in a movie. *Cleopatra*. She was a queen. She bathed in goat's milk.'

'She was Queen of Egypt, not England,' Hatter clarified. 'What do kings and queens do in England?' he demanded eagerly.

'Bathe in cow's milk?' Aggie suggested with a smile.

'It's got nothing to do with milk,' Hatter replied tersely.

'Cream?' Macy said hopefully.

'No! Absolutely not!' Hatter blurted, frustrated by our inept attempts.

'Custard,' George said mischievously. Steam began to emerge from Hatter's ears.

'No! It's got nothing to do with milk, cream, custard, blancmange or tapioca. What do kings and queens do?' he shouted.

'Chop people's heads off,' Caroline said.

'Correct.'

'It is?' Caroline queried. She, like us, found it hard to believe she had finally got something right.

'It'll do. They rule. They tell you what to do and if you don't do it, they chop your head off,' he said, bringing his hand down like an axe on the back of Mrs Bunyan's neck. She rather sportingly stuck her tongue out, rolled her eyes and pretended to drop down dead. Hatter carried on.

'Kings told the lords what to do; the lords told the knights and the knights told the peasants. You are all peasants. You are the lowest of the low, and a peasant can't become a knight, a knight can't become a lord, and a lord can't become a king. You are born to be king, born to be a lord, born to be a knight and born to be a peasant. You are your father's children. Whatever your father is, you will become.'

'So, we're fighting the Royalists so we don't have to do what our fathers did?' George enquired.

'Sort of,' Hatter partially agreed. 'Cromwell wanted parliament to be more important than the king, but most of us were probably fighting because the King is Catholic and we don't like Catholics.'

'That's a rubbish reason for having a fight,' Evy said.

'Yup, but people fight for stupid reasons,' Hatter advised with a shrug.

Winston and Josephine both looked at me and nodded.

'Maybe the motives were stupid,' Hatter continued, 'but the Civil War wasn't a bad thing. It led to the primacy of parliament, which led to voting for MPs, which led to parliament doing what voters want, which led to them doing what we want.'

I should point out at this stage that we had already had our own Battle of Marston Moor at Harribold the year before, so we understood the context. There was a Catholic secondary school near to Harribold School, and well-connected fifth formers had organised a fight between the rival establishments. The housing estate between the two was on a valley dipping down to a green space at the bottom. Between the houses, on both sides, was a series of narrow footpaths, or ginnels, leading down to the green. At an allotted time, the Harribold Roundheads lined up in the ginnels on one side; fifth formers in the front, fourth formers behind, and third, second and first formers behind them. On the other side, the St Patricks Cavaliers were arranged in a similar way. We all walked tentatively, nervously, slowly down the ginnels towards the centre, then suddenly a shout rang out, the cavaliers turned tail and ran, and we chased after them. Nobody was caught and not a punch was thrown, but at least we had made a stand for parliament and democracy, although we didn't know it at the time.

Hatter carried on. 'And it is parliament doing what we want that led to this school.'

'You mean this,' Macy pointed all around the room, 'is all Oliver Cromwell's fault,' she said.

'Yes!' Hatter agreed.

'Bastard!' she muttered under her breath.

'Maybe,' Hatter said, disregarding the foul language, 'but this school is the reason you don't have to be your father's son.'

'I'm not my father's son anyway,' Simon said.

'Hmm, yes, well, what I mean is this school gives you the opportunity, the education, to do what you want to do. If you're born a peasant, you don't have to be a peasant anymore. This school and all the other schools mean anyone can be whatever they want to be if they have the ability. You all have an equal chance.'

'Can I be Queen?'

'No, George.'

'If we all have an equal chance, why are there private schools, like Rugby School?' Peter asked.

They all looked rather pointedly at Tarquin and Quinlan. Hatter continued, ignoring the potential turmoil.

'Aah, well, things aren't completely equal. Whereas once there were lords and knights, now there are the haves...' he rather casually gestured towards Tarquin and Quinlan '...and the have-nots,' when his arm embraced the rest of us.

'Private schools are an attempt by the rich to give rich kids...' again, he casually waved his hand towards our guests '...a head start, by giving them the best education.'

'Hey, that's not fair.' By now, you could sense a little nervous tension in the air. The Hatter was unwittingly stirring up an angry mob. Tarquin and Quinlan were looking a little uneasy.

'George, if you had ever paid any attention in my lessons before, I might agree with you, but as you continue to waste the education you have been given, I find it difficult to sympathise. It is, after all, not Tarquin and Quinlan's fault they are educated at Rugby School.'

'But it's still not fair,' George said.

'Parents will always do the best for their children,' Hatter said, as if it answered everything.

'Not mine,' George stated.

'Most parents will do the best for their children,' Hatter said. 'Rich parents can buy more than poor parents.'

'That's not fair,' Roger joined in.

'For it to be equal,' Hatter continued, 'everyone would have to be paid the same, from bankers to bin men, from pop stars to police.'

'That'll never happen,' Peter said.

'So there'll always be private schools,' Hatter concluded. 'We've just got to make the best of what we're given. It's like there are two ladders to the top. Students from Rugby School and Harribold School have the same ladder. It's just that someone has smeared a little grease on your rungs. You can still get to the top. You've just got to try a little harder.'

Somehow reassured, the tension eased, and the lesson continued.

Hatter and his friends named each item of clothing they were wearing, and what they were for. Then we were given samples of cold food from the civil war cookbook. Apparently everyone always wore a hat, so it's no wonder it was Hatter's favourite period.

Eventually, the bell rang out once again, and it was time to go. We thanked the Bunyans as requested and filed out of the room.

'For a moment, I thought you were going to get lynched in there,' Josephine said to Quinlan and Tarquin, as we entered the corridor.

'I thought you might end up on Bunyan's pike stick,' Winston added.

'So did I,' Quinlan replied, sounding relieved.

'I reckon Hatter's almost as stupid as you when it comes to saying the wrong thing,' Josephine said to me.

'Oh, come on. Nothing was going to happen really,' I said dismissively.

'If he hadn't shut up about Rugby School,' Josephine continued, 'it might have kicked off in the playground.'

'Only if they were Catholic,' I said cheerily.

'I am,' Tarquin replied.

'Oh! Er... well, it wouldn't have made any difference really. I was just joking,' I spluttered, embarrassed.

Karen rolled her eyes.

'So who have you got left to tell about the moose?' Josephine asked Karen.

'Everyone in our class, which I'm going to do in geography, and then Mirabel and Flossy in 3H, I'll tell them at break.'

'Looks like you're in the clear,' Winston said to me. 'Once all the witnesses are primed, you'll be fine. We'll all be fine.'

25 MOOSE ON THE LOOSE

It was difficult to see how Mr Swan got his surname. He didn't look like a swan. Maybe, many moons ago, in the dim distant past, the people of Mud Huts-on-Marsh were handing out surnames according to family attributes. They'd got through all the useful ones: Mason, Carpenter, Thatcher, Farmer, Potter and Cook; but when they got to the family at Dog End, they didn't know what to do. They were a good-looking bunch, that's for sure, with a neat way of walking too. Local inhabitants could watch them for hours at a time, they looked so good, and no matter how shabby the animal skin, it always hung just right on them. But what name would suit? They didn't do anything useful. 'I know,' they said, 'we'll name them after those pretty white birds, the ones with the small brains… swans… that's it, we'll call them Swan.' It was all going swimmingly, and the Swans were almost ready to book themselves modelling careers in a few thousand years' time, when Sammy Swan married Wendy Warthog and the family business went to rack and ruin.

Mr Swan was more Warthog than Swan, but still retained that natural ability to avoid doing anything useful. He was definitely not the world's best teacher. 'Today,' he'd say, 'you're doing earthquakes. Read about it in your textbook, write about it in your exercise book, and at the end of the lesson, you can tell me what you've learnt.' We had all learnt Mr Swan was a lazy bastard, but didn't think we'd get away with that. The ensuing confusion, combined with sharing a textbook between two, made for a lively lesson. Half of us tried to figure out what the book meant, and then teach it to the other half. It was less of a class and more a self-help group. We wandered from desk to desk asking questions whilst the teacher swanned around, leaning back in his chair, looking up at the ceiling, an inane smile on his face. Funnily enough, we often learnt more in these lessons than we did under the whip of the strict disciplinarians.

In the crazy free-for-all, Karen was ostensibly wandering from desk to desk explaining how the slow steady flow of magma beneath our feet can rip the earth apart and cause mountains to tumble. Instead, she was carrying around a folded piece of paper with a picture of a moose. The moose was magnificent, standing regal and proud on a rocky outcrop next to a tumbling stream. Its head turned to the camera, antlers erect, eyes staring down the lens, powerful and defiant. It was a noble beast. A suitable subject for a tattoo emblazoned across the bare skin of an imaginary intruder.

There were five members of the netball team in our class, so Karen was fairly busy unfolding the paper, showing the picture, explaining where the tattoo was supposed to be and what it was supposed to look like. She was particularly good at describing the moose. Her acting was so accomplished she didn't need a picture at all. She was the very essence of moose; strong, noble, dignified, and with her hands as antlers, the animal was unmistakeable. She had become quite engrossed and ignorant of everything else around her. Her actions became so animated that even the Swan spotted something was afoot. He slid out of his chair, slinked around the desk and slowly and silently crept up behind her. We were all waving, pointing and shaking. If gestures made a noise, it would have been deafening, not that there weren't an inordinate number of loud coughs and sneezes, but to no avail. Just as the folded piece of paper was being handed back, just before it was fully in her grasp, he snatched it and held it aloft.

'And what is this doing the rounds?' he asked.

'It's a picture of a moose,' Aggie said in her strong Scottish accent.

'A what?' he asked, trying to unravel the accent in his head.

'A moose!' she repeated.

'A what?' he questioned again.

'A moose! Antlers!' She put her hands to the side of the head to explain.

'Oh! A moose,' he said. 'Like the one that was supposed to be on the back of that intruder. Oh, I see. I hope you're not leading the witnesses, young lady. I hope you're not putting pictures in their heads.'

'I was just showing them a picture, to see if they recognised the animal,' Karen said anxiously.

'I don't believe that for one moment. If this picture resembles the image they all describe to Mrs Stubbs on her way round, then we'll know it is a complete fabrication, and you... you will be out on your ear, missy.' He tried his hand at menacing but was more unctuous slimeball. He slipped the folded paper into his back pocket without looking at it. 'You, dear lady, will accompany me to the library after this lesson. We will check with the librarian whether this picture came from one of our sacred library books. If it did, I can't imagine the consequences.' He couldn't, but unfortunately, we could.

Karen looked at me, tears in her eyes. It was all my fault. I'd got a girlfriend and got her expelled in less than twenty-four hours. That was some achievement. I had to say something. I stood up, but before I'd spilled the beans, Winston kicked me so hard that I fell to the floor clutching my ankle.

'What the hell is wrong with you?' the Swan demanded.

'Cramp. It comes and goes,' I groaned. Winston helped me to my feet and whispered in my ear.

'We can sort this,' he said. 'All we've got to do is get that picture out of his pocket and replace it with something else.'

'But it has to be another moose,' I said. 'He knows it's a moose. But where are we going to get a picture of a moose that looks nothing like that moose? It was hard enough getting that one last time.'

Winston smiled.

'No!' I said.

'Yes!' he replied.

'Okay.' I thumbed through Thidwick in the deep, dark depths of my bag till I got to the centre pages. I gently tugged on the pages, tearing through the cotton binding until they were completely loose. Then I folded them up till it resembled the piece of paper Swan had recently held aloft. I showed Winston a glimpse inside my bag; he nodded. Stage 1 complete. Josephine had also been watching and nodded her assent. The game was on.

'What do we do now?' I whispered to Winston.

'You distract him, and when I'm close, you need to kick him or something.'

'Kick him?' I queried.

'So, he doesn't feel it when I take the picture out of his pocket and put in the new one.'

'How should I distract him?' I said.

'I don't know,' Winston answered, 'cramp maybe?'

I passed Thidwick to Winston and limbered up for my stage appearance. Swan was wandering back to his desk from the back of the class. It was now or never. I stood up then rolled into the aisle, clutching my leg.

'Not again, Baker,' he said as he bent over me, and then, with one apparently involuntary movement, I kicked him on the shin. At the same moment, Winston grabbed the folded piece of paper from his back pocket and tried to insert the new one, but unfortunately, I had kicked too hard. The Swan dived right over me before the exchange was completed, landing with a splat on the asbestos tiles. He rolled around on the floor, grabbing various parts of himself before settling on his shin as the primary source of pain.

'Sorry, sir. Sorry, sorry, sorry. It was an accident, sir, honest, sir. Sorry, sir.' I was genuinely concerned. I'd never seen anyone travel through air with less elegance and hit the ground with more force. If pigs could fly, this was probably how they'd land. It wasn't pretty. I turned round to sell my concern to the rest of the class, but they weren't buying. The laughing had died down, but the smirks were so wide, they almost stretched unbroken from wall to wall.

Josephine immediately strode over and took control.

'Let me help, sir. We can't have you lying on the floor like that. It's just not right,' she said, offering her hand to the prostrate teacher whilst winking at Winston.

'Thank you, thank you, my dear. Very kind,' he said, reaching up.

My God, she could sell, and he was definitely buying. He scrambled to his feet, taking the opportunity to climb up Josephine as he rose. When he was almost on his feet, she gave him a gentle nudge off balance, so he leaned forward and grabbed hold of her, and she, rather forcefully, grabbed hold of his arms to steady him whilst Winston slipped the folded paper into his back pocket. It was a master class in diversion and deception. If Josephine ever ventured into a life of crime, she could have hustled the pants off an archbishop in the middle of a sermon.

'Whoa,' he said shakily. 'Sorry, my dear, I'm a bit unsteady. Thank you for your help. I'm fine now. Thank you. You can leave me now.'

'Are you sure you are all right, sir?' she asked, concerned.

'Yes! Yes! Just fine. But thank you,' he smarmed.

Josephine wandered back to her table a heroine. The Swan slumped back in his chair, took a deep breath then rocked forward, leaning over his desk with his head on his forearms whilst he regained composure. After a few minutes, he started an inventory of injuries, rolling up his trousers and lifting his shirt to check for cuts and bruises.

We just carried on with the lesson as we were, though a little bit quieter. The bell rang out. The Swan raised his head and looked over us. He had missed his opportunity to interrogate us about earthquakes and was clearly disappointed. We packed our books away. And waited for a few unnecessary seconds in silence.

'You can go,' he said reluctantly, and we filed out towards the exit.

'Not you, Karen Hannah. You will accompany me to the library,' he said, smiling triumphantly.

'Yes, sir,' Karen replied timidly.

We all wandered out of the class.

'C'mon,' Winston said, 'we're going to the library.'

'D'ya think she'll be all right?' I asked nervously as we descended the stairs.

'Karen can deal with things just fine, no thanks to you,' Josephine said, sending daggers my way. 'But we need to be there to support her.'

Winston added a sense of urgency: 'C'mon, we've got to get down the stairs and back up the other side. Swan will cut through the classrooms.'

We walked quickly down the corridor like penguins on speed and climbed the stairs to the library. We slipped through the door and plonked ourselves down around a table just before Swan walked in with a glum-looking Karen walking behind. He walked up to the counter with a fierce look on his face.

'Mrs Wilder.'

'Yes, Mr Swan. Can I help you at all?' she asked.

'I am concerned this girl may have taken a picture from one of our library books. A picture of a moose,' he announced like a master detective.

Mrs Wilder raised an eyebrow. She looked across at Karen without a change of expression and then looked back at Mr Swan.

'And what is your evidence?' Mrs Wilder asked patiently.

'I have in my pocket the page in question,' he declared loudly.

'And why do you think it was Karen that took it?' she asked once more.

'I caught her passing it to another pupil.' He looked accusingly at Karen. 'I think she was telling them what to say to Mrs Stubbs when she asks them about the tattoo.'

'Oh. I see. Well, that is a very serious accusation, Mr Swan. We had better have a look at that piece of paper, hadn't we?'

The Swan whipped the paper out of his pocket and held it up, as if displaying the definitive piece of evidence in a court case. He briefly looked around the library, soaking up the imaginary applause. He knew he wasn't well respected in the staff room. This was his moment of glory, his time to shine. A crime had been committed and he, ever-vigilant, had caught the perpetrator red-handed. Nothing could get in the way. He wondered if he would get his name in the papers. He slapped the piece of paper down on the counter.

Mrs Wilder carefully unfolded the paper with her nimble fingers and opened it out flat. Mr Swan was still looking around, taking the applause.

'Mr Swan, this page isn't taken from a book in our library,' she advised the puzzled teacher.

'But it is a moose.' he said, clinging to the crime of misleading the witnesses.

'Oh yes. It is a moose, but surely there must be some mistake. I am not sure I would use this picture to mislead a witness,' she said.

Mr Swan looked down. Spread out before him was a cartoon moose with a wide range of cartoon animals arranged within its antlers. His world came crashing down.

'Are you sure this is the same as the moose described in the tattoo?' she asked.

He stared at the picture in silence.

'Er… I'm not sure. I don't know. Probably not. No, probably not,' he said despondently.

'Mr Swan. You may find your little joke very amusing, but I don't find it funny at all. And I'm not sure it was necessary to put Karen through this charade either. I will be having words with the headmaster.'

'But, but I… how… that's not fair,' Mr Swan said angrily.

'Mr Swan,' Mrs Wilder said, looking at him intently, 'you have clearly caused considerable distress to this young lady and wasted my valuable time. I suggest you leave Karen here with me and return to your work.'

'But… but—'

'Mr Swan!'

'Yes, Mrs Wilder.'

He wandered off, tail between his legs, and a look of disbelief on his face.

Karen looked at Mrs Wilder with apprehension and apology. She had felt guilty about removing the real pages ever since she had done so, and wasn't sure what to do now. Mrs Wilder observed Karen with those sharp, shrewd eyes, weighing up what to do next.

'Karen. Come into my office.'

Mrs Wilder led Karen into the office and gestured for her to sit down on one of the office chairs, whilst she occupied the other.

'Karen. Mr Swan is by no means my favourite teacher, but he has a point, doesn't he?' she said.

'Yes, Mrs Wilder,' Karen replied, full of remorse.

'I found this book this morning disturbed on the shelves, and it opened at this very page.' She let the book open. There were roe deer on one page and reindeer on the next. 'There seem to be a couple of pages missing, where I would probably have expected to find an elk.'

Karen burst into tears. 'I did it for all the right reasons, Mrs Wilder. I did, I did. You know I wouldn't damage a book for no reason. I love books. I love books. I had to do it, I had to. I'm sorry, I'm sorry.' Karen put her head in her hands and cried her heart out.

'Now, now, my dear. That's enough now. It is because I know you that I know your actions, no matter how foolish, would be well intentioned. But you do realise, you will have to repair the damage, after school with me, don't you?'

Karen flung her arms around the diminutive figure of Mrs Wilder and sobbed on her shoulder.

'I'm sorry, Mrs Wilder. It won't happen again.'

'I know. I know. Come on, dear, we can't carry on like this, can we?' Mrs Wilder said in a calm, reassuring manner. 'Now. Please pass me the real picture.'

Karen opened her bag and removed the picture from within and passed it over.

'You have been very foolish, Karen,' Mrs Wilder said, observing her with those sharp, intelligent eyes.

'I know, Mrs Wilder,' Karen accepted, head down, unable to look the librarian in the face.

'All is not lost. Nothing more will be heard of this and no one else will get to know. Now go, but I expect you back here this afternoon as usual, and we will talk about repairs.'

Karen got up and left the room. Instead of walking over to us, she turned and went straight out of the room. I jumped up and ran after her. Winston jumped up at the same time, but Josephine pulled him back.

'Give them a second.'

Winston looked curious. 'Are they... you know... an item?'

'I don't know. I don't think they know. But give them a second before we catch up.'

'When did that happen?' Quinlan asked.

'Yesterday,' Josephine replied. Quinlan was aghast.

'Yesterday, I thought I had fitted more than any normal person could fit into one day. When did he find the time?'

'Things happen,' Josephine said.

I followed Karen down the steps and caught up with her at the bottom, but she wouldn't look at me.

'Er... Are you all right?' I asked nervously.

'No!' she said, still facing away.

'Why?' I said, which was far and away the worst word I could have chosen.

'Why! Why!' she said back. 'I've betrayed the trust of someone I respect, I've done things I should never have done, I've lied and cheated, and I've nearly been expelled. All because of you!' She pushed me backwards with both hands. 'All because of you. You dick. Do you know what you've put me through? Do you? Do you?'

'I... I... I'm sorry,' I stuttered. 'I didn't mean to. I didn't know. It was a mistake. It got out of hand. I didn't want to hurt you. I like you. I really like you.'

She burst into tears again and buried her head against my chest. I didn't know what to do. We weren't big huggers in our family, so it wasn't a natural instinct. Gradually, I tentatively folded my arms around her and held her slackly towards me. Just as I thought things were calming down, as her breathing returned to normal and her body relaxed, she suddenly stiffened, raised herself up, grabbed my blazer with both hands, shook me then violently pushed me away.

'I wish I'd never met you,' she shouted, and marched off down the corridor.

I stumbled back into the trophy cabinet, shaking the glass and rattling the trophies.

'Careful, boy,' cried a passing teacher. 'We've not got many. We don't want to break the ones we have got.'

'Yes, sir', I said as the teacher continued down the corridor. The rest of the gang had caught up by this time.

'Is she all right?' Josephine said, looking concerned.

'No, she's upset. I'd go after her, but I don't know if she likes me, or hates me.'

'That means she likes you,' Josephine said. 'But you've done enough damage for one day. I'll go after her.' She dashed off down the corridor.

'What do we do now?' Tarquin asked.

'Go to the next lesson, I guess,' Winston said.

'Which is?' Quinlan asked.

'Physics,' I said.

'Oh good. I like physics,' Tarquin replied.

26 THE SOUND OF SHIT HITTING THE FAN

Professor Bodkin, the physics teacher, was old and dangerous. He had that wild white sticky out hair that can only be achieved by sticking your fingers in an electric socket, and he was the sort of person that would do that, just to find out what happened. He followed in the footsteps of the great Isaac Newton, who was mad enough to stick a blunt needle into his eye socket for exactly the same reason.

Someone said he was a member of the Manhattan Transfer, but they had recently been on *Top of the Pops* singing *Chanson d'Amour*, and I didn't recall seeing a mad scientist amongst them. I guess they meant the Manhattan Project, but I doubt they would have let him in; Bodkin was not the safe pair of hands they needed for developing the atomic bomb. However, Harribold was a good place to hide someone who had been involved in top-secret research, so who knows?

He was not a cosy-slippers-and-cardigan theoretical physicist; he was an out-and-out experimental physicist and proud of it. He wore a white lab coat at all times, even at lunch. We suspected he wore it in bed. Mrs Bodkin probably had her own. We assumed they indulged in experimental lovemaking all night, and in the morning, they'd record the results in a detailed report. The back pages of my science book were full of diagrams, graphs and charts from these imaginary reports, conjured up with Winston during a quiet moment in class. They often involved the dashed arc traversed by Mr Bodkin as he leapt from various objects, was fired from a cannon, or landed by parachute onto the awaiting Mrs Bodkin. If he ever opened my exercise book from the back, I was in big trouble.

For Bodkin, the experiment was everything, and in the pursuit of knowledge, accidents were bound to happen, and they did. He once dropped a bowling ball and ping-pong ball out of the second-floor science studio to prove they fall at the same rate. He sent dopey Jane down to witness the outcome. She lost concentration (if she ever gained it) at the critical moment. She was probably admiring her reflection in the window, when she saw the ball land on her head, the ping-pong ball, that is; the bowling ball whizzed past and embedded itself in the lawn.

I liked physics, despite the danger. It was interesting and entertaining. You were never quite sure what was going to happen. It had been a tough morning, so I was glad an enjoyable lesson was next… or so I thought. We lined up outside the lab. The door creaked open and Bodkin invited us in.

'Come in, come in, my little lab rats,' he said cheerily, his eyes sparkling with intrigue and a slightly sinister smile upon his lips.

The science classrooms were big. All around the perimeter were dark wooden worktops with white pottery sinks, swan neck taps and electrical sockets. In the middle were three rows of high wooden benches and tall metal stools. The teaching desk was set up a step, as if on a stage, with a large roller blackboard behind. Everyone shuffled in and found a stool. Me, Winston, Quinlan and Tarquin worked our way round to the back row, but Karen and Josephine went to the front at the opposite end to us. They clearly wanted to be as far from me as possible. Every now and then, they would look round at me with glaring eyes, followed by some secretive chatter. I didn't think they were talking about my better qualities. Bodkin gave them a withering look, but it didn't have the desired effect.

'Girls! Stop talking. This is a laboratory not a gossip shop,' he said crossly. They shut up quickly then glanced back at me. Even the telling-off was all my fault. Bodkin continued.

'Today, we are looking at sound. What is wrong with that sentence?'

'You hear sound.'

'Quite right, Macy. You've got your thinking cap on this morning. There are lots of interesting things about sound. To start with, you need an emitter. Laaaaaaah,' he sang out a long note, 'in this case, me, and you need a receiver, in this case, you.'

'Sound can be low. Looooooooow…' he sang out a long low note '…and it can be high. Miss Hannah, I hear you've got a good voice. Can you sing me a high note, please?'

Karen squawked a response.

'Clearly, I made a mistake. Your voice was getting so much practice this morning I thought it would be suitably warmed up by now.'

Karen and Josephine glared at me again. I was even getting the blame for that.

He turned to Jude. 'Miss Pringle, can you oblige?'

'Laaaaaah,' Jude sang high and clear.

'Beautiful, Miss Pringle. With a voice like that, you really should be in the choir.'

Jude blushed, embarrassed by the compliment.

'Another thing is volume. For instance, if I stand here and shout, "Mooooose!" it is not too loud.'

'It is, sir.'

'Yes, well, you're on the front row, Macy. For those on the back row, it is quieter.'

'Did he say moose?' Tarquin whispered.

'Why did he say moose?' Quinlan muttered anxiously.

'Why does Bodkin do anything?' Winston replied.

'It's probably the word circulating in the staff room,' I said quietly.

'Yeah, probably,' Winston agreed.

'Boys! Are you talking in my class, in the middle of a demonstration? What is wrong with you all today?'

'Sorry, sir.' We all mumbled our apologies.

'I should think so,' he said sternly. After a brief pause, he returned to his experiment. 'If I stand here, however,' he got down from the stage and squeezed between the first and second row, 'and I shout "Mooooooose!" it is a lot louder, at least for those on the back row. Why is it quieter the further I am away?'

'The air absorbs the sound?' Simon suggested.

'Good idea, Mr Johnson, but no, well, maybe a tiny amount. Air is actually very good for transmitting sound. It is the things around us that absorb sound. Spongy things, like your jumpers, absorb sound, and hard things, like walls, bounce it back. But there is not much between me and Mr Baker over there. Yet it still sounds quieter further away.

'If I get this long pipe...' He brought out a long plastic pipe and laid it across the benches so that it stretched all the way from the front row to the back row. 'Mr Grahame, can you put that end to your ear, please,' Winston obliged, 'and I shout down this end, "Mooooooose."' Winston recoiled at the far end, rocked backwards on his stool and toppled to the ground. We burst into laughter.

'My apologies, Mr Grahame,' Bodkin said, once the laughter had died down. Winston clambered back onto his stool.

'I think we can see that if the sound is contained in a pipe with very reflective sides, then the volume at that end is almost the same as this end. But if we let it spread out, the sound diminishes.' Bodkin spread his arms out as if casting sound to the far corners of the room. 'I need a volunteer. Mr Baker, you seem to be spending a lot of time looking over to the far corner. Now is your chance to see what it is all about.'

It was then I noticed the polythene sheet, pinned to the notice boards. I wandered over, wondering what he was up to. There were three rows of chairs set out from the teacher's desk to the polythene: one chair in the first row, two in the second, and three in the third.

'Mr Baker, can you please sit on the chair in the first row?' I sat down, perplexed.

He then dragged out what looked like a giant water pistol with a swivelling nozzle. It did look slightly comical in the hands of an elderly man in a lab coat.

'I think I filled this with water,' Bodkin said with a sly smile. 'Mind you, there are so many big bottles of strange liquid in the prep room, it's easy to make a mistake.'

I know he was joking, but he had a reputation for making mistakes, so I was feeling a little uneasy. He stood beside me, squirted the gun once and a long, narrow stream of water shot out, hit the polythene and dribbled to the floor. I was glad to see the polythene itself didn't fizz and disintegrate or catch fire. He twisted the nozzle and squirted again. This time, the water sprayed out to form a cone. Bodkin explained his experiment.

'Now, imagine the water in this water pistol is actually sound. The amount of water represents the volume of sound. Each squirt of the gun provides the same total volume. If I stand here on this mark and fire at Mr Baker here in the front row, what happens?' He pulled the trigger and almost all the water squirted over my face and ran down onto my clothes. Everyone laughed loudly. He beckoned me up. 'Thank you, Mr Baker. Please stand here next to my desk. Now I need two volunteers for the second row.' No hands went up. 'Hmm… Miss Hannah and Carter… you'll do.'

'But, sir!' Karen blurted. 'It's not fair.'

'Can't the boys do it?' Josephine pleaded.

'Miss Hannah and Miss Carter. This is your opportunity to champion the role of women in science. To be pioneers. To show the boys how it's done.'

'But I don't want to get my hair wet,' Karen moaned. The prof did not look impressed.

'That's not the spirit of the great Marie Curie, is it? She wouldn't let wet hair get in the way of a good experiment.'

'Didn't she die young, sir... from her experiments?'

'Mr Bourbon? Was that you? Are you alive?'

'Yes, sir.'

'Shame. I had been contemplating an experiment with electrodes to shake you from your slumbers. Now you're with us, yes, she did indeed die young from her experiments, but I can assure you that wet hair had nothing to do with it. Come on, you two.' Mr Williams waved them up out of their chairs. Karen and Josephine stood up but stayed safely behind their bench.

'Come on! You've spent all morning discussing this experiment. Now's your chance to take part. You have been discussing *this* experiment, haven't you, not Mrs Garland's interesting experiments with a slipper? Would you prefer to volunteer for that instead?'

'No, sir.'

'Well, come out here then... come on.'

Josephine and Karen reluctantly took their seats in the second row. They braced themselves for the soaking to come. This time, the cone of water sprayed wider to cover them both. They leaned back and looked away, but they still got a reasonable drenching. They wiped the water off their faces and squeezed it out of their hair, flicking it onto the floor. They glared back at me, whilst the rest of the class giggled loudly. My heart sank. I was pretty sure this was going on my list of crimes as well.

Bodkin looked at the grumpy faces and raised an eyebrow. 'Girls, you are now pioneers in the mould of Marie Curie. Isn't that worth a little wet hair?'

'Not really,' they grumbled. Bodkin sighed, clearly disappointed they did not share his enthusiasm.

'Stand over there next to Baker.' They got up and walked over, looking none too pleased to see me. I smiled inanely through the water dripping down my face.

'Finally, can I have three more volunteers…? Aah yes, the chatty back row boys. Come on, Mr Grahame, and please bring your guests with you.'

Winston, Tarquin and Quinlan slipped off their stools and made their way to the front.

'Take a seat… not the second row, numskulls… third row… right… let's see… comfortable?' They all nodded. He picked up his gun and took aim. 'That's lovely… don't move,' he said, as if taking a group photograph. The three amigos tried to look unperturbed.

Once again, he pulled the trigger. Despite the bravado, all three flinched, raising their hands to fight off the fine mist. The audience laughed; some even applauded. The prof took a bow then turned back to his latest victims.

'Thank you,' he said. 'Please stand next to the others.' They shuffled round onto the end of the line.

'Okay, everyone, let's see what you notice about the amount of water on our three sets of volunteers. Firstly, how wet is Mr Baker?'

The eager audience stuck up their hands.

'Yes, Miss Campbell?'

'Soaking wet, sir.'

'Yes, he is, isn't he?' I did look like a drowned lab rat. 'So, if this was sound, he would have been drenched in sound.'

'Next, how wet are the misery twins?' Karen and Josephine glared angrily. The hands went up again.

'Mr Thomson?'

'Quite wet, sir.'

'Yes, they are still fairly wet, aren't they?' He assessed the damp dribbling over their angry faces. 'They would have received a good level of sound, but not as much as Mr Baker here.'

'And finally, what do you notice about our last three victims?'

'Hands shot up once more.'

'Miss Clarke?'

'They're not that wet, sir.'

'Is the correct answer. Yes! As you can see, they are much drier. So Mr Baker here got the full force of the sound, whereas "The Grumps" shared it between them, and our three on the back row shared it between them. So, the reason it is quieter is not because it has travelled further. It can travel quite a way in my narrow tube without getting quieter. The reason it is quieter is because it is spread out more thinly.'

'Now can you please give a big round of applause to all our willing volunteers?'

The audience clapped and cheered. We bowed and waved, apart from Josephine and Karen, who scowled angrily.

'Please go back to your seats. Oh, wait. I forgot to keep a record. I should have stood you on paper so that we could draw round the size of the puddles. We'll have to do it all again.'

Karen and Josephine were about to explode. Steam was coming out of their ears, though it could just have been the water evaporating.

'Just joking,' Bodkin said mischievously.

At that moment, the door opened, and Mrs Stubbs poked her head in. She always seemed a little nervous in the realm of academia, away from her beloved sports.

'Professor, er… do you mind… could I have a word?'

'Certainly, Mrs Stubbs. Come on in.'

'Oh. Yes, well, er… I need to speak to the netball team, if you don't mind.'

'The netball team? Here?' he asked.

'No! No! No! Not here. I... I need to take them down to the deputy head's study.'

'Oh, I see. Do you want to tell them?' he queried.

'Yes! Yes! I er... think that would be best.' She drew herself up tall to make the announcement.

'Can all the members of the netball team that were training last night please follow me?'

Josephine, Karen, Aggie, Martha and Jude walked over to Mrs Stubbs.

'Karen, you're all wet,' Mrs Stubbs noted.

'I know,' she said, looking over in my direction.

Mrs Stubbs shrugged. 'Come with me,' she said, and they all left the room.

Bodkin regained control: 'Okay, you four, return to your seats.' He waited till we were back on our stools before he continued. 'So, back to sound...' He carried on with an explanation of how sound travels through air, the Doppler effect, frequency and amplitude, and a number of other interesting facts, but rather disappointingly no one else got soaked.

A little while later, the netball team returned with Mrs Stubbs, who wandered over to the back row and quietly mentioned to me, Winston, Quinlan and Tarquin that the head wanted to see us straight after physics. We nodded our understanding and she left once again. Shortly after that, the bell rang for lunch. We waited patiently for everyone else to leave before we grabbed our bags and got up to go. Josephine came over to join us, but Karen left with the others. I watched her leave, but she didn't look back.

'I guess we'd better go and see the head,' I grumbled, somewhat dejectedly. We grabbed our bags and trudged down the steps to the staff corridor.

27 THE BITCH IS BACK

We waited outside the headmaster's office once again.

'I'm hungry,' Winston moaned, rubbing his stomach. 'I hope this doesn't take too long.'

'He can't keep us hanging round,' Josephine said, 'we've all got to eat.'

'C'mon, let's get it over and done with,' Tarquin urged.

'What do you think he wants us for?' Quinlan asked.

'Don't know. A lot's gone on,' I replied.

'Maybe he's just checking how the newbies are getting on,' Winston said hopefully.

'Or maybe you're gonna get an award,' Josephine said, looking at Tarquin.

'What would it be?' Winston quizzed. 'The "Swimming in Sub-Zero Temperatures" award or the "Chasing Imaginary Intruders" award?'

'I'd happily settle for either,' Tarquin admitted.

'I guess you're not going to get the "Off-Road Go-Karting" award,' Quinlan said to Winston.

'That was amazing,' Winston said. 'I could hardly see a thing piling through that grass. I can't believe I didn't hit a tree or something.'

'Did the car survive?' Tarquin asked.

'Yup,' Winston said. 'I reckon they're bombproof, they're so strong. The army will be using them for reconnaissance next year. They'd be in and out in a jiffy if they did.'

'I reckon that was the bravest thing anyone did yesterday,' Quinlan stated, impressed.

'Or most reckless,' Josephine suggested.

'Or that,' Quinlan agreed.

Despite the chat, the mood was fairly sombre. Nobody said it, but everybody was thinking, *Maybe we've been found out... maybe it's all unravelling... maybe we're in big, big trouble.*

The door to the headmaster's study opened, and he beckoned us through.

'Come in, come in, everyone. Take a seat. Sorry about the mess. Put those books on the coffee table. Quinlan and Tarquin, how are you?'

'Fine, thank you, Headmaster,' they both chorused.

'Good! Good! Splendid. And how did you find your time with us yesterday?' he asked cheerfully. From his tone, we weren't there for a telling-off. We began to relax a little.

'I... I...' They both started, talking at the same time then paused.

'You go first,' Tarquin said to Quinlan, who immediately took up the batten.

'It was great. Andy, Josephine and Winston helped us out a lot. We had lots of fun.'

'Good, glad to hear you had fun. Did you learn anything as well?'

'Yes, loads,' Tarquin cut in. 'Lessons have been good. I admit we have covered most of it already at Rugby School, but it is good to go over it again in a different way.'

'There are more people in a class,' Quinlan said, 'so there is a bit more chatter, but we have still learnt a lot.'

'It has been good,' Tarquin concluded. 'I am really glad we are on the exchange.'

The head smiled and nodded appreciatively. 'Well, I must thank you for your valiant effort chasing away those intruders yesterday.'

Tarquin glanced across at me and shrugged apologetically. It seemed I was not destined to receive any of the praise for my imaginary acts.

'I'd also like to thank you, Josephine, and your netball team for their part in the affair.'

'Thank you, Headmaster,' she said politely.

'And, on another note, Winston, I am so glad you came through yesterday's experience unscathed.'

'Thank you, sir,' Winston said.

'To be honest, we didn't really believe the story that came to light last night that one of the intruders had a tattoo of a moose on his back. It sounded so far-fetched.' The others glanced at me and raised an eyebrow or two. The head continued: 'But Mrs Stubbs has been to all the classes apart from 4H and spoken to those who were at netball practice yesterday and they've all described the moose exactly the same way, although Karen Hannah said it might have been an elk. I think moose and elk are the same thing though, aren't they?'

We all nodded. We knew our deer by now.

'And you saw the moose tattoo as well, didn't you, Tarquin?' the head mentioned.

'Yes, sir,' Tarquin confirmed.

'So I guess it must be true. I've asked Mrs Garland, the deputy head, just to check with 4H, but I can't imagine anything will come out of that. It just goes for me to say thank you once again and—'

At that moment, the deputy head walked in and stood to attention by the door.

'Well,' she said, 'something is rotten in the state of Denmark.'

I have to say, it wasn't what I was expecting. We hadn't studied Shakespeare; most of us were only just out of *Janet and John* books, so the quote was meaningless to all of us except the head.

'Really?' the headmaster replied, obviously *au fait* with affairs in Denmark.

'Both Flossy Chippendale and Mirabel Berkeley in 4H have a different idea as to what the tattoo was of.'

'Well, I guess a moose could get mistaken for something else.'

'Not a tortoise and an octopus,' she said.

'Hmm. Yes, you are quite right. A moose could not be mistaken for a tortoise or an octopus.'

He turned his gaze back to us. 'Well... have you got an explanation?'

'Actually, Headmaster,' the deputy cut in, 'I have an urgent problem I'd like to deal with first if you don't mind.'

'Urgent?'

'Yes, urgent... in private, please.'

'Very well. Out, all of you. Wait outside, and when I call you back, I expect you to have a good explanation for all this.'

We filed out like naughty schoolchildren, which is exactly what we were, and stood outside the door. From inside, we could just about hear something about Mr Swan, locked in a toilet cubicle, shouting 'F**kin' moose,' at the top of his voice.

'Now what?' Tarquin asked. 'I had just got used to being a hero, now it looks like I am a zero.'

'I think we've run out of options,' Josephine said. 'Maybe we are going to have to tell the truth.'

'We can't do that now,' Winston said. 'We've wasted police time. We'll be crucified. Out on our ear.'

'We need Mary,' I said.

'Mary! Mary Tideswell? How the hell is she going to help?'
Josephine looked at me as if I was out of my mind.

'She just will. I know she will. She's like Goldfinger,' I tried to
explain.

'Goldfinger? You are mad,' Winston said.

'Yes, Goldfinger,' I said. 'She's our only chance. Where is she
likely to be?'

'Lunch, I reckon,' Josephine said.

'We need her. We need her here. We need her now,' I pleaded.

There was a short pause, but nobody could think of any other
possible avenue to explore. This was all that was left. Maybe, just
maybe, Mary was our escape route. We had to move fast.

'Right then,' Winston said, 'you and Quinlan try the dining
room. Me and Tarquin will search out the playing field and,
Josephine, you try the north playground. Back here in five
minutes max.'

'Okay,' everyone agreed. We all shot off in different directions.

Me and Quinlan walked as fast as our legs would take us. The
smell of the school's signature dish, toad in the hole, meant we
were heading in the right direction. We skipped past what was
left of the queue in the corridor and cast our eyes over the sea
of hairy heads, bobbing around at the dining tables. The hair
we were looking for was big and blonde. In a sea of brown, it
was easy to spot. 'There,' I said, pointing to a table at the far side,
where Mary sat alone. We weaved our way around the tables and
plonked ourselves down next to her.

'Well, boys, my popularity seems to have suddenly improved.'

'We need you, Mary,' I said with urgency.

'Well, it's nice to know someone does,' she said, looking
around.

'We need you now,' Quinlan confirmed, though I'm not sure
he knew why.

'Well, you are eager, aren't you?' she said coyly.

'We need you to come with us now. Right now,' I said. 'Please! Please! It's urgent.'

'Well, how can a girl refuse such enthusiasm?' she said. 'I'll just finish the food. The toad in the hole is excellent.' Her implacable composure was driving me nuts.

'There's not enough time. We need you now. Now! Please!' I begged.

'Why?' she asked calmly.

'It's a matter of life and death,' I said. 'Mine, yours and the netball team.'

She pushed the plates away, removed some crumbs from round her mouth and got up from the table.

'This better be good,' she said.

'It is,' I replied.

We worked our way through the tables to the corridor, where I provided a recount of everything that had happened.

'I told the police one of the pretend intruders from yesterday had a tattoo of a moose.'

'I heard, dickhead,' she replied, looking at me and shaking her head.

'We showed a picture of a moose to all the witnesses so they could describe it the same, but we missed out Flossy and Mirabel.'

'From 4H, my new class?' she queried.

'Yup,' I said. 'When they were interrogated, they said the tattoo was a tortoise and an octopus, not a moose.'

'So what can I do?' she asked.

'You can save us all,' I said confidently.

'How?' she asked, looking at me like I had lost the plot.

'I don't know, I just know you can,' I said. 'I believe in you.'

'Why?' she asked.

'Because you're amazing, because you're brilliant, because you're Goldfinger,' I explained.

'Watch it, lover, or I'll kiss you again,' she said, threatening me.

'You kissed her as well?' Quinlan asked. 'When did you find the time?'

'Yesterday,' Mary said. 'Came on to me on the bus. He was all over me. It was embarrassing.'

'No, I wasn't,' I said, hoping Quinlan would believe me.

'But you did kiss?' he said.

'Yes! Yes! We kissed. So what?' It didn't seem too important at that moment in time.

'Was yesterday just too boring for you?' Quinlan asked. 'Did you really need to spice it up some more?'

'It just happened,' I said.

'It might have meant nothing to you, but it did to me,' Mary mocked.

Quinlan shook his head in disbelief.

We turned onto the staff corridor. Everyone was coming back at the same time. They looked pretty relieved that we had come back with the prize. Winston and Tarquin were panting heavily.

'That is a big field,' Winston said. 'I wish I'd chosen the dining room.'

'Hi, Mary,' Josephine said.

'Hi,' Mary said, a little more muted than normal. 'I hear you need me.'

'Do you think you can save us?' Josephine asked.

'I dunno. I'll give it a go. See what happens.' She looked across at me. 'They shouldn't let this dipstick out of his cage. Moose! What a moron.'

'I know I'm a dick, but at least I didn't force someone to swim the pool in the middle of winter.'

Mary gave me what can only be described as a hard stare; the sort of stare that has a physical presence; the sort of stare that pushes you back and pins you against a wall. For a moment, I thought I'd blown it. I thought she was just going to walk away. Instead, she slackened her stare and nodded.

'Yeah, I'm a bit of a bastard,' she said. 'Runs in the family. It's all I know, all I've ever known. It's what I do. It's what I am. I don't think I know how to be nice. I've never been shown.'

'You don't have to be nice,' Josephine said. 'You just have to be less nasty.'

'Okay. I'll give it a go,' she said. 'Try it on for size. Can't be that difficult, you lot seem to manage it all right.'

'I don't think Andy does,' Winston replied. 'He's got us into enough trouble being nice. We might be better off if he was nasty.'

Voices grew louder on the other side of the door. The handle turned and the deputy head came out.

'You can go in now,' she said in a rather huffy manner, turned abruptly, and strode off in the direction of the next crisis.

We filed into the headmaster's study, looking nervous and uncomfortable. We stood around the coffee tables and lounge chairs, not knowing what to do. The head was standing at his desk, looking over some papers.

'Sit down, sit down,' he said, without turning around. 'I'll be with you in a second.'

We all sat down, apart from Mary, who remained standing. She looked confident; she looked relaxed; she looked like she knew what she was going to do.

The head turned round like a radar scanning the occupants until he reached the bleep.

'And why on earth have you brought Mary Tideswell in here with you?' he said gruffly.

'I'm the reason they're all here, sir,' Mary stated clearly. The rest of us looked very anxious. Was she actually going to tell the truth?

'What do you mean exactly?' he growled.

'I'm the reason for all of this,' Mary continued.

'Go on.'

'You know my dad, don't you?' she said conspiratorially.

'I've heard,' the headmaster replied, but didn't elucidate.

'He's always doing deals. Well, he had some people comin' over from Canada for something, don't know what, but, the big guy, the leader, the one they call Moose...'

'Moose, you say?'

'Yeah, Moose,' she confirmed. 'Now he goes swimming in lakes in Canada. He was askin' if there were any lakes around here. Anyway, my dad says there ain't no lakes, but there's an outdoor swimming pool at the school.'

'Our pool?' the head queried. Mary nodded then continued with the story.

'My dad's brother, Joe, he asks why not use the baths like everyone else, and Moose says he's got a tattoo. Got it when he was young, bit easy to spot, says he might as well write *Moose was here* on the wall.'

'Uh-huh,' the headmaster nodded.

'Well, Dad says, "But it's f**kin' freezing," ...sorry, sir,' Mary apologised.

'All right, Mary. Just keep it clean from now on, please.'

'Yes, sir. So Dad say, "It's freezin' swimmin' outside, you must be mad," and Moose says, "You got no balls," so my dad says, "Neither will you if you swim out there." So Moose says, "We're goin' swimming in the pool at the school," and looks at his two mates, the ones that came with him, the woman and the man.'

'Have you got any idea as to their names, Mary?' the head asked.

'No, sir!' Mary stated.

'Think, Mary, think,' the head coaxed.

'The other guy, the thin, ugly one, might have been called Bear,' she said, 'but I don't know the woman's name at all.'

The headmaster nodded and waved for her to carry on.

'The other two didn't look so keen, but I don't think they could back down then. So my dad says, "Well, if you go swimming in that school pool, I will sign the deal." Then the three Canadians looked at each other and nodded. Then Moose says, "Okay, but you'll have to get us in." Then my dad says, "You don't have to worry about that. Mary'll get you in, won't you, Mary?" He wasn't really askin'. My dad doesn't ask people to do things, they just do them.'

'I've heard that was the case. How did you get the key to the gate?' the head queried.

'I got it from the caretaker's store. They're all labelled on a board by the door. The caretaker leaves the door open, so it was easy,' she explained.

'I see.' The head made a note on his pad. Mary continued.

'I arranges it on the karting night because there's so much noise around. I thought it would cover any noise in the pool. I forgot about the netball practice. You see, there's normally no one over that side of the school. They waited till most of the kids had gone, then climbed over the fence into the nature reserve. I showed them to the pool and helped pull back the covers. I was outside the gate. I was to knock if anyone came that way.'

The headmaster was nodding along with Mary's account. It was all checking out.

'If you remember, the go-kart went out of control and half the school went racing past the pool, so I panicked and knocked on the door real loud, opened the door and shouted, "Get out, quick!" So they ran out, still in their swimming trunks, and raced through the trees towards the fence, but then Tarquin comes from one direction, and they trip over Mandy.'

'Trip over Mandy?' the head enquired.

'Yeah. She was lying in the grass, with Hollocks.'

'Oh! I see.' The head noted it down.

'Then the netball team come racing over, and Andy, but by that time, they had leaped the gate and headed off down the road.

THE BITCH IS BACK

'In the panic, they'd dropped the bag of clothes, so I picked it up, but it slowed me down getting away, so I bumped into everyone else, but that didn't matter 'cos I'm a pupil anyway, and I'm kinda respected.'

'Respected, hmm… I wouldn't necessarily have said respected… but carry on,' the head urged.

'I suggested to the netball team they didn't mention the moose tattoo to anyone.'

'And they agreed?' the head queried.

'I was quite forceful with my suggestion,' she said.

Josephine nodded, shamefaced in the background. As if she had succumbed to Mary's persuasion.

'Josephine. I might have expected the others to kowtow to threats and intimidation, but not you,' the head growled. 'Really, it's not good enough.'

'I'm sorry, Headmaster,' Josephine said apologetically. 'I thought if I said something, one of the other girls might get hurt.'

'So, what made everyone change their mind and mention the tattoo today?' the head demanded.

'Well, sir,' Josephine said, 'when Andrew let the cat out of the bag, I told the team they'd better mention the moose. Otherwise, it'll all get too confusing.'

'So what happened with Mirabel and Flossy then?'

'They were in my class, sir,' Mary said. 'I strongly persuaded them not to mention the moose. I thought they'd just say they didn't see it. I didn't think they'd choose a tortoise and an octopus.'

'Yes, well, with Mirabel and Flossy, anything's possible,' the headmaster said. 'So, what happened to the three Canadians?'

'Dad said they'd scarpered, back to Canada. He said the last thing they needed was a load of coppers on their backs.'

'I see. And you are sure they have gone?'

'I reckon so. They ain't gonna hang around here, are they?' Mary said, as if stating the obvious.

'No. I suppose not,' the head accepted. 'Now, I need to ring the police and tell them everything you've told me. I want you all to stay, in case there are any questions they raise that I need to ask you.'

Mary responded anxiously, 'I didn't know you were going to the police! Don't let them talk to my dad about it. He'll know it's me. It would be tricky.' She spoke with real fear in her voice.

'I have to speak to the police,' the head stated. 'They've got men out all over the town searching for those three. I can't ignore it. I will ask them not to speak to your dad, but I can't guarantee anything.'

'Sir! You don't know what he's like,' Mary pleaded, on the edge of tears.

'I will do my best,' he said, consoling her.

We all sat back in the lounge chairs, whilst the head made the call. He referred to a note on his desk pad, before lifting the handset and turning the dial on the receiver, once round for each number, waiting for it to whirr and click back before dialling the next. We waited whilst electrons whizzed down the line and reached their destination.

'Hello. It's the headmaster of Harribold School here. Could you put me through to Inspector Munroe? Yes, Munroe. Thank you. Ah, Inspector, so glad you're available. I've got some more information on the pool business from last night. It seems Mary Tideswell's father is involved... Yes... Quite... She says the three people were business acquaintances of her father... One was called Moose and another Bear, but she doesn't know the woman... Very unusual, I agree. Canadian apparently... According to Mary, they were just swimming. Some kind of bet with her father... No! She believes they've left the country, gone back to Canada... Mary Tideswell let them in, under orders from her father... We had another incident here last night. One of the go-karts went out of control and veered off into the nature reserve. Everyone ran past the pool shouting and screaming. They were spooked. Ran off. Left their clothes and everything... No, they were wearing swimming costumes... I guess this means case closed... Mary did say don't speak to her dad as he will know it was her that told you... He did what? Good grief, is he that bad? Oh dear. You won't mention it to him then? Good. I don't suppose it would help anyway if they've already disappeared... I don't know... She did let a group of criminals onto school premises. I can't just ignore it. I'm going to have to do something. I think she's already been to all the other schools... Thank you, Inspector. Glad it's cleared up at last. We can all sleep safely in our beds. Goodbye.'

He replaced the handset on the receiver, paused for a minute as if considering a conundrum, then turned to face us.

'Well. What can I say? I am very, very disappointed that you all lied to me,' he said gravely.

'Sir, they didn't lie. They were just economical with the truth,' Winston suggested in their defence.

'True. But still, it is very disappointing. Very! And Mary Tideswell. There will have to be repercussions, serious repercussions. We can't have an incident like this go unpunished. I will have to talk to the deputy head, but I think, like me, she will feel the most serious punishment will be required.'

'No!' Mary blurted. 'It's not fair! I had to.' Her eyes welled up with tears. She turned away.

'Sir!' Winston blurted, 'it's not Mary's fault. She was forced to do it. We'd have done the same, you'd have done the same, and you can't punish us all.'

'Winston! Do not, I repeat, do not shout at me. I am well aware of the circumstances, but we are all individuals, capable of shaping our own destiny,' the head barked angrily.

'No, we are not,' Winston continued. 'We are our fathers' children. Tarquin'll be a lawyer, Quinlan a banker, we'll work the factory floor, and Mary'll end up in prison.' Josephine and I glanced at each other. We were still hoping to avoid the factory floor if at all possible, but we said nothing. It was Mary who complained.

'No, I won't!' she shouted. 'I'm not going to prison. I'm better than that.' But whether she meant too clever to get caught, or too good to be a crook, we weren't sure.

'This is not the time for a philosophical argument,' the headmaster growled. 'I decide on the punishment, me alone.'

'Surely this is exactly the right time for a philosophical argument,' Quinlan stated. 'You intend to punish someone without taking into account their circumstances. How can that be fair?'

'Fair doesn't come into it,' the head stated forcibly.

'If fair doesn't come into it, then why are you a headmaster?' Tarquin asked, emboldened by dissent. 'Surely it is your job to teach what is fair. If fair doesn't come into it, we might as well all commit crime.'

'That is ridiculous. The person who does the crime should do the punishment,' the head argued.

Quinlan chipped in again. 'Clearly, if I committed a crime, I should be severely punished. I have had all the advantages. Parents that loved me, that taught me right from wrong, lavished me with gifts, gave me great opportunities…'

Then packed you off to boarding school and didn't have anything to do with you, I thought to myself.

'…Mary has not had those opportunities. It is not a level playing field. She deserves another chance.'

'How dare you! This is not open for discussion,' the head barked.

'So, this is not a school that encourages discussion,' Quinlan responded. 'This is not a school that encourages debate. This is not a school preparing pupils for the white heat of technology.'

'This is a great school, a fine school. This is a school righting the wrongs of the education system. Without this school, they would all be working the factory floor...' he pointed to us Harribold pupils '...but this school gives you the opportunity to make more of yourselves, to become more than you would otherwise be.'

'Only if it encourages you to think,' Tarquin stated.

'This school does encourage you to think. This school will get you the qualifications you need to make the most of your life,' the head proclaimed loudly.

'Then give that opportunity to Mary. At the end of this experiment, when we are interviewed by the *Telegraph* and *The Times*, we want to say this is a truly great school. That unlike Rugby School, not everyone has had the best start in life, but it gives everyone the best opportunities it can, and that we were proud to be students here.'

It was obvious the head knew he was defeated. Tarquin and Quinlan had him by the balls. To be honest, I suspect he had been convinced by their argument anyway. Blackmail was probably the best result for him, a suitable exit strategy. Giving in under duress meant he did not have to admit defeat. I think he quite enjoyed the cut and thrust of a lively debate, which would explain why he started a debating society the following term.

'Okay, Mary. You get one more chance,' the head decreed. 'An opportunity to turn your life around. They clearly think there's more to you than meets the eye. Do not disappoint.'

'Yes, sir!'

Mary looked across at us and smiled a surprisingly warm and friendly smile. Even the head seemed pleased. 'Great! I'm glad that is all sorted. It's been a hectic couple of days. Maybe things can return to normal now. Tarquin and Quinlan, I hope you continue to enjoy your stay with us. Now I suggest you go and get your lunch.'

'Sir, I think they'll probably have stopped serving by now.'

'Yes, very true, Winston,' the head acknowledged. 'Here, take this note and pass it to the dinner ladies. They'll make sure you have something to eat.' He scribbled a note on headed paper, signed it and passed it to Winston.

'That's all for now. You can leave.' He opened the door, holding the handles as if desperate to get us through so he could slam it shut again.

We lifted ourselves up out of the low chairs and filed past the headmaster. As soon as Tarquin was over the threshold, the door shut behind him, the handle jabbing him in the back.

There was a massive communal sigh of relief. 'You were fantastic,' we all said to Tarquin and Quinlan at once. 'You were brilliant. How you had the balls to say what you did, I don't know.'

'It's not our school,' Quinlan said. 'We knew we could get away with it.'

'Even so. You were amazing, just amazing,' Josephine confirmed.

'Yeah, you were pretty amazing,' Mary said to the new boys. She was more controlled than the rest of us, but underneath, maybe more passionately felt. 'Thank you.'

'No problem,' Tarquin said. 'We only had a bit part. You were incredible.'

'You ought to write stories,' Quinlan continued. 'How did you make that up in the time we had?'

'I'm a good liar,' Mary confessed. 'I've had to be. Dodgy parents.'

'What are you going to do now?' Tarquin asked.

'Well, firstly I'm going to get some lunch,' Mary said.

'You've already had some,' I reminded her.

'But I didn't get to finish it, did I?' she pointed out.

'Then what?' I asked. I wanted to know if she had changed.

'Then, I'm not sure,' she said. 'You lot seem to lead dull and uninteresting lives. Maybe I'll join you.'

'All right by me,' I said. To paraphrase President Lyndon Johnson, Mary was certainly one person it was better to have inside the tent pissing out, than outside the tent pissing in. She may not have had the physical advantages of the man he was describing at the time, but I suspected she was still quite capable of either.

'Yeah, fine by us,' Winston agreed.

'C'mon. I'm starving,' Josephine said.

28 THE TONGUE THAT TORE OUT TONSILS

We all wandered off down to the dining room, chatting about everything that had happened in the last two days. We handed in the note at the servery, and the dinner ladies grumpily put together a plate of food for each of us. They'd run out of jelly and ice cream, so we had leftover Manchester tart from the day before.

We sat around chatting for the rest of lunchtime. Tarquin and Mary seemed to get along remarkably well, all things considered. There might even have been a tiny little spark there somewhere. That would be a remarkable outcome of the day's events, if they got together. I'm not sure his parents would have approved.

This was the best of times. We had weathered the storm and survived the shipwreck. It is true we had been clinging to the wreckage for quite a while, buffeted by events, but we had all washed up on a sweeter shore. At that moment, I got the feeling this was going to be a good year, maybe a great year. There was only one thing left to resolve, and that was Karen.

We headed for the first lesson of the afternoon: double maths. A replay of yesterday's class, with double the time and double the fun. Mary joined us as we walked down the corridor, chatting about this and that. When we got to the class, Karen was waiting for us. She looked apprehensive.

'It's okay,' I said. 'Mary played a blinder. We got off scot-free. It's all sorted and everyone is happy.'

She looked mighty relieved. I might even have seen a spark of affection, which Mary stamped on quickly before it caught fire.

'You've got be careful with that one,' she said. 'Snogged me on the bus last night. Randy bugger, that tongue nearly tore my tonsils out. When we got off, he chased me down the street, he did. Couldn't get enough.'

Mary flashed her eyes at me as though she was after some more. I knew she was only playing, but it put a dampener on any chance of reconciliation with Karen, who was now seething.

'I chased after her because you said we had to be friends,' I said in my defence.

'I didn't say you had to stick your tongue down her throat though, did I?' she said, and stomped off into the classroom.

Josephine was now Karen's constant companion and confidante, sat at the back, as far from me as humanly possible. We took up our places at the front, same as yesterday.

Simon, Tom, George and Stephen were beating out a rhythm on the desks behind us. It was one of the coolest things. Layers of rhythm dancing over each other, and all it took was a couple of desks and four pairs of hands. They made it look so easy, so natural, so... groovy. It would normally have been a welcome distraction from my current predicament, but today was different.

'So,' Simon said over the skippity beat, 'is it true you snogged Mary?'

'Man, you've got balls,' Tom added.

'Balls of steel,' George chipped in.

'So, when you gonna shag her?' Stephen asked.

That was the last thing I needed. Rumours that I had been

shagging Mary Tideswell circulating round the school would improve my reputation no end, but ruin my chances with Karen.

'I am not shagging Mary Tideswell,' I shouted.

That neatly dragged in the whole class. Shortly, everybody was asking whether I'd shagged Mary Tideswell. I looked over to the back of the class and tried to combine an innocent look with a plea for help. It is a difficult combination to pull off, and I can't have got the mix quite right, because the response was not a friendly one. In fact, the look I got back was heavily laced with venom. If looks could kill, this one would be high up on the danger list. I might not have survived if Mr Samson hadn't walked in at that moment and taken control.

'So, George,' he said, glaring at him from the doorway, 'would you like to repeat the question I heard just outside the door?'

'Er... no, sir.'

'Good. Because I do not want to hear that kind of language in this school ever again. It is demeaning, it is disgusting, it is disgraceful. Do I make myself clear?' Mr Samson demanded, walking over to his desk.

'Y...yes, sir,' George replied, stumbling over his words.

'That applies to the rest of you as well. Do you understand?' He scanned the whole class.

'Yes, sir,' we all replied.

'I am not entirely sure who was involved, so by rights, I should keep you all in after school. However, I will leave it to you to consider what is appropriate language and abide by it. And, if I ever hear that kind of language again in this class, you will all be taken down to see the headmaster.'

There was an uncomfortable silence, during which everyone tried to avoid eye contact with the teacher, or anyone else.

'In the meantime, I would like you all, at home, to write out one hundred times, *I must not use inappropriate language in the maths lesson*.'

Karen harrumphed and grimaced at the unfair treatment.

'Apart from Karen Hannah, who will write it out two hundred times.'

Karen looked down, avoiding the teacher's gaze. I guessed all this was not going to help my cause one bit.

'Right! Where were we? Oh yes, squares.' His attention turned to the blackboard as he laid out today's challenge in chalk.

The lesson continued much like the day before. I worked through the sums without talking to anyone. Talking just got me into trouble, and I wasn't in the mood for chatting, even if the opportunity arose. Eventually, the bell rang and we all headed for the door. Josephine and Karen were holding back, making every effort not to come into close contact with me. I loped along with Winston, feeling dejected.

'Cheer up, y' miserable git. It's not the end of the world,' he said, trying to coax a smile.

'Howdaya know?' I asked.

'Lack of hell fire, no aliens, no asteroid,' he advised.

'I could be possessed by an alien,' I suggested.

'Oh, come on,' Winston replied.

'What do you mean, "Come on"?'

'As if they'd choose that body when this one's close by,' he said, wafting his hands over his "perfect" form.

'Fair enough.' I certainly wasn't any competition.

'Hey, it's the madness of Madame Oublions next. That's always good for a laugh,' he said cheerfully.

'I guess so,' I said. 'I could do with a laugh.'

29 AMOUR

'*Bonjour, mes amis. Entrez, entrez.*'

We took our seats at the front and Josephine and Karen sat at the back as before. Madame Oublions was wearing a towelling headband, and on the table in front of her was an assortment of rackets, bats and balls, shots, discuses, and leaning against the wall, a javelin.

'*Aujourd'hui, nous sommes tous des sportifs,*' she announced, walking on the spot, her black hair swinging from side to side.

'*Non, ne vous asseyez pas. Levez-vous, nous devons exercer,*' she decreed.

We didn't know exactly what she was on about, but we got the gist from her actions.

'*Levez les bras comme ça.*'

We raised our arms above our heads.

'*Et penchez-vous d'un coté puis de l'autre.*'

We leant to one side and then the other.

'*Levez un genou, puis l'autre.*'

We raised one knee and then the other.

'*Et courez sur place.*'

We ran on the spot.

'*Et sautez en étoile.*'

Star jumps was when it all went wrong. People slapped each other, some accidently, some on purpose. Chairs got kicked along with tables and bags, and the work-out disintegrated into a combination of laughter and distress. But it did brighten our day.

The rest of the lesson largely comprised pupils going up to the front and play-acting their favourite sport, using the array of props available. Madame Oublions would translate into French whilst we copied the actions and repeated the words.

The bell rang out. We started to pack our books away, ready to go. Madame Oublions asked me, Winston, Tarquin and Quinlan to stay a second, and called Josephine and Karen over.

'Josephine,' she said, 'I thought you were supposed to be accompanying our guests, showing them around, helping with their work. You can't do that sitting at the back of the class, can you?'

'I'm helping Karen,' Josephine explained.

'Karen is one of my brightest pupils. She has been here three years now. She knows the ropes, she doesn't need your help. Do you, Karen?'

'No, Madame Oublions,' Karen replied despondently, then flashed me the Laurel and Hardy look, the one that says, *This is another fine mess you've got me into.* That was all Madame Oublions needed.

'Oh! *Vous êtes amoureux.* You are in love. Such anger only comes from passion. You have had a lover's tiff. You have fallen out,' she said enthusiastically, clutching her hands against her heart.

'We are not in love,' I said vehemently, 'we've only kissed once.'

'Aaah, but you have kissed,' she said. 'That is all it takes. One little kiss, one little spark and the fire is burning.'

'We are definitely not in love,' Karen said sharply. 'We hardly know each other.'

'And yet you have kissed,' Madame Oublions said, as if it was all the proof she needed.

'It just happened. We didn't intend to, it just happened,' I tried to explain.

'It was an accident,' Karen said.

'Aah, an accident is but a chance encounter enflamed by passion,' she said softly.

'No!' we both cried together. 'Absolutely not!'

'*Mais oui. C'est vrai. Vous êtes amoureux.*' She nodded her head and smiled sweetly at us.

'We are not *amoureux*,' I announced.

'I don't even like him,' Karen stated angrily. 'He messes up everything.'

'I don't!' I said, defending myself.

'Time to go,' Madame Oublions said. 'But, my advice is to kiss and make up. You are in love. That much is certain.'

All this time, Winston and the others were draped in an embarrassed silence. They weren't sure whether they should stay or go. This level of embarrassment was almost too painful to observe, so they skulked in the background as if they weren't really there.

As soon as we got out the door, Karen turned on me angrily.

'How could you! How could you tell her we kissed? You moron. It'll be all round school. All the teachers will know. Oublions will tell everyone we kissed. You've seen what she's like, she loves this kind of thing. She'll tell everyone we're in love.'

'Is that so bad?' I asked.

'So bad? So bad? Of course it's so bad.' Karen was fuming. 'You saw how quickly your snog with Mary Tideswell got out of hand. Just think where this is going.'

'I didn't snog Mary Tideswell. I kissed her. It's different,' I said.

'You kissed her! You kissed her!' Karen shouted.

'She kissed me, I had no choice,' I argued.

'Aaagh! How could you! You… you… bastard!' She burst into tears.

'I'm sorry, I'm sorry. I'm really sorry. I didn't know it was going to end up like this.'

I was getting the gist of that old saying; Hell hath no fury like a woman scorned. I wasn't sure how my dreams could sink so far, so fast. A master fisherman couldn't reel this one in. This needed more than a fishing rod; this needed a trawler. Then, one turned up, in the shape of Josephine.

'Look, Karen, we know he's an idiot, a dipstick, a grade 1 moron, an imbecile and a fool.'

Then Winston cast out his nets:

'He can't help himself. He's accident-prone. It's like walking next to a crumbling cliff face. You're never sure when it's going to fall on you.'

And Quinlan helped to haul it in:

'He really should not be let out on his own. Look at him. He needs twenty-four-hour attention.'

And Tarquin:

'I've known him for just over a day, and I'm lucky to be alive.'

Winston heaved:

'He's been declared a disaster area. He should really be fenced off with barbed wire.'

And Josephine reeled:

'He's on the world's most unwanted list.'

Winston dragged my dreams back to the surface:

'But, and it is a big but, despite all that, despite all his flaws, despite all his failings, we love him dearly.' He tried to give me a big kiss, but I dodged his flailing arms, tripped up and fell back on the floor. It seemed to be the trigger that was needed. Everyone burst out laughing. Even Karen smiled. I was now a figure of ridicule and a figure of fun, but at least I was back on board. Opposite ends of the deck maybe, but we were in the boat together.

'C'mon, Karen, he's not bad enough to hate,' Winston said. 'Despise maybe, but not hate.'

'I know.' Karen looked down at me and shook her head absent-mindedly. If looks could talk, this one would probably say, *What was I thinking?*

'You are going to come down with us to the entrance tonight, while we wait for the car, aren't you?' Quinlan asked.

'I wasn't going to,' Karen said.

'You have got to,' Tarquin added. 'You've been such a big part of today's miraculous escape. You have simply got to come.'

'Go on,' Josephine said. 'I'll be there.'

'Okay,' she said. 'I'll come.'

We traipsed off to English. I was keeping a low profile, avoiding getting too close and avoiding speaking at all. It seemed like the safest thing to do.

30 BRIEFCASE AND THE BARD

We were late for English again. It was beginning to be a habit. Mrs Penn was none too impressed.

She had saved the front row for us and we slid into it as discreetly as we could. As soon as we sat down, Mrs Penn got up.

'Today, we are going to look at England's most famous playwright. Can anyone tell me who that is?'

Quinlan stuck his hand up.

'Yes!' She pointed at Quinlan.

'William Shakespeare,' Quinlan answered.

'Correct. Does anyone know when the plays were written?' she asked.

There was a whole host of guesses from fifty to four thousand years ago. In the end, Mrs Penn gave up on the guessing game and gave us the answer instead.

'Shakespeare's plays were written four hundred years ago. No television, no radio, no cinema, no books; well, not many, and most people couldn't read anyway. After working your butt off in the fields all day, the only entertainment available was to stick some bells on your shoes and pop down to the village green for a spot of folk dancing. Compared to that, theatre was all your wildest dreams rolled into one.

'But what was theatre really like? Everybody up, we need to rearrange the desks. Put all your bags at the back. We need a row down this side, a row down that side and a row at the end. If we've got any desks left, we'll stack them up... over there.' She pointed to the back corner of the room.

With a lot of pushing and pulling, the desks were rearranged into a large horseshoe. Most sat behind the desks, but we landed up on the few loose chairs in the middle.

'The Globe Theatre, where Shakespeare's plays were performed, looked like this.' She held up an artist's impression. 'The audience were arranged around the stage, just like we are here.

'Catch!' She threw out sweets with wrappers to everyone in the class. 'Don't unwrap them yet.' Then she handed out some glasses of water. 'And don't drink these either,' she said. 'The audience was allowed to eat and drink beer during performances. You'll have to pretend it's beer.' She then placed some soft rubber balls on the tables. 'And, the audience sometimes threw things at the performers.'

'John, George, Simon and Tom, stand up.' They got up out of their seats. 'The audience could walk around, so that's your job, and they could also boo or cheer, so you can do a bit of that too.

'Right, I need two actors to read a bit of Shakespeare. Andrew and Karen, you're convenient so it might as well be you. Come on, up you get.'

We reluctantly dragged ourselves up out of our seats and turned round to face the audience. I got the feeling they were not going to be an appreciative bunch. Mrs Penn selected a couple of books from the shelves and flicked through to find the dialogue she wanted. She passed them to us, pointing to where she wanted us to start from.

'This play is called *Much Ado About Nothing*. It's a romantic comedy. Not many laughs really, and this bit is no exception. Benedick and Beatrice have just discovered they love each other. However, Beatrice is absolutely furious with a guy called Claudio. She thinks he's been spreading malicious gossip about her female friend Hero, and she won't let it lie.

'Karen is Beatrice and Andrew is Benedick. As soon as they start speaking, you can begin unwrapping, drinking, throwing, walking round, cheering and booing. Andrew, you start.'

The play went like this:

Benedick:	*By my sword Beatrice though lovest me.*
Beatrice:	*Do not swear and eat it.*
Benedick:	*I will swear by it that you love me, and I will make him eat it that says I love not you.*
Beatrice:	*Will you not eat your word?*
Benedick:	*With no sauce that can be devised to it. I protest I love thee.*
Beatrice:	*Why then, God forgive me.*
Benedick:	*What offence, sweet Beatrice.*
Beatrice:	*You have stayed me in a happy hour. I was about to protest I loved you.*
Benedick:	*And do it with all thy heart.*
Beatrice:	*I love you with so much of my heart that none is left to protest.*
Benedick:	*Come, bid me do anything for thee.*
Beatrice:	*Kill Claudio.*

The audience weren't stationary, quiet, or friendly. They were unwrapping sweets, guzzling "beer", booing and cheering, wandering around and pelting us with a hail of balls. A love scene would normally be the most embarrassing thing to do in front of a group of school friends, but this was ludicrous; this was ridiculous; this was funny. We laughed.

'Okay. You can stop now,' Mrs Penn said to everybody. 'Please return to your seats,' she said to us.

We sat down. Karen looked at me, and I looked at Karen, and she smiled. Maybe that icy hostility was beginning to thaw. Then Winston chipped in from behind.

'It's a good job there isn't any snogging in Shakespeare, what with your reputation an' all.'

The smile turned to a grimace and my heart sank again. Was I ever going to get a clean break?

'Now, did anybody hear anything that was going on?' Mrs Penn asked.

'No!' everyone replied, apart from George, who had his hand up.

'Yes, George?'

'I think Beatrice told Benedick to "Kiss Claudio."'

'That would have been an interesting twist in the plot,' Mrs Penn admitted, 'but unfortunately she said, "Kill Claudio." So, we can see from that, if anyone was going to make head or tail of what was going on, the actors needed to be loud, very loud. But, even if they were loud, would it be easy to follow, with all the distractions?'

'No!' was the audience response. Aggie had her hand up this time.

'Yes, Aggie?' Mrs Penn responded.

'You could tell they were in love.'

Quite a lot of giggling followed that remark.

Mrs Penn turned to me and Karen. 'Well, the acting must have been pretty good then, though I guess when any man and woman are on stage together, alone, if they are not hitting each other over the head, they are probably in love, and sometimes, when they are hitting each other over the head, they are still in love.' A few more giggles erupted from the audience.

It does, however, make the point that the setting has to be clear and obvious, and so do the actions and expressions of the actors.' At this point, she mimicked various extravagant poses to portray anger, love, confusion, courage and disdain.

'Has anyone ever read any Shakespeare?' she continued.

Tarquin put up his hand.

'How easy was it to read?' Mrs Penn asked.

'Really hard. It is all in old English. There are words you can't understand. It sounds all wrong.'

'Thank you. Well put. The language is hard. But four hundred years ago, with all the chaos in the theatre, they wouldn't have been saying, "What the hell does that mean?" They would have lost the plot. But, most importantly, they would have missed the jokes, and you can't have a comedy without laughter. It must have been easy for them to understand.

'So, to your average Elizabethan theatregoer, Shakespeare wasn't difficult. It was easy, simple and obvious. A bit like *Coronation Street*. They didn't struggle with the language, because they were familiar with it. If an Elizabethan gent turned up today, and we took him to see James Bond, it wouldn't make any sense at all. They would struggle to understand James Bond just as much as we struggle to understand Shakespeare.'

'A car with an ejector seat would be a bit of a shock, miss,' Simon said.

'A car would be a bit of a shock, Simon, without the ejector seat,' Mrs Penn pointed out.

'Oh yeah.'

Mrs Penn went on to explain how pronunciation had changed over time, so words that should rhyme no longer rhyme and puns go unnoticed. She also explained how the meaning of words had changed, so you need an old English dictionary to understand some bits. I wondered why we bothered to learn Shakespeare at all. Maybe that was in the next lesson.

The final bell rang out.

'Before you go, can you please put the desks back where you found them?' Mrs Penn instructed.

There was some frantic rearranging of desks and chairs before pupils darted out the door. We hung around and tidied things up a bit. Mrs Penn thanked us and then we wandered out at a more leisurely pace than the rabble before us.

We plodded down the stairs and along the staff corridor to the main entrance, where we sat on the steps outside, like we had in the morning.

31 THE LONG GOODBYE

'I thought yesterday was mad enough,' Quinlan said, 'but today may have been madder.'

'Oh, c'mon,' I said. 'Yesterday was much madder. Nobody had to swim in ice-cold water today.'

'Or drive across the nature reserve in a go-kart,' Winston recalled cheerily.

'Or run across the field in underpants,' Tarquin added.

'Or kiss Mary Tideswell,' Winston mentioned unhelpfully.

'Or kiss Karen,' I said, in a desperate attempt to balance the books.

'I hope it wasn't a chore,' Karen sniped.

'No! It was nice. I liked it… a lot,' then sensing I hadn't gone far enough, added, 'a very lot.'

Josephine put her hand over her face and shook her head in despair at my feeble attempt to win Karen round.

'So, when did you two kiss?' Quinlan asked, trying to rekindle the flame.

'After I ran in to get dry. Karen was helping sort me out, looking after me. We were both a bit emotional. I… and she… '

'It just happened,' Karen said, dismissing it out of hand.

'Still, you must like each other,' Josephine said, 'to kiss each other.'

I blushed bright red and turned away. 'I like Karen... a lot,' I admitted, hoping she might say the same.

'I'm not sure,' Karen said, anything but affectionately.

'Let's get that book out again,' Winston said, deciding it was a good time to change the subject. 'I can't believe you thought we could use it.'

I got the book out of my bag and opened it on a page with all the animals in the antlers.

'It would have been funny if the netball team had to remember all those animals,' Tarquin said.

Winston started to mimic the scene.

'Er... well, if I remember rightly, there was a bear, a bird, a tortoise, an octopus, no! No! It was a fish, no, a whale...'

'I wasn't expecting them to include all the animals,' I said grumpily.

'Just some?' Quinlan asked.

'None of the animals,' I corrected.

'If Karen hadn't got that picture, we'd be lumbered,' Josephine said.

'I know,' I said. 'It was an amazing thing to do.' I looked at Karen in what I hoped was a conciliatory manner.

'Landed me in the shit though, didn't it?' Karen gave me a sideways glance and shook her head.

'Yeah, but you'll be all right. Wilderbeast loves you,' Winston chipped in.

'And now you've got lessons in book binding, she'll love you even more,' Josephine added cheerily.

'I have to admit, I do quite like the idea of book binding,' Karen acknowledged. She gave me another sideways glance, but this time she nodded some form of reconciliation.

At that point, the silver Mercedes entered the gates once again and pulled up adjacent to the steps. We all stood up as Mr Pickering opened the door and got out.

'Have you had a good day?' he asked us all, but mainly targeting Tarquin and Quinlan.

'Brilliant day,' Quinlan advised.

'Fantastic day,' Tarquin confirmed.

'Oh!' Mr Pickering responded, somewhat surprised by the enthusiasm. 'Less exciting than yesterday, I hope.'

'A little,' Quinlan answered.

'Not much,' Tarquin added.

'Well, you'll have to tell me all about it in the car on the way back. In you get,' he said, opening the back door.

'Goodbye,' they said. 'See you tomorrow.'

We waved them off then sat back down on the steps; Josephine and Winston, Karen and me. No one was officially going out with anyone; we were just two couples chatting. Karen shrugged off her animosity and we were soon laughing and joking about the insanity of the last few days. It felt great; it felt grown up; it felt special. After a while, Josephine had to leave to catch the bus. Winston got up and walked with her over to the bus stop, leaving me and Karen alone. We chatted for a second or two then she grabbed her bag, threw the strap over her shoulder and stood up to go. She gave me that goodbye look, but I didn't want to say goodbye.

'Can I walk you home?' I said.

'You've got no idea where I live. It could be miles away.'

'It's a sacrifice I'm willing to make.'

'Haven't you made enough rash decisions for one day?'

'Where do you live then?'

'Over there.' She pointed out over the car park.

'What, at the end of the drive?'

'No! In Bilton.'

'I can walk you to Bilton.'

'You don't know where Bilton is, do you?'

'Over there.' I pointed in roughly the same direction.

'You can walk me to the end of the drive.'

We both got up, slung our bags over our shoulders and walked out across the car park and through the main gate. Dotted around were the dribs and drabs of daydreamers, slow coaches, scaredy-cats and the reluctant few for whom school was better than home.

'If you want, I could walk you back a little bit further every day until we reach your house,' I said.

'I don't think so.' She gave me a sideways glance and shook her head.

'You're just embarrassed by your home, aren't you?' I said.

'No!'

'I bet you live in a castle with a moat and a drawbridge and a portcullis, and a dungeon, and turrets and towers and ramparts and a keep and a gallery and—'

'I know what a castle looks like.'

'That's because you live in one.'

'Do I look like a princess?'

'Er... yes and no.'

'Hedging your bets?'

'It's a tricky question.'

'I don't live in a castle.'

'A lighthouse then?'

'In Bilton?'

'A boat?'

'There's no water.'

'A kennel?'

'Really?'

'A mansion? An enormous mansion with huge gates and

stone pillars with lions on the top and a gold carriage with six
white horses and a footman and a butler and a scullery maid and
a… plumber.'

'A plumber?'

'Lots of toilets in a mansion.'

'I don't live in a mansion.'

'Well, you don't need to be embarrassed if I walk you home then.'

'It's not home that's a problem.'

'It's your parents, isn't it? They're evil villains.'

'They're not evil villains!'

'They're hippies then, naturists, bird watchers.'

'No! It's not my parents.'

'Well, what is it then?'

'…It's you.'

'But I thought you liked me.'

'Like you? You are a f**kin' disaster area. I don't know anyone
who could f**k things up as much as you. You are a danger to be
around. In a war, you should be dropped over enemy lines and
left to f**k things up for the enemy.'

'I'm accident-prone.'

'You're not prone to accidents. They don't just happen to you.
You throw yourself at them. You're the guy with his head in the
lion's mouth. In a swimming pool full of shit, you would choose
the deep end to dive in. You have no idea of the chaos you cause.
You manage to put your foot in your mouth with your head up
your arse.'

'So, I'm not perfect.'

'Not perfect! Weren't you in a fight last week because of
something you said?'

'He pushed in front of me in the dinner queue. It was a matter
of principle.'

'Yeah! But what did you call him?'

'Shit on a stick.'

'Shit on a stick? What does it even mean?'

'I don't know.'

'See. You don't think. You don't think things through. Georgina Roley said you almost did the same yesterday.'

'He pushed in.'

'And you kissed Mary Tideswell, half an hour after you kissed me.'

'We were on the same bus.'

'Do you kiss everyone on the bus?'

'She kissed me.'

'She was pretty emphatic that you kissed her back.'

'It wasn't like that. She grabbed me.'

'Just an accident?'

'Yeah. Just an accident.'

'You're a basket case. I don't know if I could survive another day like today.'

'I'm sorry. I'm sorry. I made a hash of things.'

'With all the trimmings.'

'Okay, I messed up, but ignoring the briefcase, the fights, the moose, Mary Tideswell and the Wilderbeast...'

'I could kill you for that alone.'

'I know, but... putting all that to one side... do you like me?'

She said nothing for few seconds. She looked up to heaven as if it was too difficult a question for her alone, then she stopped and sighed. She looked down at her feet.

'I really like you,' I said. 'I really, really like you. I just hoped you might like me too.'

There was an uncomfortable pause.

'I like you,' she said, looking up. 'I do like you, but I'm not sure I want to be your girlfriend.'

'Why not?'

'You're too difficult. I'm not sure what it would be like, with you as a boyfriend.'

'It'd be great,' I stated enthusiastically.

'Really?' She was more sceptical.

'Look! There's Mandy. She's had loads of boyfriends. She must know why it's good to have a boyfriend. Hey! Mandy.'

'Yeah?' she called back.

'We need to ask you something,' I said. She came over to join us.

'Okay! What is it?' she asked.

'What are the good things about having a boyfriend?' I asked, expecting a positive answer.

'Why? Are you two…?' she queried.

'Not yet,' Karen said.

'Oh! But you like each other?'

'Yeah, kind of,' Karen said.

'Well, that's the difficulty,' Mandy advised.

'How can liking each other be a difficulty?' I asked. 'Surely it's a benefit.'

Mandy explained: 'You start off kissing. One of you wants to go further. Because you like each other, one goes too far, sacrifices too much, loses themselves, becomes dependent. The other drifts away. One is left feeling guilty and the other is left feeling hurt.'

'You're really not selling it, Mandy,' I said, hoping for something a little more encouraging.

'You're better off as friends,' she replied, 'honest.'

'I didn't know you'd got hurt,' Karen said, surprised by Mandy's tale of woe.

'Not me. I don't get attached. I'm a slapper. It's the others.' She shrugged and walked off.

'Sounded bleak,' Karen said.

'You don't want to listen to her,' I said dismissively.

'Maybe we are just better as friends,' Karen suggested.

'Okay. But if we are going to be just friends, can I kiss you one more time before we break up?'

'I didn't know we were ever together. But all right. One last kiss,' she agreed.

We stood facing each other. I put my hands on her waist. She moved closer; I could feel her heart beating. I could feel my heart beating. I looked into her eyes. I felt myself drowning in her scent, her touch, her breath, and then we kissed, and the world no longer existed.

'Can I walk you home?' I asked when at last we came up for air.

'Okay,' she said.

32 BAGS

Friday 24th October 1975 was the last day before the half-term holiday and Tarquin and Quinlan's last day at Harribold School. Me, Winston, Josephine, Karen and Mary sat on the steps to the main entrance, waiting for the silver-grey Mercedes to turn up for one last time. We'd had a good time and we would be sad to see them go, but we could tell they were ready to return to their former life.

Following the craziness of those first two days, life fell into a steady routine. After the lunacy, we were more than happy with mundane. Mary was still inside the tent pissing out. She had taken it upon herself to provide a counter-balance to male sexist behaviour across the school, becoming a sort of feminist vigilante. Josephine would feed her the names of badly behaved boys, and Mary would do what Scary Mary did best: terrorise them. Ursula and Rain had even been conscripted as suitable sidekicks. We pointed out there were plenty of red capes with SM on should she feel the need for a costume, but I don't think Mary could stomach the wholesome apple pie goodness of Superman. She was more the moral ambiguity of Catwoman.

Me and Karen were an item of sorts. I had walked her home a few times, but I wasn't really welcome. Karen's father was sorely disappointed. He was really hoping his girl would fall for a practical sort of guy; a plumber, carpenter, mechanic or muck man; somebody who could do something useful, rather than a wannabe accountant. He considered 98% in a maths exam as a significant failing on my part. Karen was still writing; mainly romantic, mushy, lovey-dovey stuff, the sort of thing that couldn't possibly happen in real life.

Josephine and Winston were lining themselves up to be future world leaders, having wiped out bullying at Harribold with their ARSE, as well as leading the school teams to glory. They had formed a close friendship, only coming to blows whenever Winston called Josephine Glasshopper. To be honest, we had all become close friends and spent much of our time chatting to each other on the benches around the school. I had finally discovered talking to girls can be good fun, and not something to be scared about, although I was still a little nervous when it came to Mary. As we sat on the steps waiting for the car to arrive, we talked about those first two days; how terrifying, amazing, exciting and utterly ridiculous they had been.

The limousine slowly made its way down the drive and circled the car park, coming to rest by the steps. The housemaster jumped out and opened the rear door for his prestigious passengers. Tarquin and Quinlan emerged into the sunlight with wide smiles and a cheery wave; somewhat more relaxed than their arrival three weeks before. Quinlan was wearing his trademark pink jumper, which I can only assume was some kind of protest against the fashion bullies. All I can say is, it was a good job ARSE was around. Tarquin had decided he was, after all, the natural successor to Roger Moore as James Bond and was as meticulously turned out as ever.

'Hi, guys,' we said as they came up the steps. 'One more time.'

'One more time,' they replied.

We headed into the foyer and paused outside the big oak doors to the assembly hall. 'Ready?' Winston asked.

'Ready,' they agreed. We pushed open the doors and stepped inside. It was already packed with row upon row of students: squabbling, joking, chatting, crying, sitting silently, and laughing their heads off. The sound echoed around the hall, filling every corner of the space. Karen and Mary sidled off into one of the rows, sitting next to some friends from the netball team. We carried on down the central aisle all the way to the front, up the steps and onto the stage. We took our place in the five awaiting empty seats, alongside the teaching staff and dignitaries. The headmaster was already up on his feet, whirling his cane with gusto. He raised his hands and the chattering gradually declined to a whisper, and then silence.

'Ladies and gentlemen, girls and boys. Rugby School and Harribold School. Two very different schools. One serving the needs of the rich and one serving the needs of the majority. Even ignoring issues of equality, it is a shame these two schools exist as wholly separate institutions, because, if we are to stand a chance of creating a society where everyone is valued and everyone can thrive, we must start by understanding each other's experience of life. We need to reach through the railings and shake hands. It is with this in mind that an exchange was organised between our two great institutions, so that two students could experience life on the other side. Those students are now in a position to describe their experience to others in their respective schools and help foster the understanding we all crave.

'Tarquin and Quinlan have spent the last three weeks here, and I believe you have both had a good time, haven't you?' Tarquin and Quinlan nodded enthusiastically. 'To say thank you for being such good students, we have a present for each of you, and I think you'll find something selected by our students inside. Please come to the front.'

Tarquin and Quinlan moved to the front of the stage. 'And the rest of you as well,' the headmaster instructed, beckoning us up. We joined the two of them at the front, looking out over the huge audience. 'Winston, can you present the gifts?' Winston nodded. From under the seats, he pulled out two Adidas sports bags and handed them to Tarquin and Quinlan. They beamed cheerily and shook Winston's hand as he passed them over.

'Go on then, open them up. Let's see what's inside,' the headmaster encouraged.

Quinlan opened his first and drew out a pair of toy binoculars. He smiled and nodded at the reference to his role as lookout in the briefcase adventure. The headmaster ran a commentary over the event.

'For those who cannot see, they are a pair of binoculars, presumably for bird watching.'

Tarquin opened his bag and drew out a pair of swimming trunks and a picture of Sean Connery as James Bond, sporting a similar pair in *Dr. No*. He laughed and nodded knowingly to the rest of us. The headmaster continued with his role of reporter.

'Tarquin has received a pair of swimming trunks and a picture of James Bond. Well, I can see the likeness.' The audience laughed.

'I believe Tarquin and Quinlan also have some gifts for our students, so if this is a good time, feel free to hand them out.'

Quinlan went and grabbed three canvas sport bags emblazoned with the school logo, *Orando Laborando*. He had a quick look inside to check the contents then passed them out to each of us.

'It seems these bags also have gifts inside, selected by Tarquin and Quinlan,' the headmaster announced. 'Go on then, open those and show the students as well.'

Josephine opened her bag first to reveal a *Thunderbirds* annual. She smiled graciously.

'Josephine has received a *Thunderbirds International Rescue* annual, presumably for the netball team's heroic acts three weeks ago,' the headmaster continued.

The three of us laughed, and the rest of the netball team in the audience joined in.

Winston opened his bag and removed a pair of driving gloves. More laughter and smiles.

'Winston has received a pair of driving gloves, presumably a reference to that fateful day when the go-kart went out of control and he ended up halfway across the nature reserve,' the headmaster explained. There was sporadic laughter in the crowd.

Finally, I opened up my bag and pulled out a framed picture. I turned it to face the audience. It was a picture of *Thidwick the Big-Hearted Moose*.

THE BIG THANK YOU

It would be impossible to write about childhood without thanking my kind, caring, creative and occasionally amusing parents. A happy childhood is something positive you can look back on with affection, whatever adult life throws at you. A big thankyou to my brothers and sister for all the games we played and adventures we shared, and thanks for putting up with my inability to pick up a phone, email or use social media. I also thank all my friends from school for making my young life a happy one.

I raise a glass to all the good teachers that put in a decent shift to help me on my way, and one special thank you to my infant school headteacher who is just great.

I thank my son for reminding what it is like to be young again, and for all of the Lego, drawing, imagination and games of Octopus.

Finally I would like to say thank you to my darling wife, who I love dearly, for putting up with this writing malarkey when there are a hundred DIY jobs awaiting my attention.